Waiting

'Round to Die

Waiting 'Round to Die

Chris Grant

atmosphere press

For Glen,
I will see you when I get there.

TABLE OF CONTENTS

Act I

LITTLE ROCK, 2016

After a decent dinner consisting almost entirely of pimento cheese and alcohol, I retired to the bar at the Doubletree to continue my drinking. A few rounds of bourbon in, and I was feeling great. I had not felt this disconnected from my myriad responsibilities in years. No one, save the person who checked me into the hotel, knew where I was. I kind of wondered if my wife cared. I suspected she didn't. She told me to leave. I was just taking her advice. I slept quite soundly that night and, after a brief stop at Bill Clinton's favorite McDonald's for an Egg McMuffin, I returned to the road.

By this point I had a vague idea where I was going. I was headed east. The pine trees form a curtain along I-40 as you head from Little Rock to Memphis. If you just look straight ahead as you go you may very well think you are driving through a canyon, because you can't see anything to your left or your right. Eventually you emerge from this forest to find the Mississippi River attempting to stop you from crossing over into Tennessee. Fortunately, there are plenty of bridges and I did not have to swim or take a ferry.

Once across the muddy river you are in Memphis, a dirty city with a very fancy hotel and a couple famous landmarks. I figured this was as good a place as any to stop and have a look around. And it seemed like, since I was already there, I might as well pay a visit to the King.

SAN DIEGO, 2000

"As we were, so perfect, so happy. They'll remember only our smiles, 'cause that's all they've seen." "The Approaching Curve" by Rise Against is a fantastic song with an ending you can see from a mile away, but you may still be a bit surprised when it gets there. Not unlike this very tale I am telling? Hmm, I don't know about that. Perhaps there is going to be a big twist coming up soon. I guess you'll have to stick around to find out.

"I think I'm done," she said. Her eyes distant. Her hand no longer holding mine, as we sat in our favorite bookstore/coffee shop in the Kensington section of "America's Greatest City."

"You want to go home?" I replied, matter-of-factly.

"Yeah. But so should you."

Her words slapped me back to reality. They were not shocking, but they stung all the same.

Claire Grace Taylor was an intern at the newspaper when I met her. She was in college at the time, young and bleached blonde with blue eyes and a body most men would daydream about. Maybe she was too young, but that didn't stop me. The pursuit did not take that long because in some ways she needed to be chased even more than I needed to chase her. At first, it seemed like nothing more than a harmless fling. She was headed back to college in the fall, and I did not have that much interest in driving over the mountain to San Diego on a regular basis anyway.

So we hooked up for a month or six weeks. Taking midnight drives into the darkness. Fucking on the beach at two a.m., or in a Las Vegas hotel room, or in her room at her parents' house. It didn't matter. Like I said, it was a summer fling. Then she was gone, back to school. By this point I was in love with the idea of us and so that long trek over the mountain no longer seemed that long. That does not mean I was making it weekly. No, I was going out and drinking with my friends most weekends, but when things slowed down I would go spend a fairly chill time on the beach, or in the bars and restaurants of the Gaslamp, with Claire. But then disaster struck and as my friends began to disappear like the money from my wallet on a drunken Friday night, Claire became more and more important to me. Soon, she was the last remaining piece of what I had regarded as the best time of my life. And that is how she became everything.

Soon, I began going to San Diego every chance I had. This meant every weekend, every day off. Hell, sometimes I would just drive over there after work and come home the next morning. We were happy. At least that's how I remember it. She lived in a small rental house in Kensington where I spent the better part of the next seven hundred days. I want to regale you now with flowery stories of love, and I suppose I could, but here's the thing, Claire was super fucked up. More than I am now, I think. She was the youngest child of some very old, very rich parents. She had siblings who were older than me and, despite her parents' good intentions, she felt they did not give her the love or attention she needed. I am sure this is why we were together. Were you going to point that out? Well, you are probably right. But I needed her just as much. Because without her, I was alone. Abandoned by my friends, left in a place I loathed. She was all I had. Everything there was.

So when she would tell me about the guy she "accidentally" made out with at some party. I didn't really care. I would just ask her if she wanted to stay together, she would say yes, and we would go on with our little charade. It didn't bother me the first time, or the second, or the third. There may have been a fourth too, but I don't recall. Even when I found myself hooking up with other girls on my nights in the Valley, I did not think about ending it with her. Like I said, we needed each other. Right up until she no longer needed me at all.

The night before the final night of our time together had started off like any other. Then she went off to some study group and never came back. Not until six the next morning. Turns out the group had decided to go to Tijuana after they finished studying. I have no doubt she went with some other guy. Maybe he was number five? Shit, I should quit counting. She came home, cried, and then we went to sleep. The next day we woke up early and fucked for what would be the final time. After, we took a long drive up the coast to Carlsbad where we had what would turn out to be our last meal together. She ordered a forty-dollar lobster. I will never forget that. It was a baller move.

When we got back to Kensington we went to that aforementioned bookstore. By this point I was pretty sure what was coming. We had been in this situation many times before and every time it ended with her in my arms, crying and both of us agreeing to soldier on. This time was different. There was a resolve in her eyes that I had never seen before. So yeah, I knew what was going to happen, but I was not ready for where it would all end up.

We silently walked back to her small house, which was two

blocks away, both of us looking in different directions, trying our best not to look at each other. The night was overcast, and you could feel the ocean in the air. There were no stars, but we were in the middle of the city, so it was not really dark as we trudged past the park that spans one block in the middle of Kensington. I could smell the salt water and the trees as we passed them. Soon we were across the street and in front of her apartment. I followed her inside so I could get my things and leave. Once in the house, her tears finally came.

"I guess you can stay. If you want," she said. Still trying not to look at me. "It's late. I don't want you to have to drive all that way this late."

"Fuck you if you think I'm going to stay." I was angry. She was breaking up with me? What the fuck was she thinking? This was not the way it was supposed to happen. I bought her a forty-dollar lobster, for God's sake!

"Just. Don't," she responded, trying to touch my arm, which I quickly pulled away from her. "I think this is for the best." Her words came through her muffled tears. "I just need some time."

"I guess you'll have all the time you want then." I grabbed my bag and stormed out the door.

I did not know then that I would never see Claire again. I honestly figured we would get past this too. Just like all those other times. In the weeks that would come, I would try. I would get drunk with whomever I could find to drink with me. Or by myself. It didn't really matter. Then I would go home and call her. She would never answer. No matter when I called. Her reluctance to take my calls did not stop her from calling me though. Her calls usually came in the afternoon. Probably when she was bored. She would ask how I was doing. She would ask if I was dating anyone else. She would tell me about her life. Whatever it was she was up to on that particular day. Mostly I just listened to her and remembered our smiles and how she had left me alone. The last time we spoke was a few days before Christmas. She said she was coming to see her parents and wondered if I wanted to get together for lunch. I told her I was heading to Vegas with a friend and said we should try and meet up in San Diego in the new year. She agreed to the plan and for the first time since she had dumped me, she sounded happy. Fucking great for her—right?

Just a short time after that last phone call I was married. When we got back to the Valley, I fired off an email to Claire telling her what had happened and wishing her the best of lives. Her response was fairly brief. "Married? Fuck you! Hope you have a fucking happy life." Sometimes when I need a good laugh, I will bring the printed copy out of my desk and read it. I don't think anyone has ever hated me as much as she did in that moment. That was not the final time I heard from her though. No, that happened about a month after that email. I was at work when Yahoo! Messenger popped up on my computer with the words "hello, are you there?" typed on it. The sender of the message was Claire, and it took me a long time to decide what to do with it. I was convinced that if I replied we would end up back together. Yes, I was married and for all I knew she was in the process of fucking some other guy while she was writing to me. But it did not matter. I was certain we were damaged magnets that could not escape each other, no matter what we did. So I did not reply. I simply turned off my computer and walked away, in much the same manner that I walked away from her house that night.

"Hey, come back," she called after me.

"Fuck you," I yelled back, not bothering to turn around.

"I'm sorry," she said. "Just come back."

By this point I'd made it to my car. I could see her standing on her stoop, looking at me. I did not give her the satisfaction of returning her gaze. Instead, I got in my car and slammed the door. I think I heard her call my name one last time, but I can't be sure, because the engine noise drowned out whatever it was she might have been saying. With the radio now turned up to twenty and Morrissey singing "There Is a Light That Never Goes Out," I sped away, into the night. Alone.

AUSTIN, 2016

I think if I ever decide to jump into the pimp game, I am going to call myself White Jesus.

I don't know why, but I like the name. I may have heard it before. On that documentary Ice-T produced about pimps. You know the one, right? I can't recall the name of it. But Don "Magic" Juan is on there. They used to show it on HBO a lot. In the end everyone ends up going to some sort of pimp's ball. Do you know what I'm talking about? Lots of dudes in bright-colored suits? I think there's a white guy in it and maybe his name is White Jesus. Hell, I don't know for sure. It's a great name though, right? White Jesus the pimp? Okay, I know there's a song by the rap group The Coup and it is called "Me and Jesus The Pimp in a '79 Granada Last Night." I am positive of that. But I don't think anywhere in that song does it say anything about him being White Jesus. No, I totally stole that from that Father John Misty song, "Bored in the USA." You know, where he says, "Save me white Jesus?" Not familiar with it? Maybe you should check it out.

Fuck me. I don't know why I'm talking about being a pimp

anyway. I'm not ever jumping into the pimp game. I am an almost middle-aged man with a wife and a kid. The only whores I have ever even seen were in a brothel in Mexicali and they scared me. Never mind that they only spoke Spanish. There's a language barrier there, you know? You can't pimp someone who you can't even communicate with—right? What if they want a day off? Or need something? If you can't even understand a word they are saying, then how are you going to put them to work for you? Plus I don't look good in purple. I had a purple polo shirt once. I wore it. Because I bought it. But I never thought it looked that great. Honestly, I was pretty happy when it developed a hole on the hem so I could just throw it away. Figured it was better off in the trash than on me.

Well shit, I feel like I am rambling again. Yeah, right, like Sam Elliott in *The Big Lebowski*. I think half my thoughts are stolen from all the movies I watch. The rest just sort of come to me. Out of the blue, I guess? Thin air maybe? Like I'm a magician, right? Well, I'm not a fucking magician. No more than I am a pimp. I am just a guy with too much time on his hands. I spend a lot of that time here. In this room. On that brown leather reclining sofa. We used to have a brown leather reclining chair, but we traded up last year. This one reclines on its own. Well, not on its own. You have to push a button to make it recline or come back up. Still, it takes all of the work away from you. No pushing with your legs or pulling with your hands. I guess that is pretty cool. I do like how I can adjust it to any position I want. But sometimes, when I am pushing the button to recline (or to get up), I feel maybe a little lazy. Was it really that hard to just push the damn thing back myself?

But yeah, I spend a lot of time sitting on that thing. Sometimes all day, if you want to know the truth. Not really doing anything. I feel like watching TV all day is somehow worse than just sitting there doing nothing. Or looking at the internet on my iPad. I do that a lot too. Usually around noon I will fix myself a sandwich. Turkey and cheese for the most part. Sometimes I will change it up to ham and cheese and once a week I make tuna salad. It is usually good. Assuming I don't use too much mayonnaise and get the amount of onion powder correct. A lot of sweet relish and a touch of pepper. Those are the only other ingredients I use. So, there you have it, my personal recipe for tuna salad.[1] Give it a shot. You won't be let down.

Mostly though I just stare at the wall. The big one, covered in the art we have collected from around the world. Five, six, seven, twelve hours a day. Sitting here. Staring at the wall. Nothing ever changes.

MEXICALI, 1998

I wanted to start this story with the words "woo-hoo." I realized as soon as I began to tell it to you that seemed a bit silly. I was going to set the stage and I would have told you the people were in a club in the border city of Mexicali. It was a Friday night, and everyone was drunk, and they were generally having a good time. There was a band on a stage, and they were fronted by a beautiful girl with dyed-orange hair singing alternative rock songs in Spanish. She was a prime example of the alt-rock girl I lusted after for most of my young adult life. The girl from Lush, the girl from Garbage, the girl singing to thirty-five people in a Mexicali nightclub. If you had that alternative-girl look, you know the one—dyed hair, thick eyeliner, some sort of vintage dress, boots—then I probably had a thing for you. Didn't matter if you fronted one of the biggest bands in the world or were in my English class at Santa Monica City College. That girl's name was Lisa Machado, by the way. Her hair was orange, and she had a tattoo back when that actually meant something. We bonded once over our love of Jack Kerouac, or maybe it was the Beastie

Boys, I cannot remember which. But that was as far as that went. Probably a missed opportunity on my part. But I digress. What I'm getting at here is, it didn't even matter if you just played Friday nights at some club in a border town, if you looked that particular way then I was smitten. This girl looked like that, and there she was, singing a song I did not know, which probably made me love her even more. I watched her intently, but I don't think I ever talked to her. Not once. I think the closest I came was a smile when she walked off stage and went to get a drink. Maybe I stood next to her at the bar a couple times, but that was probably just a happy accident. I was already there, and she came up and stood next to me to get the bartender's attention.

So yeah, she was there, but she's not even the main character here. I am, dammit! This is my god-damned story and I'm not going to be upstaged by some imagined romance from the past.

I was not alone in Mexicali. I never was and that was what made it magic. Adam was there. He was my best friend. The guy who would match me drink for drink. The guy I went to when I needed something. The guy who would follow, or lead, down the night's path of debauchery. Adam was always there. Others would come and go. This one guy James. He was a photographer at the newspaper we worked at. Oh yeah, we were all a bunch of young journalists working at a newspaper in that border town. Did I forget to mention that? Doesn't really matter. This is not a story about journalism.

So Adam was there. And James. He'd driven us down there. I could probably write you an entire chapter about James. He was having an imaginary affair with this girl Natalie. She was there too, because her husband was somewhere else. But she wasn't really into James, so she was off doing her own thing. Back to James though. James was engaged to some girl we had never met who lived in San

Diego, but he insisted that he was carrying on affairs with numerous girls throughout California's Imperial Valley. That's where we all lived. Out in the desert, east of San Diego. Really lovely place. If you don't mind 120-degree days. But the setting is not really important. This is not a story about the desert.

James claimed to have all these girlfriends and he often gave us very graphic descriptions of the things he did with these girls. The descriptions were, in fact, so graphic that they made very little sense. None at all. In fact, they seemed much more like the teenage daydreams of a boy who had only seen naked girls on HBO rather than the actual experiences of a sexually active twentysomething. So James was full of shit. Still, he claimed Natalie was one of the girls in his thrall and that soon he would pick her up from the 7-11 (he was very specific about this) and that the two of them would run away together. He never said where they were going or what was going to happen to the many girls he would leave behind (or to Natalie's husband), but he promised us that soon the two of them were going to ride off into the sunset together. That never happened.

There were a couple of other people there too. There were always a couple other people. Usually my sister was around. She was the person who typically drove me home after a night of prolific drinking. If you end up enjoying this, you have her to thank for it. Or, if you hate it, blame her. I would be dead or in jail if she hadn't been there. One cannot drink and drive that many times and not eventually suffer the consequences. Thanks to her I never had to. What? Drink and drive. Well, maybe on the rare occasion she had something better to do. But that didn't come up that often. There aren't a lot of things to do in the Imperial Valley. Didn't I tell you that already? I suppose the rest of the characters don't matter. Not now. Not twenty years later. They came and went. But Adam was there. That was what mattered.

"Hey, I think Max is in trouble," Adam interrupted my intent staring at the orange-haired singer. Sorry, I forgot about Max. He was one of my favorite people at the time. A pot-head from Weed, California. He was also a photographer at the paper. Somehow he worked for James, which seemed like bullshit because he had more talent. But talent can only get one so far, right?

"Huh," I replied, pulled from my own daydream about girls and loud music and escaping to Paris.

"Look, the bouncers are fucking with him."

I tore my gaze from the singer and followed Adam's finger toward the door where I saw Max pushing one of the club's security people. We hurried over to see what the trouble was and found that Max was very close to punching someone. Adam, who conveniently was very fluent in Spanish, confronted the party in question and after some long exchange that I understood very little of, a full-on fight was averted. Instead we were all shoved out of the bar and into the warm Mexicali night.

"Now what?" Adam asked.

"As long as there are drinks involved, I don't give a shit," I replied.

James, my sister, and Natalie had figured out what happened, and they now joined us outside. "I know," James shouted. "Let's go to Las Juntas!"

Las Juntas was a regular hangout for us in 1998. One of the seediest strip clubs in Mexicali, it featured a magician who would come out to entertain the audience in between dancers. He was called "Joker" but since the "J" is silent in Spanish, his name always sounded like "Yoker" to me. And when he took the stage, performing astounding feats of illusion between two stripper poles, the club's DJ would announce him by saying his name three times. "Yoker, Yoker, Yoker," would bound on stage, intent on entertaining us. I think the only trick he ever performed was sucking the life out of the room.

Still, Las Juntas was our spot. So much so, the doormen of the club knew us, and our stack of money, and always hustled us to a table by the stage. Sometimes going so far as to relocate other customers who might have already been sitting there and bringing out our standard order of a bottle of Bacardi and Coke and plenty of Bohemia beer. Coincidentally, James claimed to be having an affair with one of the dancers at the club, a cute brunette who called herself America. I am not sure how Natalie felt about seeing one of his other conquests, or what America's feelings were about seeing Natalie, for that matter. I always hoped they would fight over him, maybe tumbling onto the stage in the process. Of course that was not ever going to happen—but I think I've already explained all that.

Into Las Juntas we strode, a low-rent, six-person, inter-gender Rat Pack. My black-and-white wing tips reflected the lights from the sign outside the bar as we made our way to our table, seated by our very own waiter who would spend the rest of the night making sure we were all able to get just as drunk as we possibly wanted to be. The girls would come and go, taking more of our money in the process. Sometimes Adam or Max or James would disappear with some of them into a back room. Every once in a while, I would join them.

Everyone laughed when America sat on my head because I had my back to the stage, but James quickly calmed her down by handing her twenty pesos, which I think was probably two bucks? I was never good with the exchange rate. After Las Juntas kicked us out at four a.m. (Can you believe bars in Mexico close? Sadly, they do.), we would head to the best taco shop in the world—Asadero Ocotlán—where we would eat copious amounts of carne asada tacos smothered in their house pico de gallo, which featured chunks of avocado. (Are you looking for something to spice up your pico? Chop up an avocado and put it in there. Trust me. I eat a lot of tacos. I know what I'm talking about.) There we relived the night's highlights and tried to sober up enough to drive back across the border.

And in that time, everything was perfect. We were kings and the entire valley, on both sides of the border, was our vast wonderful playground. Every night was a drunken adventure. Everyone knew us, most of those people loved us, and when we walked into a place people knew shit was going to go down. The heat, the dead-end journalism job, the fact I was living in my parents' spare bedroom because I had no better prospects, none of it mattered. We were young and we were free. I think that's from a Bryan Adams song. Or maybe I am paraphrasing that song by Fun. You know, the one about the sunglasses at the bar? Sorry, I have a tendency to lose myself and it kicks up from time to time. Anyway, go ahead and insert your own cliché if you want. Or your own song lyrics. You could interchange any of them I figure. Just as long as the point is made. I was young and poor and everything was better. Got it? Good. So, whatever you want to do really. Because it doesn't matter. This is not a story about the wonders of youth anyway.

MEMPHIS, 2016

Graceland is a place unlike any other. And the people who visit are a fantastic cross section of not just America, but the world. I had wanted to visit Graceland ever since the Dead Milkmen released the song "Going to Graceland" on their 1987 record *Bucky Fellini*: "Goin' to Graceland, we're going to Hell, we're gonna sing Heartbreak Hotel." The words, for some reason, had stayed with me for three decades, and now here I was. Finally in front of Elvis Presley's mansion. Let's get a few things out of the way first. The house is way smaller than you might think it would be. This is not to say it is small. But it's not that big either. Kevin DuBrow's brother has a house that is probably ten times bigger. Yes, the guy from Quiet Riot. No, his brother is not a famous musician. How do I know this? Because my wife watches *The Real Housewives of Orange County* Those people are all awful. I know. But that dude has a way bigger house than Elvis ever did. Elvis had his own plane though. I don't think Terry DuBrow has one of those. Plus Elvis was Elvis. So he has that going for him too.

The neighborhood around Graceland is not really that

great either. It's not as bad as my mother warned me it was. She called it a "bad part of town." I didn't get that exactly. That said, I found most of Memphis seemed like the bad part of the town I lived in anyway. So this particular part of the city did not stand out all that much. After what was a shorter than expected drive from Little Rock, I arrived at the Graceland visitor's center and parked close to Elvis's fleet of airplanes. You have to cross a bridge over a small creek to get from the parking lot to the visitor's center. The house itself is across a rather large road and you have to take a bus over there. I did not know this at the time, but I do now, and I figured you might be interested. In case you are planning your own trip. As I walked across the footbridge leading from the parking lot, I noticed someone had taken the time to write "Elvis was fat" on the ground in multicolored chalk. I am guessing the staff at Graceland is not amused by this sort of activity. Not only that, but it seemed sort of rude to me. I mean, the guy is buried here, for God's sake. Imagine if someone graffitied your tomb with some negative comment about you.

"Sylvia was a bitch!"

"Rhonda's meatloaf sucked!"

"Hector was an awful friend!"

"Trent was a bad dad!"

You see what I'm talking about? It stings, right? Plus Elvis wasn't really that fat. Certainly not as fat as fifty percent of the people walking around Graceland that day, filling their already ample bellies with fried peanut butter and jelly sandwiches. Yes, you can get those there and they are delicious. I should know. I had two of them.

The wait to get to the house was not a short one. I ate my sandwiches. I browsed the gift shop. I watched some sort of film about Elvis's life. Then I watched it again. Finally my number was called and I was able to board the bus that takes you across the street. I am unsure why they don't just let you walk. I guess because of the aforementioned wide road. As you may have guessed, the bus trip over was a short one and soon I found myself in the jungle room and all of the other downstairs spaces, still decorated in their 1970s glory. I was disappointed I did not get to go upstairs. The Dead Milkmen had always promised me the opportunity to see "the bucket that Elvis Presley kicked" and I did not get that because I did not get to see the bathroom where he died. Such is life I suppose. Full of all kinds of disappointments. Both small and large.

The rest of the day in Memphis was productive. I made it to Sun Studios where Elvis, Johnny Cash, and Jerry Lee Lewis (among others) all got their start. I did not see Carl Perkins's Cadillac, though. I guess it's not there. I did see a piano where the Killer put out a cigar, permanently burning a hole into one of the keys in the process. After leaving Sun I drove up Union Avenue to the park where the great Confederate Nathan Bedford Forrest is buried. I say great in the sense he was important. Not that he was a great guy. He was a hell of a cavalryman though. Don't doubt that. Even racists can be good soldiers.

Eventually I made my way back down Union to the Peabody Hotel, home of the famous ducks, which would be my stop for the evening. I had ribs for dinner at Charlie Vergos' Rendezvous, which is in an alley across the street from the Peabody. The ribs were pretty good, but maybe not as good as the hype they have surrounding them. In fact, I am pretty sure I make way better ribs in my backyard and that is all thanks to my top secret rib rub,[2] which I would tell you all about if I had the time. Not really. I said it was top secret, didn't I? Then quit asking.

I spent the rest of the night drinking on Beale Street and sometime around two a.m. wandered back up the block to pass out. Not being that tired, I decided to take the elevator up to the roof and check out the view of the river from the top of the hotel. As I expected, the place was deserted, save one middle-aged man who was standing on the opposite edge of the building with his back to me as he looked out at the river. I did not take too much notice of him as I walked over to the edge of the roof to get a better view of the bridge that was partly obscured by a rather tall building in between the Peabody and the Father of Waters. As I could not see that well, I climbed up on the ledge to get a better look and soon realized that a strong gust of wind would probably bring a quick end to my trip, and somehow that appealed to me. It's not like I hadn't spent most of my life dealing with suicidal thoughts. Honestly, before they gave me drugs, I thought about it almost every day. And here, on top of this building, those voices that had quieted themselves somewhat over the past decade were making themselves loud and clear. It would be so easy to just fall and be done with all this . . .

Yet I did not jump. I was just emerging from these thoughts of self-harm when, from the corner of my eye, I caught the man making his way toward me. I dreaded the interaction and honestly had a brief fear that I was going to be propositioned, when it occurred to me that there was something familiar about this guy. So I turned to get a better look. He was now hurrying toward me, waving for me to get off of the ledge. As I no longer had any thought of jumping, I did just that and watched as he continued his approach, which slowed noticeably once he was sure I was not planning on leaping to my death.

The man was rather nondescript really. Maybe 5'10", wavy gray hair. A belly had formed over what appeared to have once been a skinny frame. He was wearing an aloha shirt. It was black-and-white. That seemed odd. Although maybe not too odd. I saw plenty of shirts like that in the older man's section at the department stores by my house, so maybe it was nothing. But as he got closer, and his face became more clear, it became apparent to me that I did indeed know who this was, although I was not sure how in the hell he was here.

"Hello, nephew," he said to me when he was close enough to put his outstretched hand on my shoulder. "How have you been?"

AUSTIN, 2016

I wrote a book. Did I mention that? I did. About two hundred pages on a summer romance that didn't work out. It was called *A Season in Hell*. It sold about eight hundred copies. I would say you can look for it in your local Barnes and Noble, but that's not the case. Maybe you could find it at Half Price Books, but I think you'd have to get pretty lucky to pull that off. I am pretty sure the publisher burned most of them. Or maybe they sent them to poor people in Africa. You know, like the t-shirts of the teams that didn't win the Super Bowl. I wonder if there's a village of people in Africa who are familiar with my picture from the back of that book. Wouldn't it be strange if I were to ever take a safari and encounter some of them? Hell, they might even think I was famous and run after me, asking for my autograph. And I imagine I would have no idea what they were doing, this gang of hungry people in Cam Newton jerseys who think I am a celebrity and that the Carolina Panthers are the champions of the world.

But I digress. Yeah, so I wrote a book, somewhere around my twenty-ninth birthday. I finished it a few weeks after

Adam departed our two-year desert party for the beaches of Texas. I suppose his absence gave me the time I needed to complete my writing project. After about a year of shopping it around, I actually found a small press in San Francisco that was willing to publish it, which they did, to the shockingly tepid results I previously mentioned. Now, don't get too upset, because a little book of literary fiction is never supposed to lead to fame and fortune. However, there is a twist in this story. Five years after the release of *A Season in Hell*, I was contacted by some fellow who was looking for my agent. This, of course, was funny. I had no agent. I did for about six months after the book had initially been published, but when it became apparent it was going to be a flop, he figured I had no more use for him and quickly disappeared. Thus, I took the call myself. To make a long-ish story shorter, because really this is not a book about how to make it in the entertainment industry, some Hollywood bigwig had come across my tome and he simply loved it. Not only that, he wanted to purchase the movie rights to the novel which he was going to turn into a big Academy Award-winning spectacular. The amount of money they offered me was a lot more than I was making as a sports editor and, of course, I took it. They could have my book and do whatever they wanted with it. I would take their small fortune and do whatever I wanted with the rest of my life.

"Are you picking up Lucy, or do you want me to go get her?"

Eleven years later we find ourselves here, in Austin, Texas, and face to face with middle age. That person talking to me is my wife. She is the vice president of a tech company downtown. She makes a lot of money, which doesn't really matter that much to me. But it's the truth. She also provides me with health insurance, which is what she tells me every time I ask her what she is bringing to the relationship. I am mostly joking, as she is a good person and a decent wife, with a penchant for expensive handbags. Shit, we have a closet full of them. An entire closet dedicated to handbags. I wonder if those poor kids in Africa need any of them? Maybe to carry my book around in, while wearing their Panthers jerseys down to the river to get a drink of dirty water?

"I guess I will go get her," I replied. "It's not like I'm doing anything else."

Lucy is our only child. Her actual name is Lucinda Colleen, but she goes by Lucy most of the time. A thirteen-year-old girl with blue hair and glasses. By all appearances, she is a good kid, but in the privacy of our three-thousand-square foot home, she shows her true colors. When she is not calling me fat, she refers to her mother as "Turdy" and complains a lot when she can't look at her phone all day. I am not saying she is a monster, because that's not the truth. In fact, she is a pretty normal child who grew up in a world that made everything so cheap she was able to amass two rooms worth of belongings before her tenth year. This despite the fact that once a month we take a garbage bag full of her unwanted possessions to the local Goodwill. It would not surprise me if some of that ended up in Africa too.

I drove my family-sized car up the road for a couple miles to find my daughter standing outside her gymnastics studio, waiting patiently for me to pick her up. "How was your workout?" I asked as she got in the car.

"Fine," she replied. "Teacher says we have no class next week. Where's Mom?"

"Working at home," I said. "What do you want to do now?"

"Hmm," Lucy is not one to make decisions without careful deliberation. "How about getting a smoothie? I really feel like a smoothie."

My child suffers from single-child syndrome in that she is very much like a small adult. Not only in the way she speaks, but also in her choices. I am sure, at her age, I would have

27

asked to go get ice cream and never even considered going to Jamba Juice. I can also assure you that there is no way I would have ordered the superfood green smoothie or the side shot of wheatgrass. But she did.

Okay, so back to the book I wrote. I apologize for this slice of life getting in the way of my story, but that's the way it goes, especially when you have a kid. You can't just sit around doing whatever you want when there is another person relying on you for rides and food and help with their homework. You have to be a responsible parent, you know what I mean? But hell, I guess that doesn't matter. This isn't a book about parenting.

So here comes another, possibly, surprising turn. The book, *A Season in Hell,* was never turned into the movie the studio promised. In fact, nothing ever happened with it at all. The executive who was in love with it got caught up in a sex scandal shortly after my check cleared and was run out of the business less than six months later. I never heard back from anyone else at the studio regarding the book or any sort of movie production and, honestly, I didn't care all that much. I had my money and as far as I was concerned, this meant I had no more problems.

I stuck it out at my job for one more year, confusing everyone I worked with as the trappings of my life became more and more expensive.

"Is that a new car?" was a familiar refrain during my final twelve months of employment.

"What kind of watch is that? Patek Philippe? Never heard of it . . ."

"You're going WHERE on vacation?"

"Wait, you're buying another house?"

"You need to take the afternoon off to meet with your pool builder?"

Yeah, so it went on like that for a year as I tried to be

responsible. Then I decided I was done with it. No longer would I write the sports stories that made the whole world sing. (Okay, shit, I did it again—Barry Manilow, right? And that time it doesn't even make any sense. Stories don't make people sing. Well, maybe a story about a song. Maybe? Probably not. I'm going to try and stop doing that from now on. I promise.)

Now where was I? Oh yes, after a year I gave up my fifteen-year journalism career, sure I would retreat to the friendly confines of my single-family home and find my way in the world. Sure that my great idea, that one thing I desired more than anything else, was just around the corner and, given a little time to think, I would figure it out and go get it.

This is where I have been for the past four and a half years. Still in that same house, the one with the poorly built swimming pool in the back yard. The one with the semi-new cars in the garage. The one with the ever-growing art collection.

My first thought was I would go back to school. I figured I would return to my study of history. The same one that I had pursued when I first went to college. The same one that led me to a career in journalism—because jobs for historians are few and far between. I spent an entire year applying to graduate schools only to find that my more recent professional achievements did not mean as much as the very average grades I had amassed during my academic career some twenty years earlier. This meant no PhD program would have me. Thus, I enrolled in an online master's program, pretty sure that I could work my way through that and then move on to the PhD program of my dreams. (Which was the one at Tulane University in New Orleans, by the way. Just throwing that out there. Look what you missed out on, Tulane! All this could have been yours! But no—you didn't want me so now I am here, talking to these fine folks, which is fantastic. Don't get me wrong. I love you people. It's just that I am pretty sure I could be making a significant contribution to the academic record of the American Civil War had it not been for the shortsightedness of the admissions department at Tulane.)

Self-funded and self-assured, I entered the academic arena, with my focus on the Civil War because, with the exception of baseball, it had been the one thing I loved learning about my entire life, and I succeeded. I had a couple papers published, my grades were great, and after two years I had my master's degree. But I had also come to the conclusion that I did not want to go any further and, honestly, there's not a ton you can do with an online master's degree. So I stopped, choosing to sit here, chauffeur my kid around, and stare at that wall. I mean, the money is there, the bills are paid, no one is going hungry or without anything, really. We still go on our yearly tropical beach vacation. What more could you want from life? Right? How could things get any better? Fuck if I know.

LAS VEGAS,
DECEMBER 31, 2000

I got married while sitting in my car at the drive-through window of a wedding chapel on the Las Vegas Strip. This took place two weeks after I had broken up with my girlfriend, who I had been dating for two years. She was the only real girlfriend I ever had, in the two decades or so that I had been on the market. Okay, you got me; I'm not that old. I just liked the pattern of twos I was dropping on you. I mean, I guess I could have been on the dating scene since I was ten, but that seems unlikely. Although I do remember having a few "girl-friends" in the fifth grade. That mostly meant we gave each other presents at Christmas. I suppose that's not unlike the relationships a lot of adults have with their significant others.

It was not this girlfriend of two years who I was marrying. It was, in fact, a completely different girl. A girl I'd met at work. She had taken Adam's place after he headed east to Texas to become the renowned journalist he is today. Ironically, she had also taken his place on this trip. He and I

31

were supposed to go to Vegas for New Year's, but he backed out on me at the last minute because he had some girlfriend who didn't want him to go. This would soon become a recurring theme in our relationship, but more on that later. So I asked this girl to go, and we ended up in Las Vegas and on a whim decided we would get married. Hell, it's not like we were doing anything else that day.

I can't tell you that I did not know my future wife. Like I said, we had worked together for about a year and had been dating, I guess that's the word for it, for a couple weeks. Honestly, it was more like hooking up and eating Mexican food together. I don't know that we ever had any official "dates" prior to saying "I do." So the fact we decided to get married was probably a shock to anyone who knew either of us. The handful of people who witnessed the event sort of tried to talk us out of it, mostly saying that divorces were much more expensive than the fifty bucks we paid for the drive-through wedding. But we did not waver. Buoyed by alcohol and maybe a few legally obtained pills, we soldiered forth and said the words necessary to seal our union. In the process, I became just the second member of my gang to get married. I will not tell you the name of the first. This is not a book about pioneers.

The rest of that night in Vegas remains a blur to me. I know there was a small gathering at someone's apartment where my new wife called her mother, who promptly told her she better be joking and that she needed to "get her ass home immediately." I did not bother to call my family as I knew they would only be angry. I did call one person and he laughed a lot.

"Wait, YOU got married?"

"Yeah," I replied, repeatedly.

"You? Got married." Even more laughter on the other end of the phone.

"Yes!"

"Oh man, I don't know what to say. Congratulations for sure, but I hope you know what you are doing."

And one more time I said, "I do."

That person I called was Dave. He had been my best friend since I was fifteen years old. Basically half my life at that point. He will figure more into this story at a later point. But for now, this is all you need to know of him.

When we returned to our jobs the Monday following our nuptials, it seemed as if we had shocked the world. I was called into my editor's office after which I was called into the publisher's office. I am not sure that they really cared that much. They just wanted to know what the hell had happened and to hear the story solely for the entertainment value. I eventually told my parents. My mother wept. My father laughed. My uncle Glen told me that "love that blooms quickly is often the best." I don't know if he came up with that himself or if he stole it from someone (or even a greeting card), but I have always remembered it. He was a lot of different things to me. He was also a better storyteller than I am, so I apologize for that. Be assured that I am doing my best though. That's enough about him for now. Much like Dave, my uncle will return. Just be patient.

So yeah, we got married. We remained at our jobs in California for exactly one year before deciding we had had enough and headed east. I wish we had gone west. Just because it sounds cooler. But once you are in California there is not much further west you can go. Yes, we could have gone the hundred miles to the coast and that would have certainly been awesome, but even in the old days, the area of Southern California closest to the beach was too expensive for average people to move to. This meant it was way too expensive for a below-average journalist. Thus we chose to head east, to the Republic of Texas.

We kicked around the state for a little while before finally landing in Austin. It was there that I got my book published. Ironically enough, by that small publishing house in California. It was there that my wife discovered her talent for computers, and it was there that she got in on the ground floor of the start-up where she is now a vice president. It was there that our daughter was born while I did my time in the journalism mines before my windfall made that part of my life obsolete. It was also there where I realized I could no longer write. Well, except the sports stuff. That always came easily enough. But something had changed. The words no longer flowed from my head when I sat in front of my computer. The only talent I ever thought I had was gone and I eventually lost my desire to even try and get it back.

ROSEBURG, OREGON, 1987

"You really should continue with the creative writing," my sophomore-year English teacher said to me one day after class. "You are really good at it."

And so it began. The idea was planted. It would one day spring into a full-fledged tree that would more or less consume my life for a decade. I could write. I couldn't do much else. Growing up I had wanted to play quarterback for the Dallas Cowboys, like my hero Roger Staubach. But my football career never really took off. I played for three years in junior high and high school. But I was so slow that I had no chance of ever being the quarterback, even if I could throw the ball with a fairly tight spiral. Nope, they put me, at the time one of the smallest kids on the field, on the offensive/defensive line. It was there that I spent three years being mercilessly beaten by much larger members of the team. It would not surprise me if I was concussed at least once. Probably more. In fact, I am almost positive I have chronic traumatic encephalopathy, and it is to blame for my lifelong depression. I'm not sure about the general malaise, but the depression is because of the

CTE. I just know it. Don't believe me? Then cut my head open when I die and take a look at my brain. That'll prove me right! As much as I love the game of football, there is a certain barbarism to the entire experience and I was never mean enough, or big enough, to hit back with much fervor. So I just took the beatings and went home.

My fallback plan had been to play left field for the Boston Red Sox. You guessed it, I was no good at baseball either. I spent a couple years trying to get my baseball career going in the Pony Leagues of East Texas. Nothing ever came of that. Rather than stepping into the ball I usually bailed out of the batter's box, which is not the way to become a great hitter. If you don't believe me, just get yourself a copy of Ted Williams's *The Science of Hitting* and skim it. You will learn very quickly that you should step into the ball, not away from it. When you step away you screw up your swing and can't generate any power at all. Sure, Ichiro sometimes steps away from the ball before he hits it, but he is such a master with the bat that he can steer the ball anywhere he wants it to go. Sometimes he slaps it the other way and when he does, he is already running down the baseline towards first. This gives him an advantage over other hitters. He jumps out of the batter's box so quickly that even a routine grounder turns into a possible hit because he is speeding toward the bag. So yes, it can be done, but I was not a good enough baseball player to pull something like that off. In fact, I was terrible and I spent most of the two years of my baseball career sitting on the bench watching.

That was it. Two plans for my life and both of them involved being a professional athlete. Neither of them panned out. So those words from my teacher actually had a profound effect on the direction of my life. My next year of high school, I joined the school's newspaper. Later on I wrote for my college paper and then on to the newspaper in California. But it was not just journalism. No, the entire time I was also writing other things. Stories, poems, novels, journals, whatever. There were words in my head that needed to get out and so, every day, I devoted at least a little time to giving them a new home, either handwritten in an old notebook or typed on my parents' typewriter. These words were different than the ones I got paid for, because they were just for me. Or for whomever I decided to share them with. I am not going to sit here and tell you they were all good. Shit, I won't even tell you that any of them were good. At least a few hundred pages of them ended up being good enough to get published. But you already know that. And those words were good enough to make me richer than I ever thought I would be. But were they actually good? Fuck if I know. They were mine. That it is all I am claiming. And I was proud of them.

When they stopped, sometime in the summer of 2004, it was not initially alarming. There had been times where I could not write; days, even weeks, but never more than a month. So, after a month passed, I started to wonder what was going on. I would spend hours sitting in front of my computer, waiting to unburden myself, but the words would not come. Not after a month. Not after two. Not after six. Not after an entire year. Somewhere around the eighteen-month mark I pretty much gave up. By then we were expecting our little bundle of joy and my journalism career was going pretty well. A few years later I got that check and never looked back. I hate to say it, but the words never came back. I wish I could tell you where they went, what became of them, but I cannot. Perhaps I only had so many in me and once I got them all down on paper, that was it. I suppose that is a possibility. What I can tell you is that once they were gone, I missed them. I tried to fill the void with more alcohol and a whole lot of Xanax, but those were only temporary fixes. Nothing could replace them. Not the drugs or booze or the child or the money. Nothing.

AUSTIN, 2016

"What are you doing?"

"I don't know," I replied. "Watching TV, I guess. Mostly just messing around on Facebook. *House Hunters* is on. They're in Paris. God, I wished I lived in Paris."

"You should go," my wife told me, although I knew she wasn't really serious. "Just move. It's not like you're doing anything here."

"If I leave, who will pick Lucy up from school?"

"That's true," she replied matter-of-factly. Probably because she was never serious in the first place. I was pretty sure the woman I married, sitting on the couch and staring at her computer, never really heard much of what I said anyway. When I told her I spent the entire day staring at the wall, she heard the words enough to realize I had stopped talking so she could utter a "huh" before continuing with whatever it was she was doing after coming home from her job. I am not saying to you she didn't care. Because I am sure deep down, she did. She just either didn't know how to deal with it or was too wrapped up in her own life to pay me much attention. And, honestly, that was fine with me. I had been an independent entity when we had found our way to each other, and I had remained a fiercely solitary figure throughout our marriage. She had done the same and it was probably why we stayed together. We could exist as two separate beings, co-existing, but not reliant on the other for much more than companion-ship. In many ways it was my ideal relationship. I did not want to be coiled together by too much intimacy, impossible to untangle except under extreme duress. The fact of the matter is, I probably could have gone off to Paris and she would not have been that upset, assuming I continued to pay my share of the bills.

But I chose to stay. The responsibility of being a parent had consumed me, almost to the point of self-destruction, since the day I first heard my wife say she was pregnant with our lone child. Long before the kid was ever born, I would suffer periods of extreme anxiety, where my heart would race and I would struggle to breathe. I thought I was dying for the first three years of Lucy's life as these episodes became more and more frequent. Finally, I went to see a doctor who, after running all kinds of tests, told me I suffered from severe anxiety and wrote me a prescription for Xanax. I found it curious that he never referred me to someone else, like, say, a psychiatrist, to try and work on my issues. It was almost like the pills would solve all my problems. And I guess they did. At least on a superficial level. When I took them, I felt pretty good. When I took them with a couple glasses of bourbon, I felt even better. So that's what I did. For ten years, I medicated myself and when I didn't, I was fairly sure I was about to drop dead. The responsibility I felt as a parent is nothing I can ever explain to a sane person. Years of perceived neglect from my own parents had convinced me that I must give myself completely to my child, in ways they never even dreamed of doing, and so that is what I did. But it was that same feeling that wrecked me in ways I never could have imagined.

This routine played out on a daily basis with very little interruption. I suppose it only became worse once I quit my job. No longer focused on anything other than my kid and the novel I felt I should be writing, I became almost homebound, leaving only to pick Lucy up from school and chauffeur her to her various after-school activities. Most of my time was spent sitting on that aforementioned couch, watching *The Price is Right* and *Let's Make A Deal,* before I would move over to the desk where I would stare at the computer for four or five hours a day. I was simply passing the time, waiting to interact with the only two other humans who remained in my life. The days of yore were long gone. Dave had departed for distant lands and a wife who seemed uninterested in returning to the states. Adam was married too, restrained by the social mores that insist a person should not spend all their time partying with their friends when they have a spouse waiting for them at home. Of course, I too was married. Plus I had a child. Yet I felt as alone as I did the night Claire sent me on my way. Every day, it was just me, my record collection, and that wall. Yes, Drew Carey and Wayne Brady came by too, but they were just distractions. Brief interludes with an outside world I had abandoned, choosing instead the unfriendly confines of my living room and a self-imposed exile that became harder to deal with each passing day.

MEMPHIS, 2016

The thing about my uncle Glen was he was dead. At least he was supposed to be. He left this world for the next one about thirteen years earlier, the victim of some sort of cancer that had robbed the world of one of its most interesting people and me of my biggest supporter. I know this for a fact because I was there, sitting in the hospital room with my father, who kept a dutiful death watch over his favorite sibling, as the bright Hawaiian sun shone onto the golf course outside the hospital window. I was never sure if he knew I was present or not. I had hurried to Hawaii from Texas, hoping to beat his rapidly expiring clock, and I was successful, sort of, I guess. I found my uncle, once so full of life, hooked up to machines that kept him alive and not looking much like the man I remembered. For a minute he made eye contact with me, and I think he knew I was there as I squeezed his hand. That was on the first day I arrived. After that, he mostly seemed to be unconscious and any rally in his health I had been hoping for never came. He lingered this way for a few more days before finally dying as I slept in some hotel room in Waikiki.

While I did not see the actual end, I did go back to the hospital and saw his empty bed. And my father had been there, and he confirmed the news. I was there when he picked up the ashes too. And at the small memorial gathering in Glen's bookstore, where my father wept and my mother exhorted me to take his place in front of these strangers, speaking about him. I did not. I am no professional speaker, nor am I one to stand in front of people and cry. So I stayed in my chair and waited for it all to mercifully end, which it eventually did. And when it was done, I returned to Texas and my life, which I believe you know plenty about at this point. And every day I thought about my uncle, and I wished he was there. And sometimes I would write him at his old email address, almost always thinking he would actually reply, right up until they started being returned with delivery failure notices. That took a year or two, I think, for someone to turn it off. But it did eventually happen. Still, every time I drank a beer I poured some of it out for him. Because he was gone, but damn sure not forgotten. (That is part of Geto Boys song. Just FYI. I stole it and repackaged it for my own purposes. Props to the G.B. The greatest rap group of all time.) And I wished I could talk to him just one more time. Eventually I made my peace with the fact this would never happen, right up until I was standing on that rooftop in Memphis. Right up until he was standing in front of me, asking me how I'd been.

"Pretty shitty," I answered as if it was not strange at all that I was speaking to a . . . hell, I was not really sure what I was speaking to. Was he a ghost? A hallucination? Had I finally lost my mind? (And with no one to commit me!) I suppose if this was the great nervous breakdown I had yearned for most of my adult life, someone would eventually figure out I had a wife and contact her. She could sign the papers, I guess. Or maybe I'd actually jumped off that roof? Was I dead? No, that made no sense. I was almost positive I hadn't jumped, and I certainly did not feel dead.

Glen moved closer and soon was next to me with his arm around my shoulder. We were on the rooftop of the Peabody Hotel staring out at the Mississippi River and the bridge that spanned it. The ducks were behind us, but they were quiet. It was very late at night, or early in the morning, and we were the only two people up here. Or, I was the only person up here. Me and my imaginary uncle. "What's wrong?" he finally asked me. "And why are you in Memphis?"

"Shit." I turned my gaze to look him in the eye. He did not look much older than when Dave and I had visited him in Hawaii years earlier. I definitely looked older. I wonder if he noticed. Could he notice? Do imaginary uncles notice things like that?

"I don't really want to talk about it. It's the same stuff I've been talking to you about forever, I think. Just with a different cast of characters and locations. But the problems are all basically the same. At their most basic level. They have not changed since we were in that Korean bar in Honolulu. I am not sure they will ever change."

"You seem rather tense," Glen said. "Do you want to go have a drink?"

"I think the bars are all closed."

"What about your room? Does it have a minibar?"

"I don't think so. Maybe. Shit, I don't fucking know. How the hell are you here?"

My uncle laughed at my question. It was the same laugh he used to have when he would tell a funny story or when we would watch the Muppets together during one of his infrequent visits during my childhood. He liked Fozzy Bear. And sometimes he would "wakka wakka wakka," which was maybe strange in retrospect. But it delighted me when I was a child. "We'll get to that later," he told me as he gently turned me from facing the river, back toward the door that led to the

43

elevators, which would take one from this roof back their room. "I have a minibar in my suite. We can go there, and I will make you a gin and tonic. Do you still like those?"

Not really, I thought. But I was not going to turn down the chance to have another drink with him. So I followed him from the roof, into the elevator, and back to his room. He opened the door and led me inside. There were no lights on at first, save the blue lighting that came from under the beds at the Peabody. I could immediately tell his room was much larger than mine. For some reason I wondered how it was he had a room. How was he paying for it? Do dead people have credit cards? When he flipped the light switch it became apparent just how much bigger his room was. We were standing in a large living room of what was obviously a suite because there was no bed to be found. There was a bar to my left and a seating area in front of it. To the right sat a table with chairs for a lot of people. (I wasn't counting, okay? If you need an actual seating count for this room, then please contact the Peabody Hotel. I am sure they can tell you.) Glen walked over toward the bar and pulled two highball glasses from the shelf. "Gin and tonic, yeah?"

"Sure." I looked around for a place to collapse and eventually chose the most comfortable looking of the armchairs.

"You want lime in it?"

"You have fresh limes in your room?"

He laughed. "One of the benefits of the VIP suite I guess," he said as he handed me the glass filled with his favorite beverage.

"So, what's wrong with you, nephew? I was worried you were going to throw yourself off that roof. Which would have been a waste."

"What are you talking about?" At once I felt like a child talking to an authority figure and also like an adult being questioned about actions he did not want to discuss. I had the urge to explain and defend myself and also to tell him to go fuck himself. It was a strange feeling, almost as if a portion of my conscious mind had been jettisoned back into the past while the other part of it stayed in the present—and they were both trying to make sense of my uncle's question and trying to combine forces to give him an answer.

"I think you know. Tell me what's wrong."

"You tell me how the fuck you are here?" I finally had worked up the nerve to say it, so I did. "You are dead!"

"Am I?" he asked. "Could a dead man make you a drink? Or rent a hotel room? Or ask you how you've been? Or punch you in the arm?" With that he hit me. I imagine if I had been speaking to the ghost of my father or grandfather, they would have slugged me in the face, but my uncle just popped me on the arm. It stung, but it did not hurt and would not leave any lasting damage. I do like the idea though, of him just belting me squarely on the jaw and knocking me out. Think about that. Then I could wake up on the floor and he could be gone, and I would have thought it was all just some strange dream. Except for the bruise and swelling in my jaw. That would have made it all the more confusing. But I digress. This was not a dream. He was here. I was talking to him and for a second, he made my bicep hurt. Then it stopped and he kept talking. "How do you like Memphis? Have you ever been here before?"

"So you're not going to answer my question?"

"Which one?" He asked as he moved to sit down in the chair across from me.

"The one about how I am sitting here having a drink and a conversation with a dead person."

"Oh, what does that matter?" He put his glass down on the table to his right and kicked his feet up onto the coffee table in front of him. "I'm here. You're here. Let's talk."

"About what?" I was growing sort of agitated by his non-answers to my biggest questions. "Perhaps the mysteries of the afterlife?"

He laughed and a little of his drink came out of his mouth in the process. "No. Save that for another time. For now, we talk about you. Whatever you want. How is the writing going?"

"Shouldn't you know? Don't the dead know everything?" He had yet to admit to me that he was a ghost, and I was determined to get him to open up about something related to the fact I was having a supernatural experience.

"Do you remember the time you came to Honolulu, and we were discussing dead people and what they knew or didn't know? Do you remember how you said you were worried that my mother, your grandmother, would be able to see what you were doing and she would not be happy? Do you remember that?"

I did. So I nodded in the affirmative.

"Do you remember what I told you?"

"Something about a greater understanding when people are dead? Something about them not judging. Something like that. Hell, I was drunk almost the entire time I was in Hawaii. There's lots of that I don't remember."

Again he laughed. "Is that what I said? Hmm, maybe it was." He scratched his head as if that was going to jog his memory. "It's funny. I clearly remember the conversation, but I cannot recall exactly what we said . . ." His gaze drifted off for a second. "Let's just put it like this, I don't know any more about your life right now than I did the last time I saw you. So tell me about what is going on. Tell me about why you are in Memphis."

For the rest of the evening, I spun the tale of my life for him. The same one that I have already told to you. He seemed plenty interested in it, but he is my relative and has known me since the day I was born. I understand if you are not feeling the same way. I mean, really, how long have we even known each other? I cannot expect someone I just met to be as invested as a man who has known me since the day I was born. Yes, it is easy for you to sit there and tell me you care about what becomes of the people in my story, and, in some way, I suppose that is the case. When I was twenty years old I wanted everything to work out for Sal Paradise and to a lesser extent Dean Moriarty, so maybe that's how you feel now. But if things don't work out, will it profoundly change your life? Maybe? Eh . . . it doesn't matter. Glen was interested in my story. And it is why he sat silently and listened to the entire gloomy tale for close to three hours, making and consuming gin and tonics the entire time, until I had finally finished.

When I was done talking I stared at him for a minute, thinking he was, somehow, going to make sense out of it all. Instead, he set his glass down again, looked at me, smiled, and said, "Let's get some sleep."

ROSEBURG, 1995

Dave was the first one to leave. He even left our hometown before I did. Gone away on a college basketball scholarship that ended the summer after our senior year of high school prematurely. Dave left and then my other friends left and, eventually, I left too. We were supposed to be together forever, but those boyhood dreams died fairly quickly. And it was alright, I told myself. We still saw each other pretty often. Sometimes meeting back in Roseburg to get drunk on the third floor of the high school commons building. It was the biggest building in the quad at Roseburg High School. We would climb to the top floor of the massive concrete structure and sit down in front of the door to the room where I took French when I was in high school. With a good view of Mount Nebo, we would drink wine straight from the bottle and then shoot bottle rockets into the starry night, behaving much the way we had when we were teenagers and we both still lived in the small lumber-mill town where we'd grown up.

"I'm going to Japan," Dave said to me on this, the last of those nights. The encore of our teenage years had dragged on longer than most, but in this moment the band was really leaving the stage. And they weren't coming back. No matter how hard you cheered.

"Why?" I questioned, not quite sure I even understood what he'd said.

"I got a job teaching English," he answered. "It's a good opportunity for me to travel. I figure I can stay there for a couple years and explore all of Asia. You should come visit after I get settled. I think it is going to be pretty cool."

I was in shock. In one fell swoop, he was not just leaving, but leaving for at least two years? I did not know what to say to him, so I said nothing, satisfying myself with another gulp of the now-bitter wine from our shared bottle.

"I'd thought about going to grad school," he continued. "But I think I am done with all that. School, I mean. I just don't want to go anymore. You know what I mean?"

"Uh-huh," was all I could get out.

"I found this ad for the teaching job at my mom's work. I thought it looked cool, so I applied and they hired me. The pay is alright. Nothing great, but they help you with a place to live too. Like I said, I think it is going to be cool."

"That's great." I was finally able to string together a couple words to offer my support. It was not that I was against the idea of him going. But maybe I was against the idea of him going alone. What about me? What was I supposed to do? Who was I going to drink with on the third floor of the commons building during my visits to Roseburg? Shit, why would I ever come back here again . . .

Eventually we finished that bottle of wine and the other one we'd purchased at Fred Meyer and descended the stairs of the building before taking the quick, silent walk back to Dave's parents' house. It was indeed the last time I ever drank on top of that particular building, which was probably good, because I am sure it was illegal. It was not the last time I saw Dave. No, he was still around. But our frequent visits changed to yearly visits and then to every two years, until they finally became so infrequent that when we did see each other we were unsure of just how long it had been. His two-year stay in Japan turned into the aforementioned lifetime commitment once he got married. Eventually, when I had enough money, I made my way to visit him in Tokyo and it was everything he said it was. But I was not convinced it was better than drinking on top of the commons building. Even if there were more pretty lights.

DALLAS, 2016

As for Adam, well, there had been a time when we were inseparable. After he moved to Texas, I got married, and then headed back to the state of my birth—both for a job, and to be at least in his proximity. We eventually both ended up living in Austin and for a brief period, everything was as it had been. There were late nights of drinking and revelry, poker and me watching him chase girls. For close to a year, everything seemed perfect. Then the woman who would become his wife came along and soon he was gone to Mexico City for work. Shortly after, I became a father and, in the process, one of the great friendships of all time basically died.

Okay, not really. Sometimes, when I find myself listening to a little too much Father John Misty, I can get a little melancholy. It is true, we still saw each other. But only once or twice a year, despite the fact we ostensibly still lived in the same city. I can give you no specific explanation for why. It's just what happened. Things did not get any easier once Lucy was born, and after a while our twice-yearly meetings turned into a once-a-year trip to see a concert or a baseball game where, for a brief evening, we would try and recapture some part of the glory of those heady days in Mexicali. Our friendship was not dead, but it was not in full bloom either. Maybe it was just hibernating. Waiting for that chance to escape from a forced slumber and roar to life once more. And be sure, that did happen from time to time. The binge drinking would always help with my anxiety, and for an evening I would feel the way I had fifteen years earlier, responsibility-free and completely indestructible. But, when the morning came, and with it the sickness that had never occurred in my younger days, reality would set back in, and in a few hours Adam would be gone and I would find myself back where I had started.

Dallas seemed primed to be one of those trips. We had driven the two hundred miles north to see a mash-up of two of our favorite bands, and the concert had more than lived up to my expectations. I could find escape in music, much the way I found it in liquor. When I was at a concert, and the band was playing songs I loved, at volumes that were surely not good for my old ears, I could imagine I was a teenager again, raging to The Clash or Public Enemy in my bedroom at my parents' house on Corona Loop Road; and for those few hours, I felt the kind of happiness I did not otherwise know. This show had been like that. Almost three hours of loud guitars and politically charged lyrics to distract me from all of my troubles, both real and imagined.

Wait, what? Who was the band? I think you should be able to figure that out on your own, don't you? I mean, the hints are there! But no, I'm not going to tell you. So just guess, or forget about it. Because this is one name I am not dropping. After all, this exercise is a confession. Not a concert review.

Anyway, yeah, the concert was great and after a few drinks I was feeling good. "What do you want to do now?" Adam asked as we sat outside the auditorium, waiting for our Uber to show up.

"I think you know what I want to do," I answered.

He laughed in reply. "Yeah, I guess we have to."

When the driver eventually found us and asked us where we wanted to go, there was only one answer we could give. If we were in Dallas, we were going to The Men's Club.

*****

I suppose a history lesson is now in order. Many years earlier, when I was still a strapping young man (as opposed to the fat, old man I have become) Adam and I had met up in Dallas for a weekend of Boston Red Sox baseball and the kind of debauchery we had first cultivated on those Mexicali streets. This meant way too much alcohol and lots of naked women. As coincidence would have it, The Men's Club of Dallas was just around the corner from our cheap hotel. This was the only reason we ever went there. I mean, honestly, neither of us knew anything about the nightclub scene in Dallas. The Men's Club was closest, so that's where we went and that is the only reason it became such a key piece of our shared mythology.

That summer I met him in Dallas was a strange point in my life. I had no idea that I was just months away from marrying a person who I literally had met just days before flying from Los Angeles to Dallas. I was also on a timeout in my relationship with Claire Grace Taylor. She had left for the summer to study Spanish in Mexico. Somewhere during her absence, I hooked up with a leggy blonde from the University of Texas who just so happened to make her way into my favorite watering hole in El Centro. Our affair flamed out in about two weeks, but it happened, which told me I needed to officially end any relationship I may have had remaining with Claire. So that's what I did. Via email.

I know. In retrospect, this was a dick move. You may be

saying to yourself, at least it wasn't via text. Well, that's because you couldn't really text back then. Remember those early days of the cell phone? When there was no such thing as texting? Yes, it was that long ago. So I used the only medium available to me, to attempt a cowardly exit from what had been a year-long relationship at that point. The result was a very long collect call from Mexico that ended with us not broken up, although not really back together either, and with me having to pay a $250 phone bill. (Apparently, international calling is/was quite expensive.)

Further complicating matters was the fact that Claire returned from Mexico the day before I was to fly off to rendezvous with Adam. I met her at her friend's house, and we drove to Anaheim to watch the Red Sox play the Angels and see where our relationship stood. Eventually we ended up in bed together, despite me telling the man at the front desk of our hotel that we wanted two beds. This led to her spending the next day with me and even dropping me off at the airport. I was still hesitant to say we were back together, although that seemed to be the case. She very much wanted that to be the case but agreed to further discuss it when I returned from my trip to Texas.

It was with all this craziness swirling about in my life that I strode into The Men's Club that warm August evening. I walked in at the height of my powers, twenty-nine years old, the best-looking I would ever be. I had slept with three different women in the past year and my pockets were full of cash because I was making a decent salary at my newspaper job and paying no rent to my parents for living in their back room. I was a few months away from making a decision that would change and shape the rest of my life, but I had no idea about that. In that moment I was a king. I was a super-man. I was everything I ever aspired to be. And The Men's Club of Dallas was hosting my victory party.

Despite my drunkenness, our time at the club that night remains like crystal clear photographs in my memory. It all started with the standard stuff. Drinking. Dollars to the girls on stage. Trying to get the girls who wanted more of our money to leave us alone.

"I have a great idea," Adam announced at one point.

"What's that?"

"We should travel the country and compile a guide to the various strip clubs," he said. "Think about it, it could be a guide to debauchery."

"A bible of sin!" I answered, before raising my glass to toast his idea. (Honestly, I still think the idea holds up. As I am now an old man with a kid, I do not think I have the ability to do it justice any longer, so you can have that one for free. Take it and run with it, friend. Just do me the favor of a thank you at some point when you get it published and make your million dollars.)

Eventually the evening took a turn, and Adam and I ended up in a back room with two girls, one of whom was from Iran. She had the biggest breasts I had ever seen and claimed her name was Tiffany, although after a few drinks she admitted her name was actually something Iranian, but I no longer recall exactly what that was. The drinks and the money flowed in that back room and soon the girls were on top of us. Every fantasy I had ever had regarding sex, drugs, and the life I imagined myself leading pretty much came true in the back room of The Men's Club that night. Surprisingly I left with most of my money and Tiffany's phone number. It was a memento I kept up until the day after I got married.

*****

In the years that passed in between that night and this one, The Men's Club had become our go-to spot any time we found ourselves together in Dallas. I am sure you know it was never the same, but who would have expected it to be? This night was different though. Despite the fact the club was almost empty, things seemed to be more primed for retro-style fun and, in some ways, that is what happened. No, we did not end up in any back room with girls on top of us. But the booze did flow and the girls did give us all the attention we desired and that connection to my long-gone glory days was reestablished long enough for me to finally see clearly, if only for a second.

In that moment I found myself. I mean the real me. The guy who wanted to write a novel and drink himself to death before he turned thirty. Not the suburban dad who suffered from terrible anxiety because he feared he would not be able to protect his child from turning out like him. The live fast, die young, leave a pickled, bloated corpse guy who spent his best years drinking himself into oblivion on a nightly basis. That guy knew exactly what to do. To the surprise of everyone around, but mostly to Adam and the dancer sitting on my lap, I maneuvered myself from underneath her and began to get out of the chair. Rising to my feet as "Smooth Up in Ya" by The Bulletboys played in the background, I exclaimed, "I've got to get out of here," before falling back into that aforementioned chair.

"You want to leave?" Adam asked me, his eyes inferring that I was crazy.

"No," I said as I pulled the girl back into my lap, becoming one with the moment and the music. "Not yet."

AUSTIN, 2016

I returned home the next day in time to pick my child up from school. I guess I got there a little earlier than that. Early enough to post a picture of my front door on Facebook along with a line from an Alkaline Trio song. "Tonight never ends if we never go inside," it said. The feelings were true. I'd spent twenty-four hours in an homage to my past and I wanted more of it. Sadly, those anxious feelings of responsibility drew me back through the door. But I had a plan now. One that involved me escaping all of this, if only for a minute, to find myself again. To gain a clearer understanding of who I was and just what I was doing with whatever time I had left. I would hit the open road and leave all of the anxiety behind me. Maybe I would finally finish that stupid novel I'd been writing for four years. Maybe I would free myself from what was worryingly becoming an addiction to Xanax. Maybe I would find the fitter, happier, more productive version of myself I had lost somewhere along the way. But first I had to pick my kid up and make dinner.

I met Lucy at the spot where I met her every day. She came

walking down the street talking to her friends. Honestly, she appeared to be unaware of whether or not I was even there. I figured I could probably just drive off and she wouldn't notice until she got to the place where she typically got in the car. But I waited. One last time.

"Hi, Dad," she said as she climbed into the passenger seat. "You wouldn't believe what we were talking about. Cunningham was telling us about his friend Dario, who is from Argentina. Dario told him that murder is legal in Argentina."

"What?" I have to admit—even in my current state. I was a bit surprised by what my kid was telling me.

"You know, if you don't like a person, you can kill them," she calmly replied. "He says that Dario killed his sister because he didn't like her. And he didn't even get in trouble!"

"I don't think that's right, Lucy."

"No," she firmly stated. "That's what he told Cunningham. I sure am glad I don't have a sibling!"

The day was bright as we drove back to our two-thousand-square foot house in that family-friendly suburb just north of Austin. The sun shone brightly on the trees which were in full bloom. Spring turning into summer. The perfect time for a change.

After helping Lucy finish her homework and sending her off to play at her friend's house, I began preparing dinner. And packing a suitcase. I would leave as soon as we were done eating. One final step in my decade-long caregiver act. I knew the two of them would be alright without me. I was not planning on leaving forever anyway. Just long enough to figure things out. Just long enough to find whatever it was I had lost.

"How was your trip?" my wife asked as she came in from the garage. I knew she was home because I'd heard the garage door open and the rather large engine of her vehicle rattle the walls as she pulled in.

"It was fine," I answered as I began to plate the food. "Dinner's almost ready. I have something I want to tell you guys when we are done eating."

"Okay," she said as she shuffled through her stack of mail.

We had breakfast tacos for dinner that night. Eggs and bacon and potatoes topped with cheese in a warm flour tortilla. I ate three of them. I usually just went with two, but I was unsure when I would eat again. Neither Lucy nor my wife had any clue that I had put the packed suitcase into the responsible family car I drove. (It was a Volvo V60 in case you are wondering. Safest car on the road!) And neither of them had any clue about what was about to come out of my mouth.

"So I've been thinking about leaving," I said, once *Wheel of Fortune* cut to a commercial break.

"Good," my wife said. "You should go."

Lucy chimed in, "You should! You've been talking about it all the time. Go! Just make sure you come back!"

"No, really," I could tell they were not taking me seriously.

"Really," my wife said again, not even turning her gaze from the television set.

"Yeah, Dad. Just go!"

I still do not know if they believed what I was saying, but at that point it did not matter. I stood up, picked up my plate, and carried it to the sink, where I rinsed off the salsa I had spilled when I was trying to pour it onto my tacos earlier. I set the plate on the left side of the sink so my wife would know it was ready for the dishwasher and then I walked across the room where I picked up my keys, wallet, and sunglasses. I grabbed my cell phone as well, despite a momentary internal debate about whether or not to bring it. There was a lot of responsibility attached to that device and that was what I was trying to leave behind. But I figured there might come a point where I needed it. Even if it was just for the GPS. With my belongings in hand, I turned and walked toward the garage.

Pat Sajak's voice was the last thing I heard as I opened and shut the door from the house to the garage and I got in my car. Neither Lucy nor my wife said a thing. Perhaps they thought I was kidding. As I said, I still do not know.

I breathed in that Swedish new car smell as I entered the vehicle and pushed the button for it to start. I had to wait for the garage door to open so I could back out and I expected that at some point my wife would come out and ask me what I was doing, but she did not. So, I shifted the car into reverse and began to slowly back down our long driveway. As I reached the end of the concrete path she finally appeared. The door leading inside the house opened and she looked out at me. She did not look angry. I think maybe she looked sad, but I could very well be projecting how I thought she should feel onto her. I raised a hand to wave goodbye to her. She did not return my wave; instead, she reached up and pushed the button, shutting the garage door in the process.

I-35 NORTH, 2016

You have to work at the hard stuff. Like writing. It doesn't just come out of nowhere while you're staring at the wall. Well, not every time anyway. *A Season in Hell* probably came too easy. It made me money too easily. There is no disputing that. Maybe that's why I never could finish that second book. God knows I tried. I would sit down and stare at the computer. You know, when I wasn't looking at the wall. Sometimes I would stare at it for hours on end. Right up until I had to go pick Lucy up from school. Just me, staring at the computer, accompanied by the music spinning on the turntable behind me. Sometimes I did that for five hours a day. No words would come. Just music and the light from the computer screen. Should have just been staring at the wall. It would have been easier on my eyes. Writing was hard, which is why I never finished. So was raising my kid and being the subdued suburban asshole I never aspired to be. But leaving was easy. A lot easier than I expected.

I pushed the Volvo station wagon north up that stretch of hell known as I-35. If you think I am exaggerating, then you have never driven on that road from Austin to Dallas. Waco is in the middle. Did you know that? Have you been to Waco? Waco might as well be the capital of hell. Shit, even if it wasn't on I-35 it could be the capital of hell. Yes, they have a nice zoo, and they recently got an In-N-Out, but that's about it. And please don't get me started on those fuckers from HGTV and their perfect marriage. I could probably write an entire five hundred word essay on how much I hate those fucks and how HGTV pushing their supposedly happy relationship in the faces of all of us at home is doing far more harm than good to the American family. Don't believe me? Well . . . here.[3]

I had chosen to listen to "Baba O'Riley" as I fled north on my own runaway scrape. Repeatedly. Everything around me was indeed a teenage wasteland and I was escaping into the fields. Just to find out what I was missing.

I pitched the remaining Xanax I had out the window of the car somewhere around Hillsboro. I wasn't going to need those anymore. I was hopeful someone would find them and put them to better use than I had. Eventually, I reached Waxa-hachie and then DeSoto. Into the bedroom communities of Dallas I drove, past the miles upon miles of strip malls, concrete and oak trees and Whataburgers, until I started to see exits for roads I recognized.

Four hours after leaving my house, Dallas came into view. (Just FYI, that's only a two hundred-mile drive. I told you that road was awful!) The Reunion Tower, and all the other buildings my family used to drive past on our way to church, appeared on those northern plains, rising like mountains you would never find driving in this direction. Not for thousands of miles anyway.

I lived in Dallas when I was a kid. Well, Garland anyway. I like to joke that I am somehow harder because I lived in Garland. But that's bullshit. I've never carjacked anyone. Unless you count me taking the family car right now. But I

WAITING 'ROUND TO DIE

don't think that counts. The title is in both of our names. I think the fact my name is on there somehow makes this different from stealing. Plus I had the keys. And no gun was involved.

I made a hard right on I-30, right before the car collided with downtown Dallas. Interstate 30 took me past the aforementioned Garland and eventually out of the urban sprawl that is greater DFW. Driving past the exit for Kingston, which is the home of Audie Murphy (did you know he was the most decorated soldier in World War II? Well, he was. Now thank me for the brief history lesson and we'll move on.) I eventually reached Texarkana and then crossed over into Arkansas. I would like to tell you I knew where I was going, but that's not really the case. I eventually ended up in Little Rock around two in the morning. I took a room at the Doubletree Inn downtown and was so tired I did not wake up until five the following evening. That night I ate dinner in the restaurant at the Capitol Hotel, which was conveniently located across the street from the Doubletree. I later learned my great-grandfather had been the proprietor of a restaurant in that very building. I also later discovered he was buried in a cemetery not far from my hotel. I wish I had known this at the time so I could have said hello. I am a sucker for dead relatives.

HONOLULU, 1994

"I don't ever want to leave!"

"Cheers to that," Dave said as he clinked the glass holding his gin and tonic into mine. On the other side of the table sat my uncle, looking eerily like my father, a twentysomething Korean girl clinging tightly to his shoulder. He was staring intently at me.

"Shit, nephew." He raised his glass and the three of us sloppily banged all of our drink containers together. "Drinking with you is like drinking with my brother. Except you are not as uptight."

"You drank with my dad?" I asked.

My uncle laughed. "Not really. I always wanted to. I imagine this is what it would have been like."

"I was going to say . . ." My thoughts and words drifted off briefly. "I would have liked to have seen that."

The three of us laughed. Loudly. All the men at the table knew my father and we all knew he was not the type to go out drinking. The three Korean women around us did not know my father, but they laughed just the same. I suppose that is

64

what they figured they were supposed to do. We were in a bar, somewhere in Honolulu, Hawaii, that my uncle apparently frequented with some regularity. It was mostly red, with a long bar spanning one side of the building. In the back were smaller rooms where you could sing karaoke in private. In the front was a stage where you could sing karaoke for everyone. The lights were dim, as they are in most bars, and this combination of dim gold lights and red furniture made everything seem sort of orange. The six of us were packed fairly tightly into a booth, but no one really seemed to mind. I think that contact was sort of the point of the bar in the first place. The girl sitting with my uncle knew him by name and asked where he'd been when we had first come in. Her friends, who were sitting on Dave's and my laps, did not seem to know him as well but were still cognizant of who he was. He was, after all, famous in Hawaii.

I am not sure where to start when I tell you about my uncle. He has a Wikipedia page. One maintained by people other than him. I guess that's a good place to start. So yeah, he is kind of a big deal. His name is Glen. He is a renowned author and storyteller in Hawaii. And by successful, I don't mean successful like me. I mean people actually read his books. When he goes out in public people know who he is. Honestly, I have never had more success picking up women in bars than I did during that trip to Hawaii, and it was all because of this unassuming-looking man who happened to be approaching middle age. It's funny because at the time he was not much older than I am now, but he had no trouble attracting young co-eds who just wanted to hear him tell them one of his ghost stories. I, on the other hand, at this similar age would not be able to attract a coke whore if I were covered in cocaine. Okay, so maybe that's an exaggeration, but you get the point.

Glen had invited me out the year before, during a visit to our family home in Los Angeles. He was leading a tour group of Japanese students through the United States and his first stop had been to the house he'd grown up in, where he and the kids had camped out for about a week. Coincidentally I was staying in that house, the one built by my grandparents, while I was pursuing my college education. We had bonded during that time in a way we had not ever bonded previously and had promised to spend more time together in the months ahead than we had in the years that were behind us.

During my formative years, my uncle was always something of a mystery. First of all, he lived in Hawaii, so we hardly ever saw him. Second, he did not like, or know anything about, sports. As the son of a coach and a sports enthusiast from as far back as I can remember, I did not understand this. I still remember one summer when we were in Los Angeles at the same time as him. He and I went outside to play stickball in the street and, as I was still a pretty little kid, I liked to pretend I was my favorite players when I would come up to bat. Thus, when I was pitching to my uncle, I asked him who he was. He replied "Ronald Colman." I asked who he played for, and he answered, "The Hollywood Stars." I just assumed he was referring to the minor league team my father rooted for when he was a boy and did not ask him any more questions during our game that afternoon. I did not learn until later who Ronald Colman was or that Glen did not know anything about the names of professional baseball players. This did not mean I did not enjoy my time with him. He was completely different from not only my father, but from everyone else I was related to. He had the ability to tell a story that a kid could get lost in and I looked forward to any chance I ever got to see him. We spent many nights in the back room of my grandparents' house sharing a room and staying up late to watch *Twilight Zone* and *Star Trek* reruns. That said, I did not see him often, so our contact was pretty limited during my formative years.

But that fall of 1993 was a different time. I was living in that house with my angry aunt who did everything in her power to stay hidden. My grandmother had died the summer before this and my father had installed me in the house as some sort of companion for my aunt, with the idea being I could live there rent-free while I got my degree at UCLA. He never took into account that my aunt did not want me in her house, but that is a story best saved for another time. This story is about my uncle and the dawning of what would be one of the best relationships of my adult life. We spent that week in Los Angeles drinking and talking and taking the students around to see his favorite places in LA. At some point he suggested that I come visit him in Hawaii the following summer, going so far as to even write me a check to pay for my plane ticket, which he left for me on my dresser the morning he headed out early to catch his flight at LAX.

Dave and I arrived in paradise with few notions about what to expect. I think most of what we knew about Hawaii at that point had come from *Magnum P.I.* So we were thinking adventures and helicopters—obviously. Glen greeted us at the airport with flower leis and then dropped us off at our hotel, unleashing us on Honolulu in the process. These were heady times for me. I was young. My liver worked as well as it ever would. I required very little sleep and I was just beginning to discover that I had a certain charm with the ladies. For close to two weeks we tore through the Honolulu bar scene. I saw the beach a couple times too. Even slept on it once, but, for the most part, this trip was about drunken revelry and staying up until dawn. The nightlife was why we were there. We did not come for the beaches or the mountains or the ocean. We came for the Mai Tais and piña coladas, and later the gin and tonics, once my uncle convinced us to quit drinking the fruity drinks. And we came for the beautiful girls and there were plenty of them to be had as well. Honestly, I could probably churn out an entire book about those ten days in Hawaii. But this is not an advertisement for Honolulu. This is a story about a life spinning out of control. So we better get back to it.

Act II

NEW ORLEANS, 2016

I awoke at the Peabody Hotel in Memphis to my uncle handing me yet another gin and tonic. At first, I was not really sure where I was. Then I wondered if I was still asleep. Finally the sting of the lime and tonic water reassured me I was not, and I quickly gulped the drink down. I was unsure how many I had consumed by this point. It was a lot, I am sure of that. "I have a plan," he said as my eyes struggled to adjust to the sunlight and fully open.

"What's that?" I sipped the drink and the sting of the gin helped me finally get my bearings.

"We should go to New Orleans," he said. "You like New Orleans, don't you? Your other grandmother used to live around there, right?"

"Hammond. Yes. She did."

"You know I stayed with her once? For almost a week, when I was traveling the country collecting stories for one of my books. She was a wonderful host."

"Did she make you breakfast every morning?" I asked. "With those delicious little red sausages?"

I could tell he knew exactly what I was talking about, and we shared a laugh as I rolled off the couch and headed toward the bathroom to relieve myself of some of the remnants of the previous night's bender. "You want to go to New Orleans, that's fine with me. I had no reason to be in Memphis anyway."

I returned to my own room and threw my clothes into my bag and grabbed my toothbrush from the bathroom, wrapping it in some toilet paper before dropping it into the bag as well. My uncle was waiting for me in the lobby, sipping from yet another gin and tonic. The ducks were there too. We had come down too late to see them emerge from the elevators and make their march, and we were too early to see them returning to the roof. But they were there. Swimming around in the fountain in the middle of the lobby. A few kids were standing around, harassing them in the way kids do. "Here ducky, ducky." That kind of stuff. They were not grabbing them and ripping their wings off if that's what you are worried about. It was not that kind of harassment, but I have to assume the verbal calls are almost as annoying to the ducks as being manhandled by small human hands would be. Of course, that's just like my opinion man. I am not now, nor have I ever been, a duck.

"You will have to drive," Glen said to me as I made my way over to him. "I do not have a car."

"Ghosts can't drive, right?" I replied, still pretty sure I was the only one who could see this middle-aged man wearing a dark aloha shirt and khaki pants walking briskly in front of me.

That belief was quickly shattered, however, as we came to the exit. "You have a nice stay, Mr. Glen?" the doorman asked as he opened the large glass door to let us out to the portico where we could retrieve our car.

"I always do, Charles," Glen replied as he handed the man some money and walked into the steamy Memphis afternoon.

"You know him?" I asked as I made my way past Charles.

"Sure." The doorman grinned as he answered. "He stays with us all the time."

The sun was dominating the day as I pulled the car out of the hotel's driveway and onto Union Avenue and we headed toward the interstate. It was warm, as is usually the case when you are close to the big river in the middle of the year, but the air conditioning kept us cool in the cabin of the Volvo. Memphis to New Orleans is pretty much a straight shot down I-55, spanning almost the entire length of the state of Mississippi until you cross over into Louisiana around Kentwood, the childhood home of Britney Spears. You know, the pop star. Purveyor of bubble-gum pop in the '90s. Yep, that Britney Spears.

Of course, there is another way to get from Memphis to New Orleans. That would be directly down the Mississippi River. Like Huck Finn. Or was it Tom Sawyer? Or maybe like Abraham Lincoln. I am one hundred percent positive he did it. Sadly, you cannot drive a car down the river, and barge transportation is not what it used to be. So we drove down I-55. Because that seemed like the best route to take.

We sped down the interstate at unlawful speeds, through the screen of trees on either side of the road that hid whatever life there was beyond them. Past the capitol of Mississippi, Jackson, and eventually across the Louisiana state line, the Volvo carried us. We made no time to stop except for one bathroom break around Hammond. The same town my grandmother had lived in, which my uncle mentioned to me earlier. The car was eerily quiet for almost the entire drive. I did not know how to have a casual conversation with a ghost and Glen seemed happy enough to look out the window at whatever scenery he could get from behind that tree curtain. The trees do eventually give way to the lake—Pontchartrain, filled with the dead stumps of other trees, which my grandmother used to tell me about, and which are a signal of some sort of ecological disaster—which serves as your final impediment before arriving in the Crescent City. As we eased off the bridge into the outskirts of Metairie, Glen finally spoke. "I booked us a suite at the Royal Orleans," was all he said.

I just nodded and continued driving. I knew New Orleans as well as I knew any city in the country, save Austin, perhaps. I had been coming here since I was a child. As an adult I had my fun in the Quarter and then returned when Lucy was old enough to appreciate what was going on. In fact, the proximity to Austin made it the perfect place for us to take many a family vacation, and for the past decade, we had been visiting at least twice a year.

I also knew the Royal Orleans. Located on St. Louis Street, in the heart of the Quarter, it was just a couple blocks from Jackson Square and two blocks down from all the drunk tourists on Bourbon. Truth be told, it was my favorite hotel in the city. Not because it was necessarily the nicest, but because of where it was located. A venerable old building of faded white paint and black wrought iron bars, it did not feel as trapped by the crush of tourists as all the other places, and it was not surrounded by the typical drunk person you encounter everywhere else in the Quarter. The decor inside matched the weathered exterior—sort of a dingy chic that was of high quality but looked like it had seen better days . . . many years ago. In many ways, the hotel perfectly reflected the city itself and everything that it was. I swung the car into the underground garage and flipped the keys to the valet as another guy pulled my bag out of the trunk.

"Is this it?" he asked as he did. "Just the one bag?"

It was only then that I realized my uncle did not seem to be carrying any belongings.

"Ghosts don't need luggage," I replied. The guy responded with a questioning look and a slight smile.

"Don't listen to him," Glen told the guy as he handed him twenty dollars. "He thinks he's funny."

"Sure thing, sir." The bellhop tried to push the luggage cart, which was only holding my single bag, forward but I snatched the bag from the cart and told him I would carry it myself. We descended the long ramp into the basement area where you catch the elevator to get to the reception desk. The ride up was quick and silent. I tried not to look at my uncle as he stared at me, smiling. The big gold doors of the elevator opened, revealing the mostly marble lobby. We quickly dashed across it to the reception desk where we were greeted by an older guy wearing the suit that seemed to be the uniform for the male staff at the hotel.

"Mr. Glen!" He exclaimed. "I did not know you were coming back. It has been a long time."

"Indeed it has, Reggie," my uncle said as he stuck out his hand to shake the now extended hand of the desk attendant. "Too long in fact. But New Orleans is a long way away for me now."

"I hear that," Reggie said. "You want the usual room?"

"That is the one I reserved."

"Very good, sir. Do you have any luggage?"

"Just the one bag," Glen told him as he motioned toward the suitcase I was holding.

"Do you need help with it?"

"No," I said. Curtly.

"Alright then," Reggie continued. "We've got you in the Royal Suite, with a second bedroom connected to that. How many nights will you be staying and how many keys do you need?"

"Two keys," Glen answered. "And I think we'll be here a few days. I will let you know a day before we are going to check out. Will that work?"

"Yes, sir," Reggie said. "It will indeed. To be honest with

you, we're not that busy, what with it being summer and all."

Glen grabbed the keys. I grabbed my bag and we headed back to the elevators, which this time took us up to the fourth floor, where our room was located. The room itself was in the far corner of the floor. It featured more of that same furniture I was used to, overstuffed chairs, striped a faded red and white, with the occasional remnant of stain. A grand wooden bed, with noticeable chips in it, which was still plenty comfortable, sat in the middle of my bedroom. It was all nice enough, but perhaps not as nice as one might expect for the price of the room. We had balconies on either side of the corner suite. One overlooking St. Louis, the other Chartres. Across the street was the Louisiana Supreme Court building, its Romanesque columns shining in the sun, which I think added to the somewhat secluded feeling of these particular rooms. As I set my bag down on the king-sized bed in my room, I saw my uncle at the bar in the shared living room, fixing himself a gin and tonic.

"Do you want a drink, nephew?" he asked as he stirred the tonic into his cup.

"Whatever," I replied. I was exasperated by this point. What I really wanted was some answers, but he had not yet been inclined to give me any.

"Do you want to talk?" He was sitting on the sofa now. Looking at me intently.

"Do you?" I replied.

"Only if you do."

"Fuck." I made my way past him and poured myself a tiny bottle of Jack Daniels and some Coke. "How are you here? Would you please just tell me that?"

"Why does it matter?" He asked. "You needed help. So here I am. Isn't that what really matters?"

"I guess so?" I was unsure if that was really the case as I sat down next to him on the couch. "I am not really sure what the help is you think I need though. I was doing fine on my own."

"Were you?" He asked. "That's not how it looked to me. In fact, I would say you were doing far worse than fine. You abandoned your family. You drove over a thousand miles from where you live so you could get drunk and go up on the roof of a hotel in the middle of the night. What were you planning on doing up there?"

"I wasn't going to jump," I told him. "If that's what you're asking. I was just up there. To look at the river. To think. To maybe figure something out."

"Figure what out?"

"I don't know. Something. Anything . . ." I did not know what to tell him and I hated that he was asking me these questions. "Wait a second, if you aren't all-knowing, then how do you know all that stuff?"

Glen laughed. It was that same laugh I mentioned before. The one I remembered from my childhood. "I know enough," he said. "But I don't know everything."

"I never wanted any of this."

"What?"

"This." I paused, choosing my words carefully. "This life. That house. The things in that house."

"Your furniture?" Glen laughed.

"Any of it. The shit. The pictures on the wall. All I ever wanted was my friends and the night and a place to write." I stared intently at the ice in my glass as I thought about what else to say. "And then they were gone, you know? Then you were gone. Then it was gone, and I didn't know what the fuck to do. So I did what I did. I followed the best path I could and now here I am, completely lost . . . and getting drunk with my dead uncle."

Glen said nothing in response. He just sat on the ratty-chic sofa staring at me. Finally he spoke. "I think we should rest.

Then let's get some food and go out for a while tonight. Yeah?"

"Whatever." I sank down into the chair as I put my feet up on the coffee table.

My uncle picked up the remote control and turned on the TV where he somehow found reruns of the *Twilight Zone*. "Do you remember when we used to watch this show? When you were a kid and we stayed together in that back room on Oakhurst?"

I did remember. But I didn't say anything. I didn't have to.

✳ ✳ ✳ ✳

We kicked around New Orleans for the next couple of days, doing nothing in particular besides eating and drinking. Po-Boys at Domilise's, home cooking at Mandina's, Louisiana-style Mexican food at Juan's Flying Burrito, and plenty of late-night beignets at Café du Monde. For the most part, we avoided Bourbon Street. We crossed it a couple times but never ventured out onto the epicenter of tourist New Orleans. I suppose there were a couple rounds of drinks in Lafitte's Blacksmith Shop. But that was during the day. And that place is at the far end of the part of Bourbon Street the tourists frequent. In all that time we did not talk about much, choosing instead to keep our own company while physically sharing the same space. Glen seemed to be enjoying all of it much more than I was. It was his suggestions that sent us for beignets every night. He was the one who ate the large po' boys and the one who ate the entire plate of chicken parm at Mandina's.

It's not that we didn't talk to each other at all, because we did. He regaled me with many of the same stories he had told me when I was a kid. We talked about that trip to Hawaii and the various romances we had kept each other up on prior to my marriage seventeen years earlier. He never would answer my questions about how he was there, but after a while I quit caring and just enjoyed the fact he was. It's not often that a person gets to spend quality one-on-one time with one of their favorite people on the planet. It happens even less after that person has died. So I was content with just sucking it all in and for a while I forgot about why I was even here in the first place.

"I told them we were checking out tomorrow," Glen told me on the third day as we sat in our suite tossing around ideas for dinner.

"We are?"

"Yes. It's time to move down the road."

"Okay," I was puzzled. "Both of us?"

He laughed. "Yes. Both of us."

"Want to tell me where we're going?"

Again, he chuckled. "We can talk about that later. Tonight I think we should go out. Let's have a good time. Like we did before."

"So you're thinking Bourbon?"

"Yes, nephew, I am."

The Penthouse Club sits on Iberville, just around the corner from Bourbon, across the street from the Acme Oyster House, a place where tourists from the Midwest wait in line for hours to eat mediocre fried seafood because that's what people have been doing for over a hundred years. I was no stranger to the Penthouse Club. In fact, I had been there a few times with a couple different groups of people. As far as strip clubs go it is a pretty normal setup. It is dark, the music is loud, and the girls aren't wearing much clothing. Often they aren't really wearing anything at all, and this is when they draw the most attention and, of course, the money from the wallets of the (mostly) male crowd who sip overpriced drinks as they leer at them.

We actually started out in a couple of regular bars on Bourbon. They were as full as they typically are in the summer, which means they were maybe half full. The street was the same collection of drunk types who we pushed through as we worked our way toward that last sad final block. The one without any real bars on it. The one with the Krystal, which may very well be the dirtiest restaurant in the entire country. The one right before you hit Canal. We never made it to that block. No, we made the left before we crossed Iberville and walked into the Penthouse Club instead. We were greeted by a tall brunette wearing a tight black dress and an oversized fellow in a suit. They asked me for my ID which seemed ridiculous. It had been a long time since I looked under twenty-one or eighteen or whatever the age to enter such a place in Louisiana was. They just waved my uncle through, and I followed him as he was led to a table by the brunette in the tight dress. She told us to have a good night and then disappeared out the door she had led us through.

Our table was one row back from the stage, which in my opinion is usually the best spot to sit in a strip club. One row back you are under no obligation to pay any real attention to the girls dancing, which means you can get away with watching when you want and talking, or drinking, when you don't. It is also a good spot because it means you don't feel obligated to shower the girls on stage with your money. However, you are close enough that if you decide that is what you want to do then it is easy enough to get to the stage and have your fun.

We sat in silence for a minute. Glen sipping his gin and tonic. Me doing the same to my bourbon. Finally my uncle spoke. "Do you remember that club in Honolulu we went to with your friend?"

"Sure," I smiled. "The Korean hostess bar."

"No," he looked at me. The spark in his eye that came when he had a great story to tell appeared. "The other one. The Birds of Paradise."

I had not thought of that place since the night I left it, but the name brought back visions of beautiful Hawaiian women and a well-placed slap that had almost ruined my entire evening.

"Do you remember that girl?" Glen asked me. I know he knew I did. Especially now that he had brought her up. "The one who slapped you? The one you were in love with for a couple of hours?"

I did remember her, but maybe only because he brought her up. That's not to say I remember her name, because I don't. I think I remember her face. She was a local girl. Hawaiian, with incredibly large, incredibly perfect (and incredibly surgically enhanced) breasts. She had come over to our table, as the girls are apt to do, to talk to us. Of course she knew Glen, who decided to introduce me as the next great thing in the world of literature. Or maybe the next great thing in the world. He and Dave then left me alone at the table with this girl, and for close to an hour we just sat there talking. She never asked me for money, and I did not expect her to remove her clothes. I was simply enjoying having the attention of a truly beautiful woman focused solely on me. Those things did not happen that often when I was twenty-four years old, so the experience was something to treasure. We talked about all those topics that are important to people in the early stages of adulthood. Music, travel, all the bands we'd seen, books, our favorite drinks, and everything else that seems silly to me now. But then—then it was all that mattered, and during those wonderful sixty minutes the world seemed perfect. Eventually she was called away to perform and Dave and Glen reappeared, as if they had been there the entire time.

"So what happened?" Dave asked. "You get her number?"

"No," I replied. "She had to work. Said she will come back when she's done on stage." After a long pause, I added, "Guys, I think I'm in love."

Glen laughed. Dave just smiled.

"How much did you have to pay her?" Dave eventually asked.

"That's the thing! She didn't ask me for any money."

"Just wait."

"Seriously, man. I think she really likes me."

Dave slapped me on the back as he started to laugh as well. "Sure she does." He paused before adding, "you better lock that shit down then. We are leaving tomorrow."

"Yeah." At this point she had taken the stage and was just beginning her performance. Eventually she was in front of us, her perfect breasts finally free for me and the world to see. As she danced, I took the twenty-dollar bill my uncle placed into my hand and tried to give it to her. Instead of taking the money from me, her face became a mask of horror and she reached out and slapped me. I was in shock. Was our love not real? What had I done wrong? She remained on stage for two more songs but would no longer look at me. When she was done, I tried to find her in the club, but a very big man told me she was busy and did not have the time to come talk to us. Frantically, I tried to get her attention, but she chose instead to sit in the lap of some Japanese businessman and only offered me the occasional glare. We hung out in the club for another hour or so before Glen finally said it was time for us to leave. I believe I caught her eye on the way out, but by that point, she did not even bother to glare as I slunk out of the club.

"You never should have given her that money." We were back in New Orleans. The song "Back That Azz Up" was playing as a girl shook her rather large rear end on stage.

"You put it in my hand!" I protested.

Glen smiled. "I had no idea you were serious," he said before taking a sip of his drink. "Your story about just talking to her for an hour. I thought you made that up."

"Yeah. I didn't"

"I knew that as soon as you tried to hand her the money. She liked you. She didn't want you to see her as something that was for sale."

"All this advice is coming a little late," I told him. "Like twenty years too late."

"Yes. It is. What do you think would have happened if you hadn't given her the money? Do you think the two of you would have fallen in love and lived happily ever after?"

"I think we were well on our way to that. Yes," I exclaimed, my voice somehow audible above the music. "Shit. I was already in love. In case you don't remember."

Glen let loose a grand, enthusiastic laugh. "Oh, I remember. You were going to marry her and live in a shack on the beach of the North Shore. You were going to spend your mornings surfing, your afternoons writing, and your evenings making love, while the years wasted away and your many children grew up. I remember exactly what was going to happen. I suppose I ruined your life then."

"Maybe." I was just joking of course. Time had not only lost the name of that beautiful Hawaiian girl, but it had also put an end to any silly dream of happily ever after I may have had. "At the very least you probably ruined my chance to get laid. She was one of the most beautiful women I have ever even spoken to."

"Yes. That is true. I'm sorry."

"Eh." I shrugged.

"You were different then." He was looking at me now, firmly. The look of love still there, now mixed more with concern. His voice betrayed this worry as he said, "What happened?"

"Don't you know?"

"You still think I'm omniscient?"

I grabbed my glass and poured the rest of its contents into

my mouth. "I guess not."

"So, tell me what happened. You got old. I know firsthand all about that. But you have a wife. A child. You have some money. Why are you so unhappy?"

I looked him square in the eye. My mentor. My friend. My dead uncle. The man I missed every day since that day he'd died. And I felt like I wanted to explode. Either in anger or in a mess of tears. Of course, the latter would not happen. You don't cry or say you're sorry. John Wayne taught me that. I thought it was a lesson I'd learned from my father, but he cried like a baby lots of times. Like the time his brother died. So I later realized I had learned this lesson from the John Wayne movies my father favored when I was a kid. So I just assumed it was from my father, but in the end it was not. In a way, I think this means I was raised by John Wayne. But I digress . . .

"Because there's no reason to this," I finally said. "No point. To any of it. When I was young there was booze and girls and friends and fun. Then we had Lucy and she was reason enough. At least for a while. But she doesn't need me anymore. So, why am I here? I mean really. What's the point? You're dead! You tell me."

Glen reached across the table and put his hand on top of mine. It was a calming gesture, and I quickly did not feel as agitated. When he spoke, he just asked, "You are here, in this club with me, to have a good time. To drink and look at the pretty girls. Isn't that enough?"

I did not reply. Our waitress brought us multiple rounds of drinks and we did not speak other than to say "thank you" to her. All kinds of music played: '80s hair metal, '90s pop, Katy Perry, even the Pixies. As we listened to Charles Thompson sing "Where is My Mind" we were approached by a blonde dancer wearing glasses, which I found weird. She was the first stripper I had ever seen wearing glasses. Her name was Syd and she asked us if we wanted a dance, or just any company. My uncle barely looked at her, forcing the onus of responsibility onto me. "Not now," I told her. "Maybe some other time."

As she walked away Glen said out loud, "I wonder if she likes Vonnegut?"

I looked at him, quizzically. "What?"

"Never mind." Our silence was finally broken. "I think it was the glasses," he continued. "They made her look like maybe she likes to read."

"I guess they did," I said. "I have a friend who would have lost it if he'd seen her. Nothing like a stripper wearing glasses."

Glen smiled in reply. The same gentle smile as before. Then he spoke. "I cannot tell you why you are here, nephew. But I think you know that. Unfortunately, I cannot tell you the meaning of life because I have no earthly idea. Maybe there isn't one . . . you know? You just exist and then you die and that is all there is. Maybe you just make the most of the time you have and do your best not to ask the big questions . . ."

"Wait a second," I interrupted him. "You can't say that's all there is. Because you're sitting here and you died thirteen years ago! There must be something else."

He cut back into the conversation. "That is not what you need to be focused on now. You need to be focused on your life. Live it. Don't be in such a hurry to get to the next part." We both simultaneously sipped from our drinks. "Now tell me what is so bad. And then tell me why you were going to throw yourself off the roof of the Peabody Hotel."

"Okay," I was irritated and even the sight of a topless woman dancing over my uncle's shoulder could not distract me from this fact. I did not want to seem weak in front of him, thus I refused to even admit the thought of suicide had ever crossed my mind. "First off, I was not going to throw myself off that building! So quit saying that!"

"Whatever you say." Apparently, he knew better, which

CHRIS GRANT

only made me angrier.

"And secondly, I am mad because everyone left. All my friends are gone. You are gone. My wife has never really needed me and my kid no longer needs me either," I exclaimed. "That's why I'm here. Because there is no point to anything anymore. That's why I was in Memphis. That's why I'm not at that stupid fucking house I spent so much money to build. I am here and I have the opportunity to do whatever it is the fuck I want to do, but I don't know what the fuck to do! Do you understand this? Do you know what it's like to live for thirty-plus years with absolutely no purpose? Just drifting from one vignette to the next in an effort to distract yourself long enough for death to finally come and switch it all off?"

"I think I do," Glen replied. "Do you remember when I told you you remind me of myself? Back when you were younger? The things you are saying to me now sound exactly like thoughts I have had before. But you can't give into them. I found things I enjoyed, and they helped me have a relatively happy life. You have to figure out what it is you want and then you have to chase it. So, tell me, what is it that you want? Deep down inside? I thought you wanted to write. That is what you always told me."

"Yeah," I swirled the straw in my drink and wished the waitress would reappear so this conversation could, at the very least, be interrupted. She did not. "I guess. I try, but nothing ever happens when I do. After a while you just sort of give up, you know? "

"I do."

"So if that is gone, what else is there?" It seemed like he wasn't listening to me. This entire time we had been together I felt like he was just there, asking me questions I could not answer and not really giving me much guidance. And this is what it felt like right now. He was asking all kinds of questions. You might even say they were the right questions, if you are an asshole—peppering someone with questions they can't answer cannot truly be helpful to them, even if you feel those questions will ultimately lead that person to the answers they are looking for. But that's what he'd been doing ever since he showed up on that rooftop in Memphis. Asking me to be introspective when all I really wanted to do was run as far and as fast as I could and just get away from all of it. So the noise would be quiet. So I could get a good night's sleep. So I could spend an entire day without the weight of a wasted life bearing down on my shoulders. So I could drink and be numb to all of it.

"I can't tell you that," is what he said back to me. And of course that's what he said. Like I said, he was not here to provide me with any answers. Just those infuriating questions I did not want to address. As I prepared to raise myself from my seat and get the hell out of the Penthouse Club, Glen looked at me and shook his head, telling me to remain where I was. "I can help you though. Let's go out there and find it."

"What?'

"Your raison d'être."

"Shut the fuck up."

"Seriously," he continued, leaning closer to me as he spoke. "If you think you want to write, then we need to get out there and find you something to write about. And if you don't want to write, then maybe we can find something else. Some other reason for you to carry on." He paused for a sip from his glass of gin and tonic water. "I am not telling you I can help you figure out the meaning of life. Because I can't. But I know I can help you find some sort of answer. Maybe you are missing your muse. Maybe you don't need a muse at all. Maybe you need to look somewhere else. What you need to understand, though, is there is something out there for you and I think we can find it, together. So what do you say, do you want to go look for it?"

For the first time in years, I had hope that something might come together for me. "I do."

"Then let's go."

With that, Glen stood up and dropped all of the money in his pocket onto the table, forming a small pile in the process. He then turned to glance at the next girl who had taken her place dancing on the stage behind him and gave her a nod before brushing past me on his way toward the exit. I followed him out. Past the drunken frat boys and businessmen and the crazy older women who were all wearing matching hats emblazoned with glittery slogans like "flirt" and "champagne" and "hot" and finally through the door we had come in. Glen handed more money to the girl in the tight dress and the large man who was working security. We stepped onto Iberville and when I started to go right, Glen pulled me left.

"Let's go down Royal," he said. "It's quieter."

SOMEWHERE ON I-10, 2016

We left New Orleans and headed east, into Mississippi and towards Mobile. These were the same roads I used to travel when I was a child, riding in the backseat of my grandmother's Cadillac on our way to family holidays in Gulf Shores or Pensacola. While the scenery was familiar, the circumstances could not have been more different. First of all, the Volvo was no 1970s Cadillac. Believe it or not, the station wagon I was driving was actually smaller than the giant ship-sized sedan my tiny grandmother drove during my childhood. Obviously, this was not a fun-filled vacation either. No, I was seeking much more than leisure time. Although I had surely had my share of that in New Orleans, this expedition was not about relaxation, even though I must admit, I was not really sure what this expedition was exactly for. Glen hardly spoke as I drove. He had stated our purpose the previous night and I suppose that was all he needed to say. For now, he seemed entranced by the scenery. Or maybe by the Doors-only station he had found on the satellite radio. In between drumming on the dashboard, he reminded me, briefly, that when he was in college at UCLA he used to go see the Doors at the Whiskey on Sunset. I again told him that was very cool, although the truth of the matter is, I cannot stand the Doors.

We crossed over into Alabama and through Mobile. To the right, I saw the USS Alabama, the World War II battleship that baseball Hall of Famer Bob Feller had served on. It, and its companion submarine the USS Drum, had always been a highlight of those long past summer trips. To the left was the city itself, bigger than I'd remembered, its tall(ish) buildings peering out at the battleship and the water beyond it. I considered asking if we should stop but let go of the idea as soon as it had come to me. We were quickly through Mobile, and I assumed we would continue on to Florida, but my uncle had other ideas.

"Turn here," he said as we reached the other side of Mobile Bay.

"You want to stop in Spanish Fort?" (Spanish Fort is a little town on that other side of Mobile Bay. Despite its small size, it is a city with an impressive history, dating all the way back to 1712 when a trading post was established there. Battles were fought in the area during the Revolutionary War, the War of 1812, and the American Civil War. The 2010 census lists the population as 6,798.) These facts notwithstanding, I saw no reason to stop.

"No, not here," he said as he pointed to the sign for US 31. "Take 31. Let's go that way. I think I have an idea where you can maybe find some answers."

"In Alabama?" I questioned. If I'm being honest, I was completely turned off by that idea. I did not think there were any answers anywhere in Alabama.

Glen laughed, the same laugh he kept laughing every time I said something that bordered on exasperation. "Just take the road."

I obligingly turned onto 31 and headed north. Through

Stapleton, Holly Hills, and Bay Minette we drove, stopping briefly in the last town for a meal at the Waffle House where I ordered my hash browns covered, chunked, and peppered, because, honestly, that's the only way to get them. Spicy and full of pork and cheese. After filling our bellies with our daily dose of grease, we continued on 31 until it intersected with US 97 at Altmore.

"Turn here," my erstwhile navigator told me.

"Which way?"

"North. Toward the 65."

"You want to tell me where we are going?"

"North toward the 65." Glen chuckled to himself. I did not find his joke funny, but I kept my mouth shut this time.

Once we reached Interstate 65, I was instructed to continue on my north/east bound course, so I kept on driving. We passed Montgomery and I inquired about stopping, but he told me to keep going. Through the Alabama pines we sped, fueled by caffeine and the indigestion caused by all those spicy hash browns. Thanks to a stomach that did not work as well as it used to, I managed to stay awake (and fairly focused on the road) as we headed toward Atlanta. We crossed the border into Georgia, navigating the Chattahoochee River, its blue waters reflecting the green from the tree-lined shores, as we did. (Despite what Alan Jackson says, I did not find it hotter than a hoochie coochie, but it was late in the day.) Eventually we reached the outskirts of the southern metropolis of Atlanta. The skyline, notable for its time starring in the television program *The Walking Dead*, seemed to beckon us in, but we did not stop. Halfway through the city, Glen asked if I wanted to take a detour.

"A detour from what?" I asked. "I don't even know where we are going."

"Well," he said, "a detour from our final destination. We could continue on the road to get us there. Or we can turn off here and go somewhere else. We will still get where we are going, no matter what you choose. I guess the question you have to ask yourself is, do you want to get there sooner or later?"

He was speaking in riddles. But I was worn out enough from the road that I did not care. "Let's take the detour."

"Alright then. Take I-75 to Chattanooga. We will stop there."

We continued north, but now the road slanted slightly back toward the west. It was dark, so I did not see much of the Georgia countryside that we were driving through, but I knew a lot of it by heart. Kennesaw Mountain and Chickamauga were the two places I wished we could have stopped. Both were famous Civil War battlefields and Chickamauga is the title of one of my favorite songs ever written. For a moment it was where I was bound, and solitude was where I'd been. Then we were on the other side and the exact reverse was true. We finally made it to Chattanooga sometime around midnight and checked into a hotel downtown. I was surprised no one here knew my uncle, but he explained to me he had actually never been to this part of Tennessee.

"I'd like to see that train before we go," he added.

"The choo-choo?" I asked.

He laughed as he handed me my bag from the trunk. "Yes. The Chattanooga Choo-Choo. That train."

Our room had a fantastic view of Lookout Mountain, and I sat on the edge of my bed looking at the dark giant looming over the city for a while. Finally, Glen brought me out of my trance. "Get some sleep," he said. "We've got a busy day tomorrow."

CHATTANOOGA, 2016

I awoke to the smell of my uncle brewing coffee in the room's coffee pot. Never having been much of a coffee drinker, the rich smell of brewing beans did nothing for me, so I tried to roll over and get some more sleep. Glen had other ideas and a few minutes later he set a steaming cup of black coffee on the table, right next to my head. When I looked at it, I was able to see the clock. It was eight a.m.

"Why so early?" I asked.

"I told you," he casually replied. "We've got a lot to do."

I pulled myself from the bed and considered drinking the coffee, but the thought was a fleeting one. Soon I was up and dressed and following Glen down the hall toward the elevator. We rode the carriage down the four stories to the lobby and made our way outside, where we waited silently for the valet to bring the Volvo around. Eventually the car showed up and I was surprised to see my uncle make his way around to the driver's side.

"Get in," he said. "I want to drive."

I silently obliged and we slowly pulled out onto a busy

street, the name of which I do not know. Glen drove us around Chattanooga for close to an hour. The city itself was nothing to write home about. The mountains around it and the Tennessee River, which flowed through the middle of town, however, provided a picturesque setting for the residents of Chattanooga to live their lives. At one point we passed the International Towing Museum and Hall of Fame and I thought we should stop. I mean, who even knew there was a museum devoted to tow trucks? Or that tow truck drivers could somehow get themselves elected to a Hall of Fame? I wondered aloud just how that might happen. Most drivers assisted, I mused to myself. Glen looked at me and smiled but said nothing. Ten minutes later he did speak, but only to say, "I'm hungry." Five minutes after that we were in a drive-through at McDonald's and soon we were eating Egg McMuffins in silence as he steered the car toward Lookout Mountain.

The drive up the mountain is a steep one and before you reach the battlefield you pass something called Rock City, which is a very well-advertised tourist spot. As we did not stop, I cannot tell you what the deal is with Rock City. I can tell you they have a waterfall and some gardens, but you would learn this yourself if you drove up there. With all the signs there is simply no way for you to miss it. There were plenty of people at Rock City as well. A lot more than we found in the parking lot for the Lookout Mountain Battlefield Park. Glen effortlessly parked the car and hopped out. "Come on," he said as he pushed his door shut. "Let's go in."

The Battle of Lookout Mountain took place on November 24, 1863. It was part of a larger battle known as the Battle of Chattanooga which was eventually a significant victory for the Union. Following the earlier battle at Chickamauga, the Union Army of Tennessee found itself trapped inside the city of Chattanooga and surrounded by Confederate forces led by

General Braxton Bragg. Somehow, Ulysses S. Grant managed to slip through the Confederate lines and take control of the Union forces in the city. Thanks in large part to Grant's leadership, and a small seam in the Confederate siege through which supplies and men from the north were able to pass, the Federal forces eventually had the men and materials they needed to break the siege and push the Confederates back toward Georgia. Lookout Mountain was one of the key fights of that campaign and, somehow, the two sides managed to clash on a mountain that, when you are standing on top of it, seems way too steep for any such thing to occur. After a brief stop in the ranger station/museum, Glen and I found ourselves taking in that very view. It was a long way down. I will tell you that.

"They called it the Battle Above the Clouds," Glen started.

"I know," I replied.

That did not stop him. "It was foggy that day and a ring of clouds surrounded the mountain. But it wasn't foggy where we're standing," he continued. "So the Confederates watched as the Union troops pushed their way through the clouds and eventually up here."

"It is hard to imagine anyone coming up that incline," I said. "Especially under fire."

"Yes," Glen said. "It is. But I think you will find you can do all kinds of things. When you have to."

We wandered around the rather small park a while longer. There is a walkway where you can descend a portion of the mountain and we walked down there for a while before turning around and heading back to the car.

"Now what?" I asked.

"One more stop," he said. "There is someone I want you to meet."

When we reached the Volvo, Glen retook his spot in the driver's seat and proceeded to take us down the mountain.

This time he drove like he had somewhere to be. We were no longer driving around aimlessly; now he steered with purpose, heading east. We eventually reached Missionary Ridge. Unlike Lookout Mountain, Missionary Ridge is not specifically a military park but is, instead, a neighborhood populated by fairly large homes. There are plenty of plaques around commemorating what happened there in 1863, and some protected green spaces are included. However, while there you do not get the feeling you have stepped back in time. In fact, you kind of feel like you should get yourself out of there because you may very well be standing in some wealthy person's yard. Glen drove us to one of the open spaces and parked the car on the street that bordered it. "Go over there," he said. "There's someone you should meet."

"Aren't you coming?"

"No. I'll wait here."

I stepped out of the Volvo and shut the door and proceeded to walk through the small park. There was a plaque I did not bother reading, but little else here, other than grass and trees. I also did not see any people, so for a few minutes I just sort of wandered around, hoping I might run into someone who would clue me into what, exactly, I was supposed to be doing. Then I saw him. A short man in a blue coat. He wore an impressive mustache over his top lip and a funny-looking hat. As I got closer, I became starkly aware of just who he was.

✗✗✗✗

The afternoon of the Battle of Chattanooga, Grant found his attempts to break through the Confederate defenses beginning to stall. In an effort to reinvigorate the Union battle plan, Grant decided to attack the Confederate center, which happened to be on Missionary Ridge. As part of this offensive, he sent General Phil Sheridan's troops (among others) to take out the Confederate rifle pits at the bottom of Missionary Ridge. As this is not a history of the Civil War, I will shorten the tale for you and tell you that Sheridan's men did not just take the rifle pits at the base of the ridge, but they also climbed said ridge, under heavy fire from the Confederate artillery located at the top, and eventually routed those men as well. This effectively ended Bragg's hold on the city. With his center gone, the Confederates eventually retreated, and the Federal forces controlled not just the city, but the mountains that surround it.

Sheridan himself was an interesting character. Short, even for his time, he was either born in Ireland or Albany, New York. There is, in fact, a marker in Killinkere, Co. Cavan, Ireland, that claims to designate the place Sheridan was born. He eventually graduated from West Point and saw his star rise throughout the war between the states. His success at Missionary Ridge did nothing to hamper his ascent and, by the time the war ended, he was one of the three most famous Union generals. That is about all I can tell you about him right now. I am sure I could come up with some other interesting facts. If you pressed me. But this is not a book of Civil War trivia, is it?

*****

So yeah, Sheridan, interesting guy. No doubt. But, to be honest with you, I did not think about him all that much. I'd always been a Grant and Sherman guy. Sheridan and his famous horse and his ride to save the day at Cedar Creek (There's some more trivia. You're welcome!) were always sort of secondary to me. Which is why I was maybe even a little more surprised than you might expect, to find him standing in front of me.

"Hello, sir," he removed the glove from his hand and made his way toward me, that uncovered hand outstretched. "Beautiful day, is it not?"

By the time he was standing close enough to grasp my hand, I had extended my own and he shook it vigorously. I was close to a foot taller than the man holding my hand. That was all I could think. Well, that and the fact that he looked a whole hell of a lot like the diminutive general. You know, for an impersonator.

"Little Phil," I said when he released my hand, as it seemed to also free my tongue.

He did not seem happy with me calling him little. "You may call me Philip. Or Phil. Or General. Or even Mr. Sheridan. But please, sir, do not call me Little Phil. I do not care for that name."

"Sorry," I replied. "So how much do you make doing this? I've got to say your uniform is very realistic looking."

"I am paid $315 a month," he answered quickly, his words brusque and his voice deeper than one might expect from such a small man. "Although I do not think a gentleman should ask such questions."

"That doesn't seem like much," I said. "Do you have other work?"

"No, sir. I am a General in the Army of the United States of America. That is plenty of work for one man."

"I get it. You're staying in character. Nice."

"Sir, I am not sure what you are talking about. Your uncle, Glen, said I might be able to help you. So, how may I be of assistance? I do have other things I could be doing."

"Okay," I said. "I'll play along. I do need your help. I am out here looking for my purpose. I am looking for a reason to keep going. Can you help me find that?"

The small general laughed at me before regaining his composure. "It sounds to me that you have the problems of a man of your time. We did not know those kinds of travails when I was a young man."

"I guess not," I answered. "And when was that? The 1990s?"

Again, the small general laughed. "No. Much earlier than that."

"A lot of men died here." He turned from me and looked toward Lookout Mountain. "Good men. Brave men. On both sides. They were fighting for something bigger than themselves. Did you know this?"

"I did."

"Well, if you had asked them, the men in camp, day in and day out, what they were doing, they would have told you they were there for the other men. Or they were there because their country asked them to be there. Some came for the adventure. At least at first. In those days, war was the sort of adventure that could take a man away from his home and show him a larger world. Those men had no idea what they were in for. None of us did. It was nothing like fighting the Indians. Or the Mexicans. It was not even like fighting the British . . . so many of them died. More than anyone ever thought could possibly die. In the end, I don't think any of those men were worried about their purpose. They just wanted to get back home. To see their families. Even if it was just one last time. They would have given everything, just to gaze at their wife, child, mother, one final time before the end came."

"I don't know," I said. "At least their death had some meaning."

"Did it?" His eyes seemed to be filled with fire.

"They died to save the country. Even the guys fighting for the South. They died trying to protect what they perceived as being their country."

"I do not think you were listening to me," the man who might be Phil Sheridan said. "None of that mattered in the end.

Grand ideas, legacies, the honors bestowed on us by history. Little of that matters when you are bleeding to death in the mud."

I had spent a lot of the past ten years thinking I would like to take a minnie ball directly in the head after taking part in a charge on a Confederate rifle pit. It seemed like a noble way to go. Much better than being killed by the saturated fat and sugar in all of the processed food I ate. So the little general's words cut me. But I still was not convinced.

"Do you have a child?" he asked.

"Yes. A daughter."

"Is she not enough? I would think you could find your purpose there."

"She doesn't need me anymore," I told him. "She's a teenager now. She is consumed by boys and her friends and her YouTube channel. It is almost like I don't even exist as far as she's concerned. Except when she needs a ride somewhere."

He smiled at me. "It sounds to me like you have done a good job then. Assuming she is not getting into too much trouble."

"Are you really Sheridan?" I asked.

"What do you think?" he replied.

"Well, I'm on a road trip with my uncle who has been dead for thirteen years, so at this point, I kind of think anything is possible."

"And so it is," he said as he reached out and put his hand around my shoulder. "Come, let's get back to the car. I shall ride with you for a while."

We walked back from the clump of trees, past that historical marker I still did not read, and found Glen leaning against the front of the Volvo. "I see you found him," he said to me.

"Is this who I was looking for?" I asked.

"Here," Glen said. "Yes. He is who you were looking for. Here."

The three of us spent the night eating and drinking at a restaurant across the street from our hotel called the Public House. If you are ever in Chattanooga, you must eat there. Both the fried chicken and the pimento cheese are the best I have ever had. And believe me when I tell you I know my pimento cheese. It is, in fact, my favorite cheese dip/spread/ whatever you want to call it, on the planet, and I have been testing the many incarnations of the stuff since I was a small child and my grandmother in California (Glen's mother) would serve it to me on white bread. This particular incarnation was so good I can only imagine they have a secret ingredient. I am not sure what that was, and I am actually a pretty good food detective with a pretty passable pimento cheese recipe of my own. What, you want to know what it is? Fine. Combine white and orange cheddar, Duke's mayonnaise, pimentos, and a little hot sauce with some garlic and onion powder. You can also throw in a little salt and pepper. I am not going to give you the ratios. You have to figure that out for yourself because it's all about personal taste when it comes to making something like pimento cheese[4] (or that tuna salad I mentioned way back there at the start.)

So yeah, the Public House is one of the best restaurants in the South, and I sincerely mean this. Their drinks are top-notch as well. I heartily recommend the Social Old-fashioned. Assuming they still make it by the time you get there. It is nice twist on one of my favorite drinks. Did I mention they have a picture of the Dude from *The Big Lebowski* by their restroom? They do. As if you needed another reason to eat there.

I wondered what our server thought of our party. My uncle in his aloha shirt and khaki pants. The guy who might be Phil Sheridan dressed pretty much as you would expect a Civil War general to be dressed. And me, in Dickies extra-long shorts, flip-flops, and a Riverboat Gamblers t-shirt. Our server's name was Andie, and when we sat down she made some remark about us possibly going to a costume party. Glen smiled at her and gently said, "No," and that was just about it, as far as any discussion of our strange little group.

I didn't do much for the dinner conversation other than nod or add a random "uh-huh" here or there. In fact, Glen did most of the talking, telling us a story he had read once about the ghosts of Gettysburg. Sheridan added a bit about the great conflict and relayed something he had learned fighting Native Americans in the west after the war, but the details are fuzzy for me because by this point I had consumed too many of those aforementioned old-fashioneds. Eventually we found ourselves back in the room. Glen and Little Phil took the beds and I collapsed onto the couch. As my uncle said something from the other room about leaving early the next morning, I drifted off to sleep.

INTERSTATE 81, 2016

We left the next morning around eight a.m. and headed north on I-75 towards Knoxville. I was driving now. Glen was in the passenger seat, looking out the window mostly. Sheridan sat in the back, dozing. His uniform was somehow pressed, and his cavalry boots shone in the rearview mirror as he nodded in and out of consciousness. "What do you think of this horseless carriage?" I asked him at one point when I caught him looking at me.

"I am well aware of what a car is," he replied before turning his gaze back down towards the floor.

"So you're not from the 1800s?" I was having a good time needling him. Whoever he was.

"I do not believe those words came from my mouth," he curtly stated before closing his eyes.

The road from Chattanooga to Knoxville is a pretty one, skirting the Great Smoky Mountains National Park. The vast green ridges covered by trees are very visible in the distance, and they made for a nice distraction from the road which was starting to get perhaps a little monotonous. In Knoxville, we merged onto I-40 and continued on toward the east. Right around Douglas Lake, we intersected with Interstate 81 and Glen told me to get onto it.

"Just stay on this for a little while," he said.

"Right on," I said. "For how long?"

"Oh, I don't know. Four hundred miles. Something like that."

"Just a little while?" I laughed. So did he. I was glad to be able to hear him laugh again. Every time he did, every chuckle, was now a special treasure. Something to cherish for as long as it lasted and then to remember with just as much joy when he was gone again.

Interstate 81 is a busy road through plenty of smaller Tennessee towns. Past Morristown, Johnson City, and Kingsport, the Volvo pushed before crossing the border at Bristol. Into Virginia we rode, through the mountains and trees of the George Washington and Jefferson National Forests, through Roanoke and Lexington and Staunton where we made an abrupt right onto I-64, which would carry us the rest of the way to the state capital. Sheridan seemed to perk up the further we got into Virginia. Assuming he was actually who he claimed to be, he must have recognized some of the areas we were driving through, although he did not offer much in the way of conversation. For his part Glen was silent, save for humming along to the music on the radio, he seemed content to just stare out the window at the passing landscape.

"Do you think we will have the opportunity to visit Winchester?" Sheridan eventually asked. "I would not mind seeing that place again."

"You tell me," I replied. I'm just the driver. "I thought y'all knew where we were going."

"I am just here for the ride," Sheridan said, our eyes making contact in the rearview mirror.

Glen finally spoke. "No. We aren't going that far north. Just keep driving to Richmond. We'll stay there tonight."

I glanced back at Sheridan, and he looked a little saddened by the news but offered no protest to my uncle's orders.

We entered Richmond around sundown and Glen directed us to the Jefferson Hotel, located just a few blocks from the Virginia capital, as well as the old Confederate White House. We drove past the spot where J.E.B. Stuart died on the way to the hotel. Apparently, Robert E. Lee's old house was somewhere in the vicinity, although we did not stop to pay our respects. We dropped the Volvo at the valet stand and filed into the hotel in our odd procession. They have alligators outside to greet you upon your arrival, which was the one thing I noticed. I did not ever think of alligators living in Virginia, but they apparently lived at the Jefferson Hotel at some point. The live versions were long ago replaced by a couple rather large bronze statues, but other, smaller, alligators seemed to be present everywhere you looked. The lobby of the old hotel was spectacular, and I took some time to stand and stare up at the ornate ceiling. Glen handled the check-in procedure while Sheridan sat in one of the oversized armchairs and fiddled with his boot. I was content to look around as I waited for my uncle to return, which he eventually did, handing a key to me and another to Sheridan.

"We each have our own room," he said. "Let's get settled and then meet up down here in an hour. We can get some dinner. Yes?"

I nodded. Sheridan took the plastic key card from Glen and stared at it.

"You know how to work that thing?" I asked. "It's not like those big old keys they used to have."

"Yes," he replied, intent on not letting on about his actual identity.

My room was located on the same floor as the swimming pool and when I stepped off the elevator I was engulfed by the smell of indoor chlorine. Do you know the smell? It's the one you might encounter at your local health club, or the YMCA, or any natatorium really. It is not a pleasant smell, and I was not excited to find my room just two doors down from the entrance to the pool. However, upon entry, the scent seemed to fade, and after I dropped my bag in an antique-looking chair, I fell onto the bed and no longer noticed it. After the long drive, I was tempted to just go to sleep, but I wondered what new magical guests dinner might hold, so I contented myself with a Jack and Coke from the minibar and a few minutes of the local news. The time alone passed quickly, with none of the anxiety that so often consumed me when left to my own devices at home, and before I knew it, I was walking past the swimming pool and riding the elevator down to the lobby where I found Sheridan and Glen waiting.

"So where are we going?" I asked.

"I thought we could just eat here," Glen replied. "The restaurant looks nice, and they make a stiff gin and tonic."[5]

"You already had one?"

"We have had two," Sheridan answered. "Where were you?"

"I was resting." I was sort of taken aback by the implications of his question. "No one told me were having pre-dinner drinks."

"It's okay," Glen said. "There was no plan. Neither of us have any luggage so we saw no reason to go up to the room. Come on, the restaurant is this way."

I followed the pair of them across the lobby and into the restaurant which seemed to have a similar alligator theme to the rest of the hotel.

"What's with all the alligators?" I asked. "Do they even have alligators in Virginia?"

"Apparently they used to have them in a pool at this hotel," Glen replied. "People would come from all around to see them.

David Niven actually mentioned it in his biography."

"You read David Niven's biography?"

"I did. Old Hollywood. You know."

I did indeed.

We were greeted at the hostess desk by a pretty girl in her twenties. I believe her name was Holly, but I cannot state that with complete certainty. As was his way, Glen laid on the charm as thickly as necessary to make her smile, which she eventually did, going so far as to even laugh before leading us to a table in the back corner of the room. Once again no one said a word about the man dressed in Union blue. I suppose the color of his coat was not really the issue. The issue was the fact he was dressed in the garb of a Civil War general. It was a puzzling thing, really. The acceptance the world gave to this man who might be Sheridan as he strode about silently through the twenty-first century. Not one word. Ever. Just nods and smiles and every once in a while, a side-eye. But never a question, or worse, a cutting remark. I suppose all those anti-bullying campaigns really do work.

Our waiter was a younger man by the name of Michael. I do know that. I am not sure why his name has stuck with me while the hostess's name has not. He presented us with dinner menus and a communal drink menu while filling our water glasses. Not one of us bothered to look at the craft cocktails. Glen ordered gin and tonics for the table, after which I also requested an old-fashioned[6].

"Two drinks?"

"It's early."

The drinks arrived quickly, and I guzzled the G&T so I could get to the drink I actually wanted. The bourbon in the old-fashioned was a good one and it went down smoothly as we listened to Sheridan tell us of his time in Virginia. He seemed to relish the fight at Yellow Tavern that resulted in the death of Stuart.

"I said when I got here that I would solve the Stuart problem and that is exactly what I did," he explained. "Old Stuart did not last long once they put me on the job."

"Does it bother you that he died?" Glen asked him. My father was a fighter. A soldier. A man who could celebrate a death, particularly one he saw as necessary. My uncle was none of these things, and while it seemed he enjoyed Sheridan's stories of the war, he did not like to listen to the tales of specific killing.

"Not at all," Sheridan replied as he sipped his drink. "He was our enemy and a particularly good one at that. His cavalry had harassed our armies in the east for most of the war. When I arrived from the west, I set out to eliminate that problem as quickly as possible and that is what I did. Stuart knew what he was risking every time he climbed into his saddle. We all did. I am sure if the outcome had been different then he would be sitting here telling you the same thing."

I nodded. Glen looked at him disapprovingly.

"Now, let us stop all this talk of death," Sheridan said. "I am sure we can discuss something more interesting."

"Here, here," Glen said.

"I know what we can talk about," I cut in. I was now working on my fourth drink in a little over an hour and was ready to breach that subject in the back of everyone's mind. Probably even yours, yes? So let's dive in. "What the fuck are you two doing here?"

Glen laughed. Sheridan gave me a dirty look, his eyes as sharp as his saber surely was. (For the record, he had no sword with him. Or armaments of any kind really. Just his uniform and his cavalry boots. He had taken that silly hat off when he got in the car, and he'd never put it back on. But I imagine his sword would have been sharp. Had he been carrying it.)

"Seriously. What is going on?" I pointed to Sheridan and

said, "You died in the nineteenth century, but here you sit." Then I looked back at Glen. "And I saw you die. I carried your ashes. You shouldn't be here either."

Glen rolled his eyes at me, the way all the men in my family roll their eyes. It is a profound and exaggerated expression, like a person looking to the skies and pleading to God for help. "Do we have to get into this again?" he asked. "You needed me. So I am here."

"Fine. I can accept that. But what about him?" I looked across the table at the Union general. "Who is he and why is he here?"

Glen shrugged as Sheridan responded. "I am Philip Henry Sheridan, Major General in the Army of the United States and Commander of the Army of the Shenandoah. I am not an actor or an impostor. I am General Philip Sheridan in the flesh and at your service."

"Convincing," I said. Sarcastically.

"Honestly, sir, I do not care if you are convinced or not. I know who I am. What you think does not matter to me one bit."

"Fine," I replied. "Then why are you here?"

Sheridan sipped from his glass as he considered his response. "You will have to discuss this further with Glen. But I will share with you that I am here on a holiday. They let us out, from time to time . . ."

"So you want me to believe you are Phil Sheridan, on vacation in the twenty-first century?" I interrupted him. "That is the dumbest fucking thing I have ever heard. I am not an idiot."

"Guys, stop," Glen chimed in. "Nephew, why can't you just accept what is in front of you and go with it? Quit fighting this and just accept it for what it is. If someone had offered you the chance to spend time with General Sheridan a month ago, would you have turned them down?"

"No. I would have pointed out how impossible that was, however."

"And what if it wasn't?"

"What?"

"Impossible? What then?"

"Then I suppose I would say let's do it."

"Then let's do it."

I was already rather drunk and I did not feel like fighting any longer, so I did as Glen suggested. There was no disputing the fact they were there—sitting at a dinner table with me in an upscale hotel in Richmond, Virginia. The two of them eating steak while I dug around in the grilled chicken salad I ordered because I was worried about my cholesterol.

"What's next?" I asked later, after I had eaten all the chicken and croutons from my salad. "Where to tomorrow?"

"We have an appointment in the morning," Glen said. "Someone else to pick up."

I was more than a little surprised to hear this. "Who?"

"You'll see," he said. "Now let's settle the bill and go to bed. We have to leave early."

Sheridan dropped his napkin on top of his plate and took a drink from his water glass. "Goodnight, gentlemen," he said as he stood up and left the restaurant.

"You want another drink?" I asked.

"No," he said. "I am going to talk to the hostess. Maybe see what she's doing later."

I was perhaps a little surprised by the fact my dead uncle was planning on making a move on the girl I am calling Holly. At the same time, I was not. The man was a legendary ladies' man, as I may have explained before, so it made absolute sense that he would attempt to charm a pretty girl if he were given the chance. Even if it was over a decade after he had died. Still, I was curious. "Is that allowed?" I asked.

"Of course," he chortled as he slapped me on the back.

"There are no rules. Other than the ones you set for yourself. You go get some sleep. I will see you in the morning."

I watched him as he walked back up to the hostess stand and struck up a conversation with the girl working there. I heard him ask her if she wanted to get a drink and I heard her say yes. As I slowly moved out of the restaurant I looked on as the two of them strolled toward the bar. It was late and the place was completely empty, so I assumed no one would care if she was drinking with the lone guest. I imagined she would end up in Glen's bed that night and I am sure she did. But I never asked him. I figured that wasn't any of my business.

THE PETERSBURG LINE, 2016

We loaded into the Volvo around nine a.m. Glen and Sheridan were holding paper cups filled with coffee. I was a little buzzed from the two bottles of Ketel One I'd consumed before exiting my room. I noticed that the further we got into this voyage the more I was hitting the sauce. It was something I had pretty much sworn off once my daughter was old enough to ask me if I was drunk. Honestly, I usually wasn't, but I did not like the implication, so I pretty much gave up drinking more than one cocktail or two beers for most of a decade. Oh, there was the occasional exception. Like on my yearly trip into the past with Adam. Or any time we'd crack open a bottle of Costco-brand champagne with Sunday supper. But for the most part, I was sober 99.9 percent of the time. But this. This was freeing. I was consuming alcohol in a manner I had not experienced in a long time and, maybe it was just nostalgia, but I felt it made everything better. And it made me miss my long-gone Xanax a lot less. I peered at the bronze alligator as the valet arrived with the car. Glen slipped between me and the drivers-side door and got behind the wheel. He informed me he was driving, and that was fine. I had no idea where we were going anyway.

Our drive was not long that day. It took maybe an hour for us to get to Five Forks National Battlefield. Pretty much straight down I-95. There was a turn to the east at some point, but I'm not sure where. I can tell you the small park is definitely out in the middle of nowhere. There is a small ranger station/museum and some of the requisite cannon that you find at all Civil War parks. There are a lot of trees and a clearing where I imagined all the fighting took place. Sheridan pulled himself from the back seat, a look of nostalgia in his eye.

"Thank you for bringing me here," he said to Glen as he squatted down and touched the ground around his boots. "This is where we broke them."

Glen looked at me, his eyes radiating joy at the situation. "I bet you never thought that you'd be here," he said. "With him."

I just shook my head. The early morning buzz was long gone, and I was lost in the surreality of the situation.

For the uninitiated, I will offer a brief recap of the Battle of Five Forks. On April 1, 1865, a Union force under the command of my new friend Phil Sheridan defeated a cobbled-together Confederate Army led by General George Pickett. In doing so, Sheridan exposed the flank of Lee's army which, to that point, had done a good job of fighting Grant to a stalemate at Petersburg (which we passed on our way to Five Forks.) With his flank exposed, Lee knew he could no longer hold Petersburg, which was the key to taking Richmond, and the next day the Federal forces to the north broke through his lines and Lee pulled his army from the field. About three weeks later he surrendered at Appomattox and the war in Virginia was over. As far as the outcome of the Civil War goes, the Battle of Five Forks was a key one. However, it is sort of a forgotten fight. Well, to everyone except me. And Phil Sheridan, of course.

We made our way into the museum and had a look around. It was mostly the same sort of stuff you would except to find in any battlefield museum. Old guns and maps and dioramas depicting what may have happened there. They also had a life-size black horse made of plastic and fabric. I hesitate to call it a statue because it wasn't. I mean, it was supposed to look like an actual hose. Wanting to show off, I asked Sheridan, "is this Rienzi?"

"No." He was maybe glaring at me. I could not tell because the sun was shining in through the window he was standing in front of. "My horse is in the Smithsonian Museum. In Washington DC. That, sir, is a fake."

"Right. I meant, is it supposed to be Rienzi?"

"I certainly hope not," he muttered as he picked up an old rifle they had displayed and inspected it. Much as you would have expected him to inspect the rifle of one of his troops in 1865.

The man who was working in the museum eventually came out of the back room where I think he was eating lunch, because of the mustard on his shirt. "Who's he supposed to be?" he asked me as he sat down on the stool behind his cash register.

"That's Phil Sheridan," I told him.

"Huh," was his only response. "Museum's free," he then added. "We've got maps over there. Driving tour's a good one. Won't take you too long. I would recommend it."

"Thank you," I replied.

We spent another ten minutes looking around the muse-um and then drove around the park for a bit. Most things were obscured by all the trees, but the signs did a decent job of painting a picture of what took place.

"Custer was over there," Sheridan pointed out to a cluster

of trees at one point. "He was a hell of a fighter."

"Not at Little Big Horn," I chimed in. I had discovered a certain satisfaction in verbally poking Little Phil.

He shot me another one of his dirty looks. "Here he was."

I could not argue that fact. And hell, I did not know what happened at Little Big Horn. Custer probably fought well there too. After all, getting killed in combat does not necessarily mean one was not a "hell of a fighter."

Our battlefield tour did not last more than twenty minutes and, surprisingly, Sheridan did not offer much in the way of commentary. Instead, he seemed lost in a long-departed past. One he may have wished he could return to. But one he knew was gone forever.

After about thirty more minutes in the car, we were back at Petersburg and then eventually into the Petersburg National Battlefield. We drove around some there too, taking time to look at the famous crater where the Union had attempted to blow a literal hole in the Confederate line by tunneling under them and planting a whole lot of dynamite which they eventually detonated, leaving a depression in the earth that remains to this very day. The park itself was pretty fantastic. In addition to the usual cannon, they have recreated sections of the Confederate defenses, as well as the Union siege positions, which you can go out and explore. The redoubts and forts, with their sharpened sticks and gun placements, stand as if they are ready to explode into action at any minute. We spent close to an hour doing this until Glen parked the car in front of a section of the former Confederate line. He pointed over a small rise and said to me, "Go over there. We'll wait in the car."

After our dinner last night and the talking-to that Glen and Sheridan had given me, I was no longer interested in questioning my uncle's directives. If he told me to do something, I figured I would just do it. It had worked out well enough thus far. At least I was no longer sitting alone in the suburbs, high on Xanax and thinking about the pointlessness of existence. So, I got out of the car and walked in the direction he had pointed. I mean shit, the last time he'd done this I came face to face with Phil Sheridan. There was no telling who (or what) was going to show up this time.

The grass I stepped over was green because it was summer. The air was sticky and as I trudged around the ground men had died fighting over, I noticed sweat starting to bead on my forehead. As I came to the top of the rise, I looked down, and around, and saw nothing. "Keep going!" Glen yelled at me. So I did, walking farther and farther from the car as the perspiration continued to form. The buzz I had been enjoying earlier in the morning slowly had begun turning into a headache as the day wore on. I walked for about ten minutes before I came upon something out of place. But I was not sure the old man in the gray suit was what I was looking for. I slowly approached him, watching him intently, as he studied his surroundings. He appeared to be looking for something. Although I don't think it was me.

"Excuse me, sir," I hailed him as I got closer. "Have you seen anyone else around here?"

By this point I was maybe five feet away and I could clearly see his face and immediately I knew who he was.

"If only we had more men here," he sighed. "We might have held."

I grew up in the shadow of Robert E. Lee. Literally. A giant portrait of the Confederate general hung in the guest room of my grandmother's house in Louisiana and another smaller portrait, with some quote about being a gentleman or doing one's duty (I can't recall exactly what it said) was in her guest bathroom. So, every summer when we ventured east from Texas to spend a couple weeks with her, I would see him multiple times a day. Either standing in the blue uniform he wore before he was ever a rebel general, his arms crossed, his visage stern, but dignified, staring down at the little kid who was fascinated by pictures of any soldiers, or on the smaller picture. That was a black-and-white drawing of his head. It obviously did not have the same effect on me as the larger portrait because I can't even recall the words that were written next to his face. I do remember it existed though. Which should probably count for something. So when I came face to face with him in the sweltering summer Virginia heat, there was no doubt in my mind who was standing in front of me.

No longer dressed in military garb, he wore a simple gray suit. While it was dated, it appeared timeless on him, as wisps of his grey hair blew in the hot summer breeze. He looked me directly in the eye and extended his hand. "Robert Lee," he said, his southern accent flowing as smooth as a glass of the sweetest sweet tea. "It is a pleasure to meet you."

I stuck my hand out and shook his. Phil Sheridan and my dead uncle were waiting for me in my car. There was no way this was going to rattle me. "Good to meet you," I responded. "Hey, I was told to come back here. For some reason. You see anything else around?"

"No," he replied. "There is nothing else around here. Except the trees." He nodded in the direction of a grove about fifty yards away. "Besides, I think you were looking for me."

"I was?"

"Yes," he softly said. "I am here for you." He stared at me sternly. Like the man in the painting. But there was sadness in his eyes that was not in that picture.

"You are?"

"Yes," he insisted. "I believe you are the nephew of my friend Glen. He suggested you might like to meet me the last time I saw him. I was here on business, and he told me you would be here as well. So I agreed to the meeting."

"Business?"

"There are always things to be attended to." He turned away now and went back to inspecting whatever it was he'd been looking at when I'd first seen him. "Your uncle seemed to think you may be in need of some help. So, tell me, how may I help you?"

"Shit, I don't know." He shook his head at my expletive which made me smile. "You want to tell me the meaning of life?"

"You would have to ask a smarter man than I that question," he said.

"I figured."

"Anything else? I am at your service. If you have a question, please ask. That is why I am here this afternoon. If that is not the case, then please tell me so I can go. As I said, I have business to attend to up north."

I did not know what to ask him. Of course, I had the obvious Civil War fanboy questions, but I did not believe that is why he was standing in front of me.

"What were you doing here?" I finally asked. "I mean really? You had to know the war was lost. The Union had won almost every major conflict. The anaconda was strangling whatever was left of the country. So what were you doing?"

His lips turned up in a very slight, almost unnoticeable smile. "I was doing my duty," he answered. "I was defending my country."

"But your country was long gone by then," I told him. "You were just getting people killed."

The smile left as quickly as it had appeared and the sadness in his eyes flared up even more intensely. "Yes, that is true. By the time we got here, I did not know what else to do. The numbers were overwhelming and I knew that, but sometimes all you can do is what is required of you. You are right, I could have surrendered. I could have resigned my commission and gone to Richmond and sat in that house with my wife and waited for the inevitable to happen. There are a hundred things I could have done and maybe I should have done any one of them. But I did not. I did what I was supposed to do, based on my position in the army of Virginia. I was in charge of that fine group of men, and I did my best for them. You are correct that many of them died because of my decisions and, when you look at it from your point of view, with 151 years of hindsight, then you can easily say what I did was wrong. But I think, if I had to do it all over again, I would probably do the same thing."

"So you're okay with the fact that your actions prolonged the war and led to hundreds of thousands of needless deaths, on both sides?"

"No. I am not. That part has torn at me every day since the war ended. But I think you missed my point. If you are called upon, given a duty, a responsibility, then you must pursue it to the best of your abilities. Only a coward abandons his post. Even against the most insurmountable of odds."

As he spoke, I heard something in the distance. And no, it was not the sound of cannon fire. It was, instead, the sound of the Volvo's horn. Calling me back.

"I think I have to go," I told the old man. "We have somewhere else to get to, apparently."

"May I go with you?" he asked.

"Sure. We've got an extra seat."

"Good," he said as we made our way across the hot Virginia ground, back toward the rise which would lead us finally to the car. "Is Sheridan with you?"

"Yes."

"Is he still grumpy?"

I laughed, which seemed to be enough to answer his question in the affirmative.

"Good. I would hate for him to change. It will be good to see him. It has been a long time."

RICHMOND, 2016

A guy walks into a bar with Phil Sheridan, Robert E. Lee, and a famous Hawaiian storyteller, and seemingly no one gives a damn.

Yeah, there was a look when we strolled through the door of the James River Bar and Grill, but it was no different than any other look I'd gotten when I'd walked into any other bar in the entire world. I am guessing you know the look I am talking about. The one that comes from the bartender and the people on the barstools closest to the door. These people (and maybe some more toward the back) almost always turn their heads to see just who is coming in. The look on their faces is almost universally the same. It is a look that conveys the question—do I know this person? Then, basically every time, the look quickly disappears and they go back to whatever it was they were doing before you walked in. If you do not know what I am talking about then you should stop what you are doing and go to your nearest drinking establishment and walk in. You don't even have to stay. Just open the door and step inside. Then you'll know. Go ahead, I will wait . . .

As soon as we were inside, Glen headed toward the bar to order drinks while the generals and I found ourselves a table in the corner. "Mrs. Lee and the girls lived down the street during the war," the old man told us as we all sat down. "It was not a good time for them."

"I suppose not," Sheridan responded. Perhaps a little bit of scorn in his voice.

"Gentlemen." Glen was back with four gin and tonics. "Please. We're not here to rehash old history or revisit old fights. I believe we can find more pleasant topics to discuss."

The two old generals nodded in agreement with my uncle and then toward each other. The clash of ideologies, and bitter feelings, would be left for another time. For now, they would enjoy this time and this place. And, apparently, the drinks that were in front of them. Almost as soon as Glen had set them on the table, the glasses were empty and the two men were asking if we were ready for another round.

This scene repeated itself twice before Lee and Sheridan seemed content with their states of inebriation. The fourth round arrived and neither of them appeared all that interested in their glasses. Lee did not touch his, as Sheridan stirred the small red straw in his absentmindedly while surveying the bar. Glen was long gone by now. He had moved himself from our table in the corner to the bar, where he was chatting with the shapely bartender who he introduced as Jackie on one of my many trips to secure more drinks for myself. It may not be of any surprise to you if I were to tell you that at one point during the night Jackie and my uncle disappeared for about fifteen minutes. It should come as even less of a surprise that when he reappeared he seemed to be tucking his shirt into his pants, smiling at me as he did.

While Glen was sowing his dead oats, I was busy listening to the generals talk about an English Premier League soccer match that was being rebroadcast on the television. Apparently,

Lee had developed an affinity for Arsenal and, as luck would have it, Sheridan was a passionate fan of the team they just happened to be playing, Aston Villa. For most of the second half of the match, I worried the two men were going to come to blows after Arsenal's Olivier Giroud made the Villa defense appear to be little more than ghosts as he scored three goals in the first eighty minutes to lead the Gunners to an easy 4-0 victory. Actually, for most of the second half it seemed most likely Sheridan was going to punch Lee, especially after Mark Bunn's own goal put Villa behind 4-0. Time and space and wherever it was the two of them had been for the past hundred-plus years had not changed the temperament of either man. Lee sat dignified as Sheridan hurled insults, both at him and at his football club. Finally, in the closing minutes of the match, Sheridan let loose a string of profanities that would have made the early 1990s Geto Boys blush.

"I don't think it's that big a deal," I said to him. He did not reply. Either to me or to Lee's attempt to toast the victors. I clinked glasses with the old man, and he seemed pleased with the result of our subsequent toast.

"Do you watch a lot of soccer?" I asked Lee shortly after the game concluded.

"Not as much as I would like," he replied. "But I do watch when I get the chance. Of all of the sports they play now I feel like it makes the most sense. They simply kick the ball into the goal. I also enjoy studying the tactics and the formations they use. I think some of the precision, the different attacks, the flanking, is not all that different from what we strived for on the battlefield. In fact, I sort of see the pitch as a small battlefield each time I watch. The strategy is fascinating. I believe I would have liked to try my hand at it, both as a player and as a coach, had I had the chance when I was younger."

I laughed to myself at the idea of young Robert E. Lee in soccer shorts and cleats running around on a field in rural nineteenth-century Virginia. I imagined he would have been good at it. He was pretty much good at everything he did in his life, so I figured soccer would be no different.

"It's all a bunch of horseshit," Sheridan, who was standing now, exclaimed, interrupting our quiet conversation. "How did they keep allowing Giroud to get open? Three goals! I declare. And the officiating! This game was complete rubbish!"

"Perhaps the issue was with their strategy," Lee chimed in.

"What was that?" Sheridan asked.

"Their tactics," the grey-haired general continued. (Villa Coach Steve) "Clarke kept running them out in a 5-3-2, but no one was accounting for Giroud. It had nothing to do with the officials."

"Did it not?" Sheridan was indignant as he rose from his seat. "I saw at least three instances where Arsenal clearly should have been penalized. And the 5-3-2 is a tried and true defensive formation. It actually should have limited the scoring chances. You should know that."

"The tried and true does not always pan out," Lee advised.

"It does often enough," Sheridan growled. "Besides, what do you know? I am fairly certain you are typically on the losing side of things."

Lee appeared stung and quit speaking.

Sheridan, however, did not. He became progressively louder as he continued to complain about the outcome of the match. Eventually, one of the locals at the bar spun around on his stool and looked our way. "Why don't you shut him the fuck up?" the man demanded. "Or I'm going to shut him up for you."

I took Sheridan's arm and tried to force him back into his chair, but he pulled away from me. By this point Lee was standing, trying to bring some sort of calm to the situation. Glen was at the bar, still talking to Jackie, but his attention was beginning to turn more toward the table he'd left in the back.

"I would like to see you try, sir!" Sheridan was now moving toward the man at the bar. "It would take a lot more than one Virginian to get the better of me."

"Is that right?" The man had moved off his stool and was heading aggressively to intercept Sheridan. He was close to a foot taller than the Union general and probably had a hundred pounds on him. He was dressed in jeans, work boots, and a grey t-shirt. A snap-back black hat with a Confederate flag on it sat on top of his head. As soon as they were standing in front of each other, Sheridan took notice of the hat and slapped it from the man's head.

"I do not know if you realize this, sir. But that is the flag of the losing side, and you disrespect me by wearing it in my presence. I know a lot of brave men who died because of that flag."

The man, while still angry, seemed a bit confused by what Sheridan had said to him. That did not stop him from shoving him backwards, into an empty table. Fortunately, I was behind the diminutive general and was able to steady him so he did not fall over. Glen was on his way over from his spot at the bar and Lee had now joined us as well. "I must apologize for my friend," Lee said to the man. "His manners are somewhat suspect."

"I'd say so," the guy replied just before he struck Robert E. Lee in the face with his gigantic fist.

As if coming from out of nowhere, two other rather large men had joined our once solo nemesis and were in the process of putting their hands on me and Sheridan when Glen showed up and tried to calm the situation. "Come on, guys. Let me buy everyone some drinks," he said, right before a fist to his mouth stopped him from speaking any more. My uncle went down to the ground in a heap and then things began to happen very fast. The man to my right struck me twice in the head and once in the chest before I could return his aggression with a quick punch to his ample gut. It did not seem to faze him though, and soon he was throwing me to the ground. From my spot on the floor, sitting between an overturned chair and some spilled beer, I saw Lee, very much an old man, yet very much a skilled combatant, taking down the man on his left before turning his attention to the original aggressor who now loomed over Sheridan.

"Not so tough down there, are you, little fella?" the giant said to the Union general.

"If you let me get up, you will see how tough I am," Sheridan responded.

The man backed up, waving his hand in front of him as he did, inviting Sheridan to pull himself from the floor. Soon Sheridan was back on his feet, and he straightened his uniform coat and dusted off his pants. After doing so, he took one look at the giant in front of him and struck him, with all of his strength, in the throat. The big man gurgled as he fell to the floor, blood coming out of his mouth. Sheridan kicked the man once or twice in the back but did not utter another word. The giant man Lee had felled, as well as the guy who'd knocked me down, were now on their way to either check on their friend, or kill Little Phil, but Lee was there to stop the first of them, while Sheridan made short work of the second.

By now it seemed everyone in the bar had gathered around to watch what was going on. "Hey, what did the little guy do to Carl?" One of them yelled.

"Is he okay? I think he's bleeding," someone else said.

"Let's fuck 'em up," they all seemed to exclaim in unison as I was helping my uncle off the floor. Sheridan looked at Lee, who just sort of shrugged at him. Neither man was one for retreat, but I think they saw that as the only escape from this particular situation. Sheridan scooped a candle off the only table that was still standing in our general vicinity and threw it as hard as he could against a nearby wall. The fuel inside, which made the flame, exploded on said wall, and soon that side of the bar was on fire.

"What the hell are you doing?" Glen asked him as we hustled out the front door.

"I was covering our retreat," Sheridan replied matter-of-factly.

Lee looked at him angrily as we ran to the Volvo. "You cannot help yourself. Can you?" Lee was mad and his usually measured voice betrayed this fact.

"What?" The small general wondered.

"Always trying to burn Richmond to the ground." Lee sat down in the back of the Volvo and turned his head away from Sheridan.

I unlocked the car in time to see the other patrons of the bar and Jackie the bartender pour out of the front door. The large man was being helped by his friends and did not seem that much worse for wear.

"Should we stay?" I asked my uncle.

"Hell no," he replied. "I don't think they can see us over here and I told Jackie my name was Cliff. So I doubt they will be able to track us down. Besides, I don't have enough time to go to jail. Let's just get the hell out of here."

"Okay."

"You better sit up front," Glen said to Sheridan who was standing, his arms crossed angrily, next to us. "Nephew. Please sit in the back. I will drive."

I quickly ducked into the back seat. Lee did not turn his gaze from the passenger's side window as I did, neither greeting my entrance nor even acknowledging it. He simply stared out into the night as the flames from the fire that was consuming the James River Bar and Grill danced in the darkness.

I-95, 2016

Glen drove the Volvo into the darkness, but the ride did not last long. And no, we were not pulled over by the cops. Although that seemed particularly likely for much of our drive north on Interstate 95. Somewhere to the north of downtown Richmond, he pulled the car into a large parking lot—I believe it was next to the city's botanical garden—and shut off the engine.

"I'm too drunk to drive," he told us as he leaned his seat back. "We'll sleep here and get back on the road when the sun comes up."

Neither general said a word so I just closed my eyes and tried to fall asleep.

It did not take long for the sunrise to ruin a strange dream I'd been having about the small Kardashian sister and her baby daddy. I awoke to find Robert E. Lee's head resting on my shoulder as he snored through his grey beard. I bet you never thought you'd hear that sentence. Am I right? Well, I never thought I'd be saying it. I gently pushed the old man's head back toward his own headrest and noticed Sheridan wide awake, standing outside the car talking to Glen. I could not hear whatever it was they were saying, but they were back in the car soon enough, talking about what had transpired in the early morning hours of this particular day.

I was not all that interested in rehashing past events. Just as long as the police weren't on their way, I was simply relieved to be removed from that situation with my head still attached to my shoulders. "Where are we going?" I interrupted them. Just so I didn't have to listen to Sheridan boast of his fighting prowess any longer.

"North," Glen answered. Perhaps he too was tired of listening to Sheridan talk. "We've got to get these guys back."

"Back where?" I queried.

"Back north," Glen replied, a self-satisfied smile on his face.

"You drive then. You seem to know where you're going."

He pushed the button to start the car and as the car began to move, I noticed Lee was finally awake. We were quickly back on the interstate and heading north. I was not sure exactly where we were going, but the fact we were going toward Washington DC was pretty obvious, as every road sign we drove past advertised the fact. We made it to Fredericksburg and stopped at a Bob Evans for some breakfast. The hostess sat us at our table without even taking a second look at just who she was seating. And, as you probably expected, Glen quickly learned her name and struck up a conversation with her. Soon we had coffee and food on the table, which we all hungrily consumed.

Lee seemed more awake than ever as he cut into his double blueberry hotcakes. He began to tell us about Chancellorsville and the other battles which he'd fought on this very ground. At one point he paused to ask someone to pass him the syrup. I offered him the bottle of maple, but he asked for the boysenberry instead. I watched in wonder as he carefully poured just the right amount (for him anyway) of the hot purple liquid over his blueberry pancakes. When he had reached what he deemed the proper level of saturation, he smiled and handed the bottle back to me. After taking a few bites, he continued with his story about his military exploits in Virginia.

Sheridan, who was seated next to my uncle, across the table from Lee and me, rolled his eyes as the old man began speaking again, before asking Lee to stop. "You lost," he gruffly added. "Stop talking about it."

Lee looked a little humbled behind his blueberry pancakes. He set the fork down and turned away from the men across from him. I could still see the pride in his eyes, and I was growing a little tired of Sheridan's disrespectful behavior. Lee's army's performance at Chancellorsville was one of the great showings of the entire war and one of the finest examples of military strategy and risk-taking in the history of American warfare. I do not know why, but I thought I should speak up for him. Maybe it was because of that portrait in my grandmother's house. Maybe it was the sad dignity with which Lee carried himself now. Whatever the case, I confronted the Union general. "Would you have had the nerve to split your army?" I asked Sheridan. "You sure have a low opinion of our friend here."

"Of course I would have," Sheridan angrily replied. "Hell, I would have split them again and again and again. Maybe four, five times. Whatever it took! Or maybe I just would have had Custer smash their entire line." The little general was obviously upset. "And who are you to question me? What year did you graduate from West Point? How many battles have you fought?" Glen touched his arm to stop him from getting even more worked up. His tone was not as angry when he said, "Do not forget, I came here to help you."

"Okay," I said. "So did he. Maybe you should show him a

little courtesy. At the very least you should show him the courtesy due a worthy opponent."

Sheridan looked perhaps a little shamed as he scooped some hash browns into his mouth. Lee, too, had returned to eating his blueberry hotcakes as Glen smiled across the table at me. The rest of the meal went along quietly. The only words exchanged were regarding the quality of the food. Which was quite high. Breakfast at Bob Evans is nothing to be taken lightly. I cannot say the same for lunch or dinner, but luckily for you, the breakfast is served all day. So, should you find yourself eating at one, you have no excuse not to eat breakfast.

We were all plenty full by the time we left the restaurant to get back in the Volvo. We took our previous positions in the car. Glen was driving, with Sheridan riding shotgun, while Lee and I sat in the back seat. The car was mostly silent, save for the radio playing more of Glen's favorite music, as we made our way past the rows of trees that framed the road rolling north and south.

"Do you ever regret what you did?" Eventually I spoke to Lee and, perhaps, sucked all of the air out of the car in the process.

"What?" he said as Glen turned the music up in the front seat. Sheridan's eyes were closed, although I was unsure whether or not he was asleep.

"You know," I went on. "Do you regret turning your back on your country? Maybe more importantly, do you regret turning your back on your army? That has always seemed like a worse transgression to me."

He smiled at me with half of his face while the other side remained stern and dignified looking. "I do not think it is possible for a man of your time to understand what it was like then. This beautiful land was my country. Virginia was my country. Thus I chose to side with her. It hurt me every day, and in many ways I was very glad when it was all over. Of course I would have preferred a different outcome, but if I am being honest with myself, I did not ever really think we could win an actual war. My only hope was the Federals would decide to quit fighting and let us do as we pleased."

"You mean own people? Slaves? How do you reconcile that? It is one thing to turn your back on your country. It's another to stand up for something as fucked up as slavery."

My language irritated him and I could tell, but he remained measured in his response. "I think most of us knew it was wrong. But it was the way of things. I have no excuse for that and now, so many years after the fact, I wish it had been different. But you know what they say about hindsight."

"It shows you what a bunch of assholes you all were?"

Sheridan let out a booming laugh from the front seat. "Here, here!" he eventually said.

"Should we discuss you and the Indians?" Lee asked the passenger in front of him, quickly silencing Sheridan in the process. He then turned back to me, "I do not know what else you want me to say? It was so very long ago. There is part of me that is surprised you are still so interested in all of it."

His words were enough for me, and we rode quietly into Springfield before Lee finally broke the silence. "We do not have much time together, so if you have any more questions for me, this would be the time to ask them. Please though, no more about the war. I cannot add anything further to that discussion."

"Duty," I said to him. "Do you really think that's all there is?"

For the first time in the twenty-four hours we had been together, Lee laughed. "Oh no," he continued to chuckle. "I know what they say about me. I have seen the picture your grandmother had in her bathroom. All of that makes for great quotes or soundbites, but that is all those are. There is so much more than that. Love and family are probably the most important things I can think of. I spent so many years away from mine . . . and you know what they say about not getting that time back? It is true. I would often go very long periods of time without seeing my children, and every time we would be reunited it was like I was meeting them for the first time. That is a very difficult way to be a good father. I was devoted to my children. But I was not present in their lives as much as I would have liked to have been."

"So love and family and duty?"

A gentle smile crossed the old man's face as he looked at me. "There is even more than that. Although I would say those are three of the most important things to me. There are days. If you are lucky, there are many, many days. Some days are good and some are bad. On other days you lose your entire country. But as long as the next day comes then you have a chance for things to get better. I never got over losing the war, but I very much enjoyed the time I spent in Lexington. I was with Mrs. Lee and in Virginia. Those were some very good days indeed."

"So love and family and duty and . . . days?" The last part maybe made no sense to me. But, perhaps the first part didn't either. Maybe that's why I was here. Searching for whatever it was that I thought was missing.

"Just do the best you can," he replied. "That is all I can tell you."

As we spoke in the back seat on the meaning of everything, Glen had turned the car from the 95 onto the 395 and then to US 1. We followed this road to US 50, where he merged into the eastbound lanes that eventually led us to Arlington National Cemetery. As we reached the main gate Lee asked Glen to stop the car. When he did, Lee got out and went inside the visitor's center. Five minutes later he returned with a bouquet of flowers. "Mrs. Lee will enjoy these," he said as he got back inside the car. "I always like to bring her flowers when I am away longer than a day."

I watched my three traveling companions as we entered the hallowed grounds of Arlington, once Lee's home, now a somber tourist destination. It was about two in the afternoon as Glen drove the car past a security checkpoint and onto a service road that led us into the cemetery. We slowly passed the rows upon rows of uniform headstones marking the final resting places of the many members of the American military who were buried there, the white stones standing in marked contrast to the lush green grass. We headed up a hill, to a house with a fine view of the capitol to the east.

"Gentlemen," Glen said as he turned the car off. "You are home."

ARLINGTON, 2016

Glen parked the car on the service drive next to the main house. Flowers in full bloom seemed to surround us as we almost simultaneously stepped out of the car at the same time. The colors, bright reds and oranges, pinks and yellows, stood in stark contrast to the cemetery as I had a look around at the almost endless progression of gravestones.

As you may know, the house, named Arlington, was where Lee lived prior to the war. It was never really his, though. It was, in fact, the home of his father-in-law, George Washington Parke Custis who bequeathed it to his daughter, and her husband, when he died. Lee's mother was a cousin of Custis's wife, so Lee had actually spent plenty of time at Arlington during his childhood, and he also lived there for the four years between Custis's death and the beginning of the Civil War. It was the home from which his family fled when hostilities broke out and it is the home they never returned to. Following the war, the Quartermaster General of the United States, one Montgomery Meigs, so distraught with grief over the death of his own son (who coincidentally died on a scouting mission for Sheridan in Virginia in 1864) and blaming Lee for that loss of life, decided to bury the Union dead on the grounds of Arlington. Some of the first people buried were placed in Mrs. Lee's rose garden and it was from this beginning that the national cemetery was born.

Lee had a history here, but so did Sheridan. In fact, Sheridan's final resting place is not too far from the front door of the big house. Which, if I'm being honest, is not really that big. The giant Greek revival facade in front is just that, a facade placed on the front of a fairly normal-sized home. Well, normal-sized for today. It was large for the time it was built. But . . . where was I? Oh, yes Phillip Sheridan is buried in Lee's front yard, overlooking the nation's capital below. Legend has it he asked to be buried there so he could watch over the Union, even in death. I do not know if this is the case or not, as I never got around to asking him.

Sheridan and Lee milled about as Glen and I took a brief walk around to inspect the grounds. Washington was hot and sticky, as I suppose it usually is during the summer months. There were a few tourists sitting on the front porch of the house, waiting for the next tour. One of them pointed toward Lee and Sheridan and the rest of the group looked over, but none of them made any attempt to engage them. Strewn all around us, and dropping down the hill the house sits on, were the graves of Union men who died in the war. Farther down the hill were the dead from other conflicts, spreading out onto the other hills and flatter ground around us. Kennedy was down there somewhere. With his eternal flame. I wondered if he and Sheridan ever got together, during the night when everything was dark and the tourists were gone, perhaps meeting to toast their Irish heritage, or talk about Marilyn Monroe, or discuss whatever it is people who've been dead for decades, if not centuries, talk about.

"What are we doing here?" I eventually asked my uncle,

after we'd walked completely around the house and were back standing close to the generals and the Volvo.

"We brought them," he said. "I guess you could say they needed a ride."

I gave him an incredulous look. The eye roll the men of our family are known for. "Really?"

"Sure." He laughed at me. "They asked us to bring them here. So we did. It's not like we were doing anything anyway. Right?"

"I guess."

Lee had approached us as we were talking and was now standing in front of us, holding the flowers he had purchased and waiting for our conversation to end. His gray suit was rumpled from his time in the back of the car, but his hair and beard appeared meticulous thanks to the black plastic comb he seemed to always be pulling from his pocket.

"Glen, my friend." He reached out and touched my uncle on his shoulder. "I just want to thank you for the ride. I have enjoyed our time together. I look forward to seeing you again. Soon, I hope."

"Thanks for everything," my uncle replied, grasping Lee's hand and shaking it as he bid him farewell.

"And you, sir," I was now, again, face to face with the man in the portrait from my grandmother's house. "It was a pleasure to meet you. I hope that I have helped you in some small way."

I looked him in the eye and considered giving him that same patented eye roll but thought better of it. Still, he could tell I was not in agreement with his assessment of my current state. I eventually told him goodbye, but that was all I was able to say.

"Well . . . " For the first time since we'd met at Petersburg, he appeared a little flustered. "Hopefully."

He attempted to brush the wrinkles from his gray suit and

took one last look at his hair in the passenger's-side mirror of the Volvo. "If you will excuse me, I must be getting inside. Mrs. Lee is expecting me." He turned and looked at Sheridan, saying, "General," as he gave him a slight nod. Little Phil nodded back but did not bother to uncross his arms or move from his place leaning against the back of the car as Lee began walking toward the house. Glen and I followed for a while. As we got closer to the house I called after him. "What were you doing?" I asked him. "In Richmond?"

Lee turned to face me. "I was in Richmond to meet my daughter, Agnes. So I could escort her home."

"Your daughter?" I asked.

"Yes," he replied. "But . . ." Then I noticed the pretty girl wearing an antebellum dress standing next to the general.

"She has been with us the entire time," he told me. "I am afraid she did not care to be seen. I am sorry if this has caused you some confusion."

Agnes Lee smiled at me, curtsied, and then walked toward her parents' home.

Her father watched her for a brief time then turned his gaze back toward me. "I do hope you find what you are looking for," he told me before nodding toward Glen and then following his daughter toward Arlington's back door. I figured he chose the back to avoid all the people on the porch, but I can neither confirm nor deny this theory. Upon reaching the back door, he held it open for his daughter to enter, then he followed her inside where I thought I saw a small woman greet them. Then the door closed and he was gone.

Glen and I headed back toward the car where we found Sheridan in the same position as we'd left him.

"I guess it is time for me to go as well," he told us when we were close enough to speak. I do not know if the light of the day was playing tricks on me, but Sheridan looked older now. More the stout general of the army who lived in

Washington DC than the dashing cavalry officer who'd ridden his horse from Winchester, Virginia, back to the battle at Cedar Creek in order to rally his troops and save them from certain destruction at the hands of Jubal Early's army. "I have enjoyed our time." His voice was softer now as he extended his hand to Glen, who shook it.

"It is always a pleasure, Phil," Glen said to Sheridan, who eventually turned to me and asked me to walk with him.

We ventured away from the Volvo and a little ways down the hill to the marker which stood above the ground they had laid Sheridan's body in 128 years ago.

"Do you always come back here?" I asked him. It had become apparent to me in the past few days that this man, who I had been so sure was some sort of impersonator, was not that at all. But I was still unsure just what he was and was hoping for some sort of a clue to solve this mystery before he left.

"Not always," he answered. "Sometimes I return to Massachusetts."

"Boston?"

"Nonquitt," he softly said.

"Do you get out a lot?"

"No," he said. "Not very often at all. It's better that way. This country is strange to me. I prefer to remember it as it was."

"I understand that."

"Are you going to be alright?" He was now leaning against his own tombstone, looking me directly in the eye. He still looked older than when I'd first met him, but his uniform now appeared crisply pressed and his boots were definitely polished more than they'd been the night before.

"I guess."

"Let me offer you some words of advice," he concluded. "You can take them if you want. Or don't. But do me the

WAITING 'ROUND TO DIE

courtesy of listening to them. Alright?"

"Sure."

"If there was one thing I learned from my time in the army, it was that you are better off being on the offensive than on the defensive," he said. "Do you understand what I am saying?" I shrugged my shoulders. "Attack, sir. No matter what it is, what situation you are in, attack it. Give it everything you have and when you think you have nothing left to give, then dig down and find a little more. This will almost always give you an advantage, and when you have that advantage, push it. Do not just sit back and let them come after you. You hit them first and you hit them hard and then you hit them again and you continue to hit them, punish them, chastise them, until you are certain they are defeated."

"That makes absolutely no fucking sense," I replied. Because, honestly, I had no earthly idea what he was talking about.

Sheridan laughed. And then he laughed some more. "No," he told me. "I suppose not." He turned from me and I thought he might go, but soon he was looking at me again. "Do you remember a time when you were happy?"

"I don't know anymore. Maybe I never was."

"Think about it," I noticed a twinkle in his eye as he spoke. "Try and remember a time. And then try to recapture that."

I nodded. I was still not quite sure what he talking about. His advice, while convincingly given, did not really make a whole lot of sense to me, but I appreciated the fact he was trying.

"Thank you." He extended his hand to me. I took it, but not in the traditional manner. No, I took it as I would with one of my friends, sideways, and I pulled him toward me and clapped my other hand on his back—in that stereotypical bro-hug/handshake thing that I am sure most guys my age do. Sheridan smiled up at me. "Have a drink for me next time," he said as I backed away from him.

"I will." I spoke as I turned to leave. I took a few steps up the hill and then turned around to finally ask him about Cedar Creek, but he was gone.

Act III

ALEXANDRIA, 2016

We spent the rest of the day driving around looking at the monuments. We got out of the Volvo at the Lincoln Memorial, which I have to admit was impressive. I'd never had much interest in Washington DC or anything that was there, but the car tour held my attention. Glen was excited to be back. Apparently, he had been here before. More than once and, for some reason, this return trip held a strange magic for him. Our last stop was at the World War II Memorial where he looked up the name of his father on the computers they have outside the fountain. While his father's service record held no surprises for my uncle, he seemed happy just to see his name.

It was almost dark by the time he said, "I guess we should be going."

"Where?" I asked. "Or is that a secret?"

"No," he answered. "It's not a secret. It is almost time for me to go home. So we need to get to California. Are you up for that?"

It had become apparent to me that I had now been gone from my house for over a week and, as far as I knew, no one had any idea where I was. That included my wife and child. And I wondered if they were concerned. Or if they were just glad I was gone. I had a feeling it was probably the latter—and I don't say this in a sad puppy way. I say this out of empathy for people who have to live with the terminally depressed. Maybe they are better off when that person is gone. At least for a little while, they can stop thinking about them and just carry on with their lives. I realize there is probably still that worry. After all, they had no idea where I was. But still, out of sight, out of mind—right?

"Whatever," I replied. "I've got nowhere to go."

"Maybe you'll see that's not the case," Glen said. "Now let's find some place to spend the night. Tomorrow we go to Nashville."

We spent the night at a Hyatt Place in Alexandria, Virginia. It was as nondescript as any other Hyatt Place I have ever stayed in and, believe me, I have stayed in a lot of them. I only mention this because an old college friend of mine lived in Alexandria. A fellow by the name of River Buddy Mike. Okay, if I'm being honest, that's not actually his name. In fact, none of those might be his names. I'm not telling. You know, so you can't bother him. But I digress. RBM, as I have always called him, is a college professor who lives with his wife and two children on a tree-lined street a couple blocks from the site of an old Civil War fort right there in Alexandria. As we had arrived at the hotel fairly early in the evening, I decided I would send him a message on Facebook and see if he wanted to get together for drinks. No, kids, no telephone call for me. I might be old, but it is the twenty-first century. So I went ahead and DM'd him. He replied quickly enough and said sure, suggesting we meet at a pizza place downtown.

Thanks to the navigation system in the Volvo it was not hard for us to find the restaurant he'd mentioned. It is right down the street from an ice cream shop Barack Obama made famous by going there while on a date with his wife, and soon we were parked and walking inside. RBM was at the bar and caught sight of us before I could find him. He quickly got Glen's attention and waved us over to where he was standing.

"It is kind of crowded in here," he said. "Do you want to go outside?"

I agreed and we followed him out the door to a large patio area. There were tables, shade from tall trees, and a couple dartboards out back. It was less crowded, as I suppose people were trying to escape the summer humidity. We found a spot at a picnic table and a waitress hurried over to ask what we wanted to drink. Once the beers had been ordered I introduced RBM to Glen. The two of them had a lot in common as they were both doctors of something other than medicine.

RBM looked older, less like the young man I had known and more like an upstanding member of society I did not recognize. We had once been the kings of Northgate. Together we had closed down every bar in our college town, sometimes multiple ones on the same night. The list of women he had slept with was unrivaled amongst my peers, as was the amount of alcohol he could consume. Sometimes we would slip away from campus and spend countless hours floating down the Guadalupe and Comal Rivers in New Braunfels, Texas, drinking beer and chasing girls. That was where he'd gotten the nickname, which did not seem all that fitting twenty-something years later.

Now he, like me, had a wife and children. He had a job and a house payment and all the things they tell you will want when you grow up. But, unlike me, he seemed happy with it all, which was good for him, I suppose. I secretly hoped some of it would rub off on me as we briefly hugged upon first seeing each other. It did not. That would have been some sort of magic I would not have understood anyway.

Fortunately, RBM still drank beer. Not as much as he once

did; that is probably a given. But still, he drank it. So we consumed as much as he felt comfortable drinking and after a couple pints we fell into a conversation that we may have started twenty years ago, picking it up like we'd just taken a quick break so we could go to the bathroom, in that way you do with those people who are really your friends.

Eventually RBM stopped and said, "Your wife is looking for you. She posted something about it on Facebook. Asking if anyone had seen you. Are you not checking?"

I laughed. I had not even thought of Facebook since the minute I'd pulled the Volvo out of the driveway of our house. Well, not up until a couple hours earlier when I'd decided to contact him. But as you probably know, with their messenger app you don't really have to log into your account. You can just DM someone, and that was what I'd done. I had no idea what was going on with my actual profile or how many likes that last picture I'd posted—the one of the tacos I had for dinner a couple nights before I'd left—had received. Hell, up until that point, I wasn't even sure if the hotels we'd been staying at had Wi-Fi, much less what the password was.

"No," I told him. "I guess I should text her."

"Or maybe actually call?"

"I don't know about all that." I laughed. His stern look told me he did not find my comment funny.

"You guys talk," I said as I stood up from the bench. "I'm going to go take care of something."

RBM nodded approvingly as Glen slid over to occupy the space I had been in. I pulled my phone from my pocket and was a little surprised to find it charged. I suppose I had still been plugging it in when I'd been going to sleep each night, despite the fact I was not really using it. I opened the contacts and went right to the one for my wife. I considered pushing the telephone, so it would call her, but settled on the text button instead. It was interesting that she had not attempted to call or text me. Then again, she's always said if I needed to leave then I should go ahead and do it. I guess she was holding up her end of that deal.

My thumbs moved quickly as I typed out, "Hey, I'm alright. I am in Virginia, going to California. I am with my uncle. I know that doesn't make sense, but I will tell you about it when I get home. Give Lucy my love. Will try and call later." As I finished, I went to press the send button but could not bring myself to do it. Instead, I pressed delete and dropped the phone in a trash can that stood between me and complete freedom.

We spent some more time drinking. All of us told stories of our past glories and the time went by much too quickly. At some point Glen left the table to talk to a girl, and RBM and I were left alone.

"I guess it is about time for me to leave," he said. "I've got to work in the morning."

"It's only ten," I told him. Attempting to shame him into staying out later.

"Yeah. I'm old." He looked me in the eye as he prepared to stand up. "But so are you. What are you doing, man? You have a wife. You have a kid. You can't just run away from all that."

"That's not true," I laughed. "I'm here. Aren't I?"

He grinned at me. It was the same old RBM grin I'd seen a hundred times before. Maybe on the river. Maybe in the Dixie Chicken. It was the smile he gave me when we'd see a couple cute girls we wanted to talk to, or when we knew we were about to have one too many drinks, or when one of us was about to get punched. "Yeah. You are. But you know what I mean. You need to go home. And maybe take your uncle with you. Seriously, that guy is something else." His eyes turned toward where Glen was standing. I looked over and saw my uncle passionately kissing the girl he'd earlier been talking to.

"I can't take him anywhere," I told RBM. "He's dead."

He gave me a quizzical look before saying, "She's got to be half his age."

"Probably," I said. "Good for him."

"I guess." He paused. It was obvious he was trying to think of what to say next, sorting through the words in his mind, intent on making his point and trying not to offend me in the process. "Don't you think you're a little old to be running away from home? You have responsibilities, man. Go home and deal with them. Don't just hide out here in a bottle. That's no way to live."

"Isn't it?" I asked him. "Weren't we happier when we were in college? Weren't we happier when we were drunk on the river? Wouldn't you trade all this bullshit to go back and do all that over again?"

RBM looked at me and did not hesitate to answer. "No." Honestly, his words were kind of shocking. "Don't get me wrong, I loved those days and I still think about them, from time to time. But it is a rare day when I want to trade everything I have now for my past. As far as I'm concerned, all those days led up to this one and I would not have it any other way. You just need to sober up and get your head on straight. Then you will see."

"I think I am seeing clearly." I leaned in close so he could recognize the hostility in the tone of my voice. I was not going to yell at him. Not here, not now. But I needed him to know I in no way agreed with his assessment of things. "I see that I peaked at twenty-eight. I see that everything since then has been a distraction. Just random things to obscure this one fact. The fact that there is no fucking point. Honestly, man, I have been happier out here than I have been for the past ten years. Drinking every day, driving around the country, what is there not to love?"

RBM could tell he was not going to get through to me so, exasperated, he gave up. "Like I said, I've got to go. Are you okay? Do you need anything from me? Directions back to the hotel?"

"No. I will find my own way."

By this point he was standing. "Well, it was great to see you. I feel like it has been forever."

"Almost a decade," I told him.

"Too long."

We were both standing now, and he gave me a brief hug. "Good luck with whatever it is you are doing," he said as he let go.

"You too."

RBM looked at me one last time and I think he wanted to say something else. But he didn't, choosing instead to simply nod and walk back through the door that led into the bar, leaving me alone outside. I looked over at my uncle, who was completely engrossed in his make-out session with whomever that girl was, so I sat back down and finished the rest of my beer and then the rest of Glen's beer as well. If you think that's gross, don't. First off, the guy is dead. Do you think dead people have germs? Second, he'd maybe taken one sip. I mean, really, how many germs could he have gotten on that thing anyway?

Glen eventually came back to the table and picked up that empty beer glass. He looked at it like he wanted to say, "Hey! Where'd my beer go?" But he didn't say anything about it. Instead, he said, "I'm going home with Tonia over there. You go get some sleep and I will meet you at the hotel at nine tomorrow morning. We can head out then. Yeah?"

"Whatever."

Glen patted me on the shoulder as he turned and grabbed the hand of the girl who was apparently named Tonia. I considered ordering another beer but decided against it. I was already probably too drunk to drive, and while I was not against attempting to shame my old friend into breaking with his normal routine, I would have none of that myself. So I waited a few minutes and then headed out of the bar, leaving my uncle in the corner with his latest flame.

The drive back to the hotel was a quick one, and as I walked into the lobby I grabbed a free Hyatt Place postcard from the front desk. I sat down in one of the lobby chairs, one of the ones with a table, and quickly scribbled off a note to Lucy. It went something like this:

> I am sorry I had to leave. I think maybe one day, when you are much older, you will understand. I am alright though. I love you and you will always be my favorite girl.
>
> Love,
> Dad

I scribbled my address on the other side of the card and handed it, and a dollar, to the night manager. "Would you please mail this for me?" I asked him.

"Sure thing," he replied as he pulled a stamp from his cash drawer. "You want your change?"

"No."

I-81, 2016

Glen was punctual as usual, arriving exactly at nine a.m. I'd slept the sleep of the dead, again, but had stirred early enough to go downstairs for some of the awful food they serve at the free breakfast at the Hyatt Place. I had long ago learned not to eat those too-yellow scrambled eggs they put out, so I contented myself with some cereal and a stale pastry. Glen strolled into the lobby just as I was finishing my sour orange juice. "You ready?" he asked.

"Yeah. I already put my shit in the car. You want something to eat?"

"No," he answered as he rubbed his stomach. "Tonia made me biscuits and gravy. I tell you, nephew, that is a wonderful way to wake up."

It is exactly 666 miles from DC to Nashville. I do not think that has any meaning, but I like to imagine it held some deeper truth. Especially when "Highway to Hell" came on during the first part of the drive. We took Interstate 66 west to where it intersects with Interstate 81, somewhere around the town of Middleton, which is, coincidentally, right next to the Cedar

Creek National Historical Park.

"Sheridan would want us to stop," I told Glen as I pointed to the sign for the exit to the battlefield.

He laughed a little. "We don't have time," he told me. "Have other places to be. You should come back though. It is worth the trip."

We merged onto I-81 and were now looking at a straight shot all the way to Knoxville. The green hills of Virginia eventually turn into the green hills of Tennessee on this stretch of road. You pass through Shenandoah National Park and the small mountains on either side of it. Somewhere in Rockbridge County, we turned off the interstate to see the birthplace of Sam Houston. Honestly, I half expected to find the old Texan there. He was not. There were a couple markers though. And some trees leading up a steep hill. Glen seemed interested in it and I needed to piss, so I did not complain. Eventually we got to Roanoke, which I learned was not the place of the infamous lost colony of Roanoke. That was on the coast. The city, which I assume is named after that colony, is much further inland. Shortly after Roanoke, we were in Tennessee and past Johnson City. The 81 soon became the 40 and it carried us into Knoxville. I did not see much of it though. Just the parts along the interstate. It looked much like any other city you drive through. An assortment of tall buildings and strip malls. Signs for McDonald's and Burger King and local places you would actually eat at. If you were hungry. The further along on the trip I got, the more apparent it had become that all the urban spaces seemed the same. The landscape changed. Tennessee looks nothing like Louisiana, but wherever people congregate in great masses, things start to homogenize.

It did not take us long to get through Knoxville. It lacks the urban sprawl of Los Angeles or Houston or Dallas. Soon we were on the western side and speeding the 180 miles to Nashville.

"So we'll stay up here," Glen eventually spoke. Right after he'd finished singing along with Cab Calloway to "Minnie the Moocher."

"Up here?" I asked, nodding my head toward some little town, the name of which I have forgotten.

"No, smart-ass," he answered. "Not here. Up here. In Nashville."

"Okay," I replied. "What's the plan?"

"I don't know," he said. "I've never been to Nashville. We have a room at the Hermitage Hotel. It's downtown. You can use the car's computer to get directions, yes?"

"Yes."

"Good." He turned his head so he could look back out the window. He was about halfway into David Bowie's "Moonage Daydream" when he cut himself off and asked me, "Are you having a good time?"

"Driving six hundred miles?" I asked. "Without any help?"

"Do you want me to drive?"

"Not really. I can do it myself. Shit, I could drive all the way to LA if you wanted me to."

"I don't mind driving." His voice was as agitated as I'd heard it since he'd found me on that rooftop in Memphis.

"I'm just giving you shit," I said.

He quickly settled back into his calmer speech pattern. "I meant on the trip. Are you figuring anything out? At the very least you must have learned something."

"From Sheridan and Lee?"

"Yes, them," he said. "But from everything else as well."

"I learned they don't like each other. Even 150-something years after they ceased hostilities."

Glen laughed. "That's true. But look, nephew, I am not here to help you learn about the Civil War. That's why we didn't stop at Cedar Creek. What I am asking is, have you learned anything about yourself? Do you know why you were going to jump off that roof in Memphis?"

I quickly cut him off. "I was not going to jump. I was just up there to look at the river!"

"Okay." He rolled his eyes at me. "Then have you learned anything about why you are out here? Why you ran away from home?"

"Jesus fuck!" I removed both my hands from the wheel and pulled at my hair. We were fortunate that the Volvo was not only equipped with collision sensors but also with adaptive cruise control, because the car slowed itself when another car slid into our lane at that very moment. "You make it sound like I am a child."

"I say this as your uncle," Glen replied. "And as someone who never really felt all that much like an adult. So don't get mad."

"You know you can't say that."

"Well, I did. Now," he paused. "Aren't you, sort of, a child?"

I returned his eye roll, but with even more vigor. "Fuck you. I'm forty-five-fucking-years old. I wish I was a god-damned child."

"I think you know that I mean."

Few people in this world have ever known the adult version of me better than my uncle Glen. I am sure I've said this before, but he was my kindred spirit. The only one in my family, and one of the few I had in the rest of my life. So when he said I was a child, he knew what he was talking about.

"Fine," I said. Like a ten-year-old whose best-laid plans had been thwarted by his smarter parent.

"Now that we're past that, let me ask you again, have you learned anything?"

I thought long and hard about it. Other than the obvious things. Like what I said about Lee and Sheridan. Or the fact that I enjoyed getting drunk. Or that my uncle still had a way with the ladies. I could not think of a damn thing I'd learned. We'd driven across half the country and we were headed back the other way now, and everything still seemed as confusing, and as pointless, as it had been when I'd walked out of my house in Austin.

"Do you think I will discover the meaning of life out here? On the open road?"

"No," Glen said. "You still don't get it. This 'meaning of life' you keep talking about is not what you should be looking for. I don't know the meaning of life. Not that I should know more than you, but I'm just saying. I have seen things you have yet to see, and those great mysteries are still there for me as I suspect they always will be."

"So what are you asking?"

"I want to know whether or not maybe you've figured some things out?" He paused. "Besides the meaning of life."

I drew in a long breath, then exhaled what felt like a million words. "I don't think so. I mean, I'm not going to learn the meaning of life. Okay. I guess I figured that out. So then maybe someone could tell me what I'm doing here? Or maybe just tell me what I'm supposed to be doing here? Or, if that's too hard, how about telling me what I should be doing here and not in any existential way, just tell me what sort of job I should have. What can I do to be a productive member of society? I mean, does it even matter if I'm a productive member of society? Maybe I am just better off in my house staring at the wall. And while we're at that, someone tell me where all my fucking friends went? And you? Why did you leave? Am I going to find the answer to that out here? Once we've discovered those truths, then please explain to me how not to fuck up my kid. Because I don't want her to end up like me. And the anxiety attacks. Someone please make them stop. Do you have any idea how hard it is to live each day feeling like you're about to drop dead? Like at any moment, you could just fall over—dead. Don't get me wrong. I fucking love the way Xanax makes me feel, but I would like to just use it recreationally. I don't really want to HAVE to take it. Do you know what I mean? And, lastly, why can't I fucking write anymore? What the hell happened to that? I have lived most of my entire life, ever since I realized the religion I was being fed was a bunch of horseshit, with a big empty hole inside of me. But the writing, and if I'm being honest, the liquor, filled that hole. So what happened? Is my kid supposed to be my reason now? If so, then why can't I have the kid and the writing? I mean, tell me. Why, when I sit down to write, does nothing at all come out? Or, when I really force it, why is the stuff that comes out just a bunch of shit?" I stopped before adding, "I think that's it."

"Wow," was all Glen said before turning up the radio and joining Jim Morrison in singing the final chorus of "Light My Fire."

We eventually made it to Nashville. Those 666 miles behind us, I was happy to finally be at the hotel, and what a spectacular one it was. Located at 231 Sixth Avenue in downtown Nashville (right across the street from the state capitol), the Hermitage Hotel was built in 1908 and is one of the nicest places I have ever stayed. The lobby is like a palace, complete with a stained glass ceiling. We had a simple double room but found it was handsomely appointed. That night, after we'd dined in the fantastic hotel restaurant (the Capitol Grille), we came back to find slippers next to the bed placed on hand towels—so your feet never have to touch the carpet—and water bottles and a few assorted sweets next to the bed. We had hardly spoken since our talk in the car and that was fine with me.

"Maybe just focus on one thing," Glen said to me as I lay on my bed watching *The Good, the Bad and the Ugly*.

"What?"

"Maybe just focus on one thing," he repeated. "From our conversation earlier in the car. I think you are looking for too much. If you just focus on finding one thing, something, anything, I think it might be easier. And, who knows, if you can figure out that one thing, then maybe you can work on a second thing. But, for now, try and solve one problem. I'm not telling you which one—it's your life, you decide."

His words actually made some sense, so I took them to heart. I did not tell him that though. I just nodded and carried on with the movie.

NASHVILLE, 2016

Intent on finding the answer to something, I strolled alongside my uncle out the door of the Hermitage Hotel and into the already warm Nashville morning. Glen had decided we would take a day's rest from our cross-country drive and explore the capital of Tennessee. We started with a tour of exactly that—walking across the street to check out the capitol building. After finding it to be much like every other capitol either of us had visited, we returned to the hotel and had the valet bring the Volvo around so we could take in those parts of the city that were not within walking distance.

The city of Nashville is a pretty sprawling affair, at least compared to Knoxville. We drove around for a few hours before stopping at Andrew Jackson's house. The tour there took another few hours, then we returned back toward downtown. We saw an exhibition of paintings of injured Civil War soldiers at the Parthenon Museum. Yes, there is a Parthenon in Nashville and apparently, it looks pretty much just like the one in Greece. I cannot state this to you with one hundred percent certainty as I have never been to Greece. Glen had been. Once when I was a child, I'd received a letter and an envelope full of foreign currency from him. In the letter, he told me that he had put one of his fingernails behind a statue in some ancient Greek temple with the hopes that his DNA might mingle with the DNA of the ancients. It didn't make a whole hell of a lot of sense to me as an eight-year-old, but I understood it better now. He did remark that the Nashville Parthenon looked a lot like the one in Greece—only newer. So I guess you can go ahead and take his word on it, if you want. I am not saying he's an expert or anything. But he has seen both of them, so that's got to count for something.

I would like to tell you more about Nashville, but I was driving the entire day, so I did not get a chance to look at it as closely as I might have liked to. I will tell you there are hills all around it and it is very green. Lots of trees and lush grass in front of people's houses. The neighborhoods seemed interesting as well. They have White Castles and Nashville hot chicken places, which makes it unique to pretty much anywhere else in the country. As I enjoy both of these particular delicacies, I was a little saddened I had to choose one or the other for lunch. I eventually settled on the latter, which was a partial win anyway.

As it got later in the day, we made our way back to the hotel and returned the Volvo to the valet. We then marched down the hill the hotel sat on, toward the river and the bars that line Broadway. We made a special trip around the corner to look at the Ryman Auditorium and then ventured back onto the main drag, looking for somewhere to drink. As we searched for the dive-iest bar we could find, I found myself thinking about the Glen Campbell song "Rhinestone Cowboy." I had been particularly fond of that song when I was a child, and a big part of the reason why was that the street I lived on—Cumberland Drive—was right off of Broadway Boulevard in Garland, Texas. When I got older, I assumed he was singing about the Broadway in New York City. But on this day, I wondered if maybe he was singing about the Broadway in Nashville? Honestly, I have never really watched the movie, so I'm not that sure what he's singing about. Where do people have star-spangled rodeos anyway?

Eventually we found a place that looked sufficiently seedy, and Glen asked if I wanted to go in. I replied in the affirmative and soon we were camped out at a table in the back with two rounds of drinks in front of us. We did not speak for a minute or two as I chased the cherry from my old-fashioned around the bottom of the glass in front of me with a straw, while Johnny Cash sang "Cocaine Blues" on the jukebox. When the man in black was finished, I asked my uncle, "So, the fact that you're here. Can I find some reassurance from that? Can I assume there is something else? After all this."

"You know what they say about people who assume." He laughed. Alone.

I should now add that people on this particular side of my family have a tendency to make stupid jokes that only they find funny. My uncle was a genuinely smart and funny guy who could keep your interest for many hours, telling stories at the kitchen table. Still, he was not immune to this family quirk. So I did not hold his attempt at humor against him. I simply waited for him to quit laughing before I said, "Seriously."

"Oh, nephew." He finally got the picture that I did not find his joke funny. "I suppose you can take something from this. After all, I died, yet here I am. So there is that. I wish I could answer all of your questions, but the answers might not make much sense to you, because they don't make that much sense to me. I can tell you that we are here, in this day, and we have many more drinks to drink tonight. That is all I can promise you. The rest is for you to discover. On your own. Later."

"Tell me what happened after you died."

"I don't remember."

"Tell me where you've been the past thirteen years."

"Somewhere else. Somewhere like this, but different. Everything is less clear there. There are no sharp edges to things, just fuzzy, rounded corners and blurry vistas. It is almost like a haze hangs over it all and you don't hurt there, but you don't feel as much either."

Then he stopped. I waited for him to continue, but he only offered me a gentle smile and a shrug of his shoulders. "I guess that's all I'm getting." I sighed.

"Sorry. I cannot give you any more, so you might as well quit asking."

"Yeah.," I drank the rest of my next old-fashioned.

I gave up at that point. We continued to drink for the next hour or so until Glen eventually found a girl at the bar to talk to. She looked older than him, which was a change from his previous hookups. For some reason, I found this refreshing. Eventually she was joined by a younger-looking version of herself who shook my uncle's hand and then, after talking to the pair for maybe five minutes, walked over to where I was sitting. The girl was tall and blonde and maybe twenty-five years old. She was wearing a floral-print summer dress and her hair brushed her bare shoulders as she strode across the bar toward my table. She was backlit with every other step she took, from the bar door opening and letting in the last light of the day. The closer she got, the prettier I could tell she was. Soon she was in front of me.

"Hi." She thrust her hand toward me. "I'm Ashley. That's my mom over there. Talking to your dad. They told me to come over here and say hi, so I figured I would. They seem pretty wrapped up in their conversation and you looked kind of lonely."

I reached up and returned her handshake. "He's not my dad. He's my uncle." I told her. "And he's dead."

She laughed. "What do you mean?"

"Nothing," I told her. "Do you want to sit down?"

Her face gave away a bit of confusion, and perhaps apprehension, but she did eventually sit down across from me.

"You want a drink?"

"Sure," she said. "Shot of Jack and a beer. I don't care which kind. But nothing light."

I walked toward the bar and stood next to Glen, trying to get the bartender's attention. My uncle did not acknowledge my presence as I ordered the drinks for Ashley and got myself another round as well. When I returned to the table, she was lost in her cell phone and I don't think she even realized I was standing there until I put the drinks in front of her.

"Thank you," she said as she looked up at me before taking the shot glass and knocking back the amber liquid inside. "Sorry about that. It's my boyfriend. He wants me to come home and take care of our son so he can go out with his friends. Can you believe that shit?"

"Not at all."

She sipped from her beer as I played with the straw in my old-fashioned. "Do you have any kids?"

"I do. A daughter. She is thirteen. How old is your son?"

"Four," she told me.

I smiled and remembered when Lucy was four. If I am being honest, and I obviously am—look at how much I've opened myself up thus far—those were my favorite times with my kid. She was old enough to have fun with, but not old enough to cause a lot of trouble. I cannot tell you what I would give to go back in time for one more trip to the park or for one more chance to push little Lucy on the swings. "That's a good age," I eventually said.

"Yeah," she said. "It is." Her eyes lit up when she spoke about her child, and she no longer looked apprehensive about sharing this table with me. "So what are y'all doing here?"

"Drinking."

She laughed and slapped me on the arm. "Not at the bar! In Nashville. Glen told me you were from out of town."

"We're driving through. Heading out to California. I have to take Glen home."

"Does he live in California?"

"Sure." I was not sure how to properly answer this question.

"That is cool," she replied. "I went there once. Right after college. Drove the entire coast—from San Diego to San Francisco. It was a great trip."

There was a part of me that wanted to explain to her that she had not, in fact, driven the entire coast, but I chose not to. Instead I said, "Beautiful country," and let the topic die.

She smiled back at me and did not say anything else. We spent the next half hour watching as Glen and her mother grew closer and closer. The more I drank, the more I thought about trying to see if some of Glen's charm had worn off on me and if I could somehow use it on this girl. But when I took a second to consider how I must look to her, I gave up on the idea.

It was getting later in the day and I was still thinking about getting those sliders from White Castle. Ashley eventually explained that this was her girls' night out, but that her friends had to cancel on her because their children were sick. So she'd come here to hang out with her mother and was maybe a little disappointed to find her mom spending all her time with someone else. However, she did not want to go home yet because she thought her boyfriend was being a dick for asking her to give up her one free night so he could spend more time with his friends. Apparently, they had an arrangement where each of them got one night a week off from the strains of parenting and she had no intention of giving up her evening off. Even if it meant she had to drink awkwardly at a table with some guy she didn't know.

We sat quietly watching the baseball game on the TV. When it eventually ended, I figured I would attempt to resume our conversation. "What do you do?" I asked her. Choosing the most innocuous of topics. Well, besides the weather.

"I'm a nurse," she said. "I work in the ER right now. But I would like to transfer to something a little less stressful."

"That's cool."

"What do you do?" she asked me.

I could not help but laugh at her question because I did not know the answer. "I used to be a writer," I told her. "I am not really sure what I'm doing now."

She gave me the same look almost everyone gives me when I tell them that. It is sort of a cross between "huh" and "this guy's a loser," mixed with the question "is this guy rich/how does he support himself?" "What do you write?" she eventually asked.

"Oh, all kinds of stuff." I had this answer down pat. "I started out writing sports. I have written some history stuff. I wrote a novel. Some fiction. I would like to just write about baseball history, but it's not that easy to support yourself doing that."

"I bet!" she enthusiastically stated. "Your novel, tell me about it. Is it anything I might have read?"

"I doubt it," I told her.

"What is it called?"

"*A Season in Hell.*"

She nodded approvingly. "What was it about?"

"A girl."

This time she laughed and, for the first time since she'd sat down, I saw the luminous smile that had been on her face when she'd first approached the table. "Of course it was." She paused to sip her beer. "I will have to look for it."

"It's pretty hard to find."

"Oh, you can find anything on the internet," she replied.

I suppose she was right. There probably is a copy out there. Somewhere. Not that I expected her to ever look. The night unfolded in this manner for another couple hours. I could not help but notice that the more the time wore on, the closer Ashley got to me, until we ended up sitting close enough to each other that our legs were touching. Soon, she had her hand on my shoulder and it began to dawn on me that maybe some small part of Glen's charm may have actually found its way to me.

We were in the middle of a conversation about Nashville Predators hockey when Glen and her mother eventually came over and joined us. The woman, whose name was Sally, was almost a perfect copy of her daughter—or vice versa as it were, I suppose—except twenty years older. Her tall frame wore a little more weight than her daughter, but her face was virtually the same, save for a few wrinkles. Her hair was similarly blonde and hit at just about the same spot on her shoulder. She smiled at me and extended her hand, which I grasped and shook for a brief second. The pair sat down for a fairly quick round of drinks and then made plans to leave.

"I am going to go back to Sally's for the night," Glen said, after taking his final sip of his gin and tonic. "You can get back to the hotel, yeah?"

"Hey!" I was upset, but not because he was leaving me (again). "I thought we were going to go to White Castle! You said you would drive us. I've had like ten drinks. I can't drive over there."

Glen grinned and raised his eyebrows. "Sorry," he said as he stood up. "Next time." The woman, Sally, rose from her chair as well and said something to Ashley I could not hear. She then kissed her daughter on the head and followed my uncle out of the bar.

"Well shit," I said as soon as the door swung shut behind them. The girl-induced trance I had been in was broken by the fact I might not get my tasty sliders after all.

"I can take you," Ashley said to me, placing her hand on top of mine. "It's fine."

"Are you okay to drive?" I asked.

"Yeah. I only had a few drinks," she explained as she rummaged around in her purse, looking for her keys. "And I don't live that far away." She plucked the keys from her bag and held them up, shaking them as if she'd won a prize.

"Alright." I rose from my seat to walk out with her. It was the first time we'd stood side by side and I realized she was almost as tall as I am. It is not like I am a giant, but I am a bit over six feet tall, so she was a very tall woman. As we strode toward the door, she put her arm through mine and we exited the bar, arm in arm.

The night was sticky, yet cooler, as we strolled down Broadway to where she had parked. She drove a black Dodge Challenger, which I found pretty funny. "Don't you have a hard time getting your kid in and out of the back seat?" I asked.

"Sure," she told me. "But it's worth it."

"This is my favorite car," I continued. "I had one, briefly."

"What do you drive now?" She asked.

"A Volvo," I sadly answered, more than a little ashamed. "It's a station wagon."

"That's cool," she said right before she leaned in and kissed me. I was taken aback for a minute. She was the first person I had kissed besides my wife in close to two decades and the electric feeling of her lips touching mine was a jolt. She pulled back and smiled. I was unsure why someone so attractive would kiss me, but I was grateful all the same.

"Why did you do that?" I stammered.

"You seem sad," she happily replied. "And I wanted to."

I was tempted to thank her, but I just returned her smile as she whispered, "Safest car on the road," in my ear before opening the passenger door and pointing me inside.

It only took five minutes to get to the closest White Castle, which was not the nicest-looking location. In fact, there seemed to be a homeless camp in the parking lot, but it did not bother Ashley as she pulled the car into the space closest to the door. "Well, here you are. White Castle."

I opened the door to get out and thanked her for the ride. I was unsure how I would get back to the hotel but thought I could figure that out once my belly was full of those delicious little hamburgers. Once out of the car I was surprised to hear the powerful V8 engine go silent. "You want some company?" she asked as her long legs gracefully slipped out of the driver's side door.

"Sure," I said before following her inside.

Once in the restaurant, under the harsh fluorescent lights, I was able to see just how pretty she was. Her eyes were a fairly stunning shade of blue, her skin a soft shade of white and her body was as fit as any I had ever seen. In stark contrast, I stood next to her in my uniform of extra-long Dickies work shorts and the black Riverboat Gamblers t-shirt I'd been wearing for a week. I was a little taller than her, but probably fifty pounds overweight. My long beard had gone mostly grey a long time ago and I could not recall the last time I'd combed my hair. I wondered if she was shocked by my appearance, now that she could really see me. And I wondered if the people working the counter wondered why this woman had brought one of the homeless men into the restaurant with her.

There were a few other late-night diners, but we did not have to wait to order. I had my usual—twelve sliders and a Coke. Ashley ordered something much more reasonable, although I was still impressed by the fact that once the food came, she consumed her four sliders and then asked to eat one of mine. We sat side by side but did not talk much as I was too engrossed in my food. She would occasionally check her phone, but that was the only interruption of our silent repast. Once it was all gone, and we were left with nothing more than a pyramid of empty slider boxes in front of us, she again began to search for her keys in her purse. "Okay, this time I really do have to go home. I think my boyfriend is starting to get mad."

"I understand," I stood up to walk out with her. "Thanks for the ride. And for eating with me. And for . . ." Again, I wanted to thank her for the kiss, but decided against it.

"My pleasure," she said. "That was quite a feat back there!"

"Ha-ha," I said. "I don't get much of a chance to eat White Castle back home."

"I guess not," she said.

By this point, we were standing in front of her car, and she put her arms around my neck. They rested on my shoulders as I reached out and pulled her closer. Once again our lips met and once again I felt the electricity of a first kiss with someone new. I know, it was technically not our first kiss, but it was close enough. Quit being such a nitpicker.

This kiss lasted longer than the first, significantly longer. Long enough for her hands to explore most of my back and long enough for my lungs to fill with her scent. It was a mixture of whatever perfume she was wearing, bourbon, and maybe fried food. It may sound odd to you, but it smelled of heaven. And of hope.

This time I could not help myself. "Thank you," I exclaimed.

She just laughed. "Do you want a ride back to your hotel?"

Honestly, I felt like that was a foregone conclusion, but it seemed I was wrong. "You want to come back with me?" I asked. But she shook her head no. "I have to get home. My boyfriend is expecting me and I don't want to listen to any more of his shit than I have to. Plus I have work in the morning. Responsibilities, you know?"

I did. But I didn't. So I did not say anything.

"Are you really leaving tomorrow?" she asked as she pushed her hair out of her face and to the back of her head.

"I think so." I wished it was not the case. I wanted to drink more with her and make out more with her and take her back to my hotel room and do whatever it was people did in those sorts of situations. Maybe we would fuck. Maybe we would just watch Sergio Leone westerns on the television. It didn't matter. Either would be fine with me.

"You sure you don't want to come back to the hotel with me?" I tried again. "We have a pretty well-stocked bar. And a pretty big TV!"

For some reason, I really thought the television would sell it. It did not.

She bit her lip and I felt like maybe she was seriously considering my offer, but her final answer was still no. "I can give you a lift back," she told me. "But I can't say."

I leaned in and kissed her one more time and she kissed me back. The signals she was giving me were mixed, but her ultimate answer remained the same. "That's fine," I eventually said. "I can walk."

"Are you sure?"

"Yeah. The walk will do me good."

"I'm sorry," she said as she gave me one last hug and then made her way around the car. "I really wish I could." At this point she was on the other side of the Challenger, opening the door and preparing to get in. "Good luck with the rest of your trip," she said before she disappeared into the driver's seat. "Have fun in California!"

With that Ashley shut the door and started the car. She waved to me through the passenger's side window and then pulled out of the parking lot and made a right on the street that ran in front of it. Soon, her taillights were gone and I was left standing in the parking lot of the White Castle, surrounded by the homeless, but still totally alone.

I-40, 2016

Glen stumbled into the room about four a.m., drunker than he'd been when he'd left me in that bar. I was not really asleep, so it did not bother me that much. "I thought you were staying the night at Sally's?" I asked as he took off his pants in front of my bed.

"Eh," he answered, dropping said pants on the floor and then taking two steps and falling onto his own bed. "She got really clingy at the end. I didn't want to spend the rest of the night snuggling. This way we can leave early."

I would like to report we got up and left a nine a.m. as we'd planned, but that was not the case. In fact, Glen did not wake up until ten thirty and looked worse for the wear when he did. After getting a few cups of coffee in him we finally headed downstairs to get on the road.

"What happened with you and the daughter?" he asked about an hour later, as I drove the Volvo west on Interstate 40.

"We went to White Castle," I said, wary of the blind spot light in the passenger's side mirror as I attempted to change lanes. I did not feel like discussing my attempts at infidelity

170

with my uncle, so I went no further into what had happened. "Then she left."

"That's too bad," he said. "She was cute." Two minutes later he was asleep, his head resting against the window.

If you are driving west, you can take Interstate 40 almost all the way to Los Angeles. It sort of dead-ends in Barstow, California, and from there you get on the 15 and ride it into LA. I am guessing Sheryl Crow probably knows this, right? All those times she was hooking up with truckers in Barstow? She must've at least been aware of the 40. But I digress. We were heading west, through the mountains of Tennessee. We sped past Jackson and around Memphis. Then we were over the big river and into Arkansas. Driving back through the screen of trees, we ended up in Little Rock and had to follow the road north before it swung west again. We stopped to eat in Fort Smith before crossing over into Oklahoma.

It was late in the day and the sun was almost directly in my eyes as I drove across the state line into the former Indian Territory. I have never thought much of Oklahoma. A lot of that has to do with me being from Texas. We're supposed to hate our neighbors to our north. You know? So I always have. All that said, the state itself can be amazingly beautiful. In some parts, it is even prettier than my home state. While it does not have the mountains and curtain of trees of Arkansas, it does have some pretty impressive vistas and sizable rises that, while not exactly mountains, seem to me to be a little bigger than a typical hill. It was through this landscape that I drove. Glen was still falling in and out of sleep next to me with almost no words spoken between the two of us. It gave me the opportunity to control the radio and I was happy to listen to some music a little more current than the greatest hits of the '60s and '70s that he preferred. Of course, when I say current, I am mostly speaking of the music of the 1990s, which means I was listening to music that was at least seventeen years old and, in some cases, almost thirty. Not very current, right? It always amazes me when I think of those numbers because it all still sounds fresh to me. It is very sobering to realize that my younger days are so far in the past and, perhaps, even more sobering to realize how quickly it all passed.

While the scenery in Oklahoma is beautiful, the towns are fewer and farther between than they are in Arkansas. Most of the ones we drove past had Native American names I cannot remember. We did go through Shawnee as we approached Oklahoma City. I think I only remember that because both Brad Pitt and Jim Thorpe were born in, or around, there. Or maybe it's because it is the name of an actual tribe. I am sure that helps. Around ten p.m. we were in the middle of Oklahoma City and, as I was tired of driving, I decided it would be prudent to stop. After all, Glen was not going to be any help driving tonight.

OKLAHOMA CITY, 2016

I found a hotel somewhere in the downtown area and we breezed through check-in. After dropping my bag in the room, we decided to go out in search of food and drink. I wish I could tell you more about Oklahoma City, but there is very little I recall. The hotel we stayed in was fairly nondescript. The restaurant we ate at was right next to the hotel, although it was in no way connected to it, and the bar where we drank was actually attached to that restaurant. We each dined on a fairly sizable steak that was not particularly flavorful, and maybe a little chewy, and washed them down with our beverage of choice. From there we walked the fifty feet or so into the unremarkable bar section of the restaurant, ordered another round, and sat down at the only empty table in the place.

"So what are you doing?" It was my turn to ask the questions now, and Glen seemed maybe a little startled by it.

"What do you mean?" he asked. "Having a drink with my nephew?"

"No. I mean out here. What are you doing on this trip?"

He rolled his eyes. "Are we getting into that again? I think I've told you repeatedly, I came to help you."

"No. Not that," I sipped from my sub-par old-fashioned. "I don't mean in relation to me. What I mean is, what are you doing?"

"How so?"

"All the women," I said. "Are you fucking your way across the country?"

He laughed. Not a small chuckle either, but a hearty belly laugh. "Maybe I am," he replied. "I just . . . I can't explain it. But it feels so good to be here. With you. On the road. Exploring. Seeing the country. I just can't help myself. I feel so alive right now. Much more alive than I have felt in . . ." he paused, obviously thinking. "It is like the old days. You know?"

My uncle was typically more eloquent than this and I took his stunted sentences as evidence that he was truly enjoying himself.

He finished his gin and tonic and maybe found a little of his composure. "When you are gone, there is so much you miss. The people, the ones you love, are the biggest part of this. I miss our conversations. I miss the emails. The secret meetings in Los Angeles that no one else in the family ever knew about. But you also miss the sights and the sounds of everyday life. And you know a big part of that for me was the women. Oh, nephew, I doubt I can ever tell you just how much I miss the women."

"I think I can guess," I interrupted.

"I suppose you can," he chuckled. "And this chance came, and of course I took it because you needed my help. But it became apparent to me that it was a second chance for me as well. I am sure you realize I did not plan on leaving when I did. There was still so much more I wanted to do and maybe this is my opportunity to do a little of that while I help you. So yeah, if I get the chance I am going to spend as much time with as many pretty women as I can, because I have no idea when the opportunity will ever present itself again."

I could not argue with what he was saying to me. There was never a person more full of life than my uncle Glen. And now, even though he was dead, those same words seemed appropriate when describing him.

The night continued on this way, the two of us making small talk as I watched him look for an opening with any of the women in the bar. However, it did not seem like it was coming, and around one thirty a.m. I was ready to call it a night. Glen, on the other hand, had other ideas. An Oklahoma cowboy had left his girl at the bar to go shoot pool with his friends and I could tell Glen was interested as he watched her intently for about five minutes before rising from the table.

"Don't," I warned him. "She's with that guy."

"For now," he winked at me, then raised his eyebrows twice. "She might be with me in fifteen minutes."

I tried to grab his arm, but he shook loose and before I could say another word he was standing next to the girl at the bar. I watched, worried about what would happen when her boyfriend saw what was going on, yet impressed by the ease with which my old uncle charmed this much younger woman. After ten minutes or so of back and forth, her hand was brushing his on the bar while his other hand was resting on her shoulder. I watched apprehensively as the cowboy noticed what was going on and walked back over toward his girlfriend and Glen. I was especially not happy to see him still holding his pool cue as he grabbed Glen's hand and forcefully removed it from where it had been. I was quickly up out of my chair and on my way to hopefully stop the confrontation when I caught sight of the guy's friends hurrying over from the pool table as well. There were three of them and they were all about the same size as the first guy. Which is to say, they were all much bigger than either me or my uncle. In fact, if you'd told me they were members of the offensive line of the University of Oklahoma football team, I would not have been surprised.

"Get your fucking hands off my girl, old man," the first cowboy said as he shoved Glen into the corner.

We have already established my uncle is no good with his fists, so he was trying his best to defuse the situation. "It's okay," he tried to calm the guy. "We were just having a conversation. Nothing wrong with that, right?"

For a second the big fellow seemed like maybe he was just going to let it be. Then his girlfriend looked at Glen, then looked at him, and said, "Don't listen to him, Brian. He was so hitting on me."

I rose from my seat as it became apparent Brian was about to do something he should not. I bounded across the barroom floor faster than I have moved in decades and struck the big fellow in the face with as much force as my time-ravaged, alcohol-filled body could muster. The skin of his cheek seemed to melt against my fist as it crashed into him. His head turned violently to the right and something flew out of his mouth. Whether it was spit or a tooth I will never know.

The next thing I saw was the big cowboy hitting Glen, who went down pretty easily with the first punch. It surprised me he did not strike me first. After all, I'd hit him. "That was for hitting on my girl," he snarled at Glen, who now lay under him on the floor. "And this if for punching me, cocksucker." His rather large hand then crashed into the side of my head and things went black. But not for very long. I regained my senses long enough to push him away from me. Unfortunately there was no stopping the guy, as he took the pool cue he'd been holding in his left hand and broke it against my shoulder. I took another swing at him and grazed the side of his ear, but it only served to make him angrier. He landed two more big right hands to the side of my head and soon blood was coming from my mouth. I do not know if it was a good thing, but at this point I was being held up by little more than the barstool as Glen lay on the floor moaning. I threw one more punch at the guy and landed a weak roundhouse which I think hit him in the chest. He responded by knocking me down next to Glen before repeatedly kicking me in the side. Finally, mercifully, sometime before I lost consciousness, one of his friends pulled him away.

"Come on, Brian," one of them said. "The cops are here and you don't need to go to jail again."

He let them pull him away. I was pretty sure he could have broken free had he wanted to. He seemed to regain his composure as he backed up. "You're lucky," he said as he pointed at the two of us, almost in a pile, against the bar. "I should kill you."

"Not again." One of his friends got in front of him and pushed him toward the door.

"Celia, let's go," he said to the girl as he grabbed her by the arm and pulled her away with him.

I looked down at Glen and I think, maybe, he was about to say something, but when the blood from my mouth landed on his shirt he seemed to think better of it.

As the cowboys headed out the front door the bartender finally showed up with a towel that he handed to me as he helped my uncle back to his feet. "Sorry about that, guys. Those kids come in here and start shit a lot. I think one of their mothers is a waitress next door. Can I get you anything?"

I pushed the towel against my mouth, hoping the bleeding would stop. Glen was now on his feet and rubbing what must be his sore jaw. "No thanks," he told the bartender as we watched the police outside briefly stop and question the guys who'd just kicked our asses before letting them walk off. Soon enough the officers were inside and in front of us.

"What was going on here, fellas?" one of them, tiny, wiry, speaking in some sort of strange midwestern accent, flecked with insecurity and authoritarianism, asked us.

"Oh, just a misunderstanding," Glen told him.

"Right," the little cop said. "You got any ID?"

My uncle just sort of shrugged and smiled, while I fished around in my now-beer-soaked shorts for my wallet, which held my driver's license, which was soon in the possession of the officer, who took it outside.

"You going to stop now?" I asked Glen as we waited for the policeman to return.

"Stop what?"

"With the women."

"Ah," he replied. "Probably not. I figure I'm still doing pretty well. You're the baseball fan. My average has got to be pretty high, yes? This is just the first time I've gotten punched."

"That was a hell of a punch you threw back there," he added. "Thank you for that."

"Not that it did any good," I muttered. "We still got our asses kicked."

"It happens." Glen laughed as he slapped me on the back fairly hard, rattling my already jostled insides. The blood in my mouth had finally stopped flowing and I was pretty sure I was going to be okay.

The officer eventually returned with my identification. "You're clean. I did get a hit on your name though. Looks like someone in Texas is looking for you. Are you a missing person? Did this guy kidnap you?"

Glen laughed. I laughed. The cop did not laugh. "It is probably my wife," I responded.

"She don't know where you are?"

"I guess not."

I suppose the sarcastic tone of my answer was too much for officer small guy. "Don't get like that with me, mister," he said, sounding even angrier than before. "I don't like it when you out-of-towners come in and fuck with our city. You understand?"

"I do," I replied. "Can we go?"

"You can go the hell out of our town for all I care," the policeman told me. "If I were you, I would call home, but to be perfectly honest, I thank God I am not you and, as long as you are on your way back to your room and out of our fine city, then get the hell out of here."

"Thanks," I snidely responded as Glen and I headed toward the door to the bar and back up to our room, where the pair of us, bloodied and bruised, collapsed into our beds, not even bothering to take off our quite dirty clothes.

I-40 AND AMARILLO, 2016

I woke to find Glen no worse for the wear, sitting on his bed, putting on his shoes. Somehow his clothes were clean. I do not understand how, but every morning that same aloha shirt and his pants were clean and pressed, while my wardrobe just got progressively dirtier. My ear was swollen, as was my lip. The taste of blood still filled my mouth, but my side did not hurt as much as I'd expected it to. He asked me how I felt, and I told him I felt like shit and that I blamed him for my current condition. He simply smiled in reply. At least he didn't laugh. I guess that's something.

We spent the morning touring the Oklahoma City National Memorial, which is a must-see if you are ever in the area. As you might imagine the place itself is very somber, which makes it a good spot for reflection. The museum is both terrifying and fascinating and would rank right up there with the best museums I have ever been to. Also, make sure you see the survivor tree, as it is truly something to behold.

After a couple hours reliving the terrors of April 19, 1995, we got back on Interstate 40 and continued our trip west. Glen was driving, as I was still feeling a bit woozy from last night's action. This also meant we were back to listening to his music, which may have been a good thing. The loud guitars and bass-heavy rap I favored probably would have done nothing good for my aching head. So we got the hits of the 1960s and '70s. More of the Doors and Rolling Stones and whatever else it was people my uncle's age listened to when they were young. After maybe an hour of driving, he informed me we would be spending the night in Amarillo, as he planned a detour from our current route the following day. This was actually welcome news as it meant we would not be in the car as long as I'd been expecting. It is, in fact, just a little over two hundred and fifty miles from the Oklahoma capital to Amarillo, which meant we would be in the car just three hours. About halfway there, we stopped for gas and Glen decided he was done driving. My head no longer hurt as much so I did not mind getting back behind the wheel.

The car could have been on autopilot, had such a thing existed, as the road through the plains was just that straight. Glen was looking out the window at the vast open spaces when he shifted in his seat and turned towards me indicating he had something to say.

"I ever tell you the story of Sampson Altman?" he asked as I kept my gaze fixed on the interstate in front of me.

"Well?" I could tell he wanted to tell a story and there was nothing I could do to stop him.

"I guess not," I mumbled, although I was not actually in the mood to hear anything other than the music from the radio.

"Good," he said, reaching out to turn the radio down in the process.

" 'Back about eighteen and twenty-five . . .' " He laughed. "I'm just playing. I know that is the way 'Tennessee Stud' starts."

I too was familiar with the fact that the Jimmy Driftwood song (made famous by Johnny Cash, amongst others) started this way, so I gave him a complimentary smirk but nothing else.

"Okay, seriously," he continued. "I'm going to tell you the story, alright?"

"Whatever."

"It was actually sometime after the Civil War. The late 1860s, a wagon party departed the war-torn South and headed west, bound for the untouched lands of California. There were six families from Georgia and six wagons loaded with whatever they could fit in them, led by a man named Sampson Altman. He was a veteran of the Confederate Army who had fought with Lee for the duration. Fredericksburg, Antietam, Gettysburg, Petersburg; wherever Lee went, this guy was with him. Somehow, he survived the entire war only to go home and find that Sherman had burned his farm, killed his livestock, and, more than likely, murdered his oldest son."

"I am guessing Sherman did not kill that guy's kid," I interrupted. Insults hurled at my favorite Civil War general have never sat well with me.

"You know what I mean," Glen replied before continuing his story.

"Sampson Altman and his party left Georgia, crossed the Mississippi, and ended up out here, fairly close to where we are right now, in the northern part of Texas, headed west to what they hoped would be better lives. The Altman wagon was full of Sampson's wife Varina, his daughters Mary and Julia, as well as his younger son, thirteen-year-old David. They were traveling with the family of his brother-in-law, who was also a veteran of the Confederate Army. The same was true of the men who drove the other wagons, although history has sort of lost their names."

"They got this far, close to Amarillo, but not close enough

to get to the town before dark, so they decided they would make camp, again, in the general vicinity of Interstate 40. Things were going smoothly for the group that evening. As the sun set, the women were fixing dinner while the men hobbled the horses and secured the livestock, when Sampson's brother-in-law noticed horses approaching from the north. As you probably already know, in the late 1860s, riders approaching on the horizon were often not a good thing. Especially on the open plains. So Sampson sent the other men to gather up their guns while he stayed with the livestock to try and get a better look at just who was approaching. By the time the riders emerged from the sunset it was clear to him they were Indians. He did not know it, as he was from Georgia, but they were a Comanche raiding party headed for the Texas settlements to rob and loot and do whatever else the Comanche did in those days."

"Whatever they wanted to," I interjected.

"Yes," Glen agreed, before adding, "now quit interrupting."

He continued. "By the time Sampson realized who he was looking at, an arrow was sticking in his leg. He then took another in his shoulder and a third in his arm before the riders were upon him. Before he even had a chance to raise his arm, a war club landed squarely on his head rendering him unconscious.

"Now, eventually, Sampson woke up to find the Comanche gone, most of his guts outside of his body and a portion of his scalp missing. Somehow, through sheer force of will, he pushed his insides back inside his abdomen and crawled toward the camp. What he found was a grizzly tragedy. Everyone was dead. The men had been tied to the wagon wheels and set on fire, all of them scalped. The women, most of whom were naked, had been raped before they too were killed, and the children, the ones he could identify, had their heads crushed by the clubs and rifle butts of the Comanche raiders. Sampson realized, however, that not all of the children were accounted for. He could not find the bodies of Mary or Julia, and he knew there was a chance they were still alive, as Indians often took smaller children as prisoners who would eventually be traded for livestock and other things or assimilated into their tribe. He took cloth from one of the torn dresses and tightly wrapped up his midsection, then he grabbed one of the Enfield rifles the Comanches had left, and began walking, very slowly mind you, following their tracks south."

"If you're going to tell me he found them, I am going to just stop the car right now. I have a pretty hard time believing the guy is even walking at this point."

"I said be quiet," Glen admonished me before finishing his tale.

"You are correct to assume he didn't get far. No, Sampson Altman may have been a strong man. In fact, he surely was a strong man; he survived the entire Civil War. But he was not strong enough to survive his wounds and after making it maybe half a mile from the site of the massacre he collapsed and died."

"Okay?" I questioned. "Why did you tell me this?"

"Because to this day, there are reports of people driving on this stretch of I-40 who look in their rearview mirror only to see a bearded man sitting in the backseat of their car. His face is always covered in blood, and he is holding his stomach. He looks at them, through his black eyes, and asks if they have seen his daughters. And then, as quickly as he appeared, he is gone.

"This has led to this stretch of road being known as one of the most dangerous in the country. More single-car accidents happen on these fifteen miles of road outside of Amarillo than happen anywhere else in the country, and no one has any idea why. Some surmise it is the speed limit, which they think is too high. Others say it is the curve we just passed, which I will admit is fairly sharp. But it should be noted that it curves right about the same place Sampson's body was found by some cowboys a couple days after he died. Personally, I agree with other people who believe the cars wreck because of the appearance of an unexpected passenger and the shock of seeing him in their backseat."

When he was alive, my uncle traded in something he called "chicken skin." Not that he sold the skin of a chicken; no, this term is Hawaiian in origin and refers to the goosebumps a person gets when they are scared. You might say that once upon a time, he was the master of chicken skin, and I can assure you that his stories always gave them to me. This time was no exception.

"Is that true?" I asked him after giving the tale a minute or two to sink in.

"Of course," he laughed. "Well, maybe . . . Some of it anyway."

He reached down and turned up the radio and the music eventually drowned out the waning moments of his laughter.

True or not, I drove the rest of the way to Amarillo without ever looking in the rearview mirror.

*****

There is very little remarkable about Amarillo, or most of Texas's panhandle really. There are those Cadillacs parked on their front ends on that guy's ranch to the west of town. There is Palo Duro Canyon, which is the second-largest canyon in the United States, but it is almost an hour's drive away, so while you have to give it consideration when discussing the panhandle, I am not sure that it deserves that much consideration when talking about Amarillo. There are other things, sure. Like that George Strait song "Amarillo by Morning," and all the subsequent versions of that song sung by country singers in the decades since it was released. There are lots of cows too, which brings me to my favorite Amarillo landmark—the Big Texan Steak Ranch. Yep, an entire ranch dedicated to steaks. If you are unfamiliar with the Big Texan, then all I need to tell you is that it is the place where you can win a free dinner if you can consume a seventy-two-ounce steak as well as a bunch of sides. Just how big are seventy-two ounces, you may be asking? Well, it's four and a half pounds to be exact. Yeah, it's a lot of beef.

We stopped at the first hotel we came to and were quickly in the lobby. The place was your basic mid-range chain hotel and everything about it was fine. This does not mean that everything was great, or even good. It wasn't bad or awful either. It was just fine. I am sure you've stayed in similar places. But hey, sometimes fine is all you need.

We took the elevator up to our room on the fourth floor and went inside. "What's the plan?" I asked Glen after dropping my bag on the table that was holding the TV.

"I think we should have a rest," he answered. "After that let's get a couple steaks."

"Sounds good," I added. "I think I might want to try and do the Big Texan challenge."

"The seventy-two-ounce-steak?" Glen asked.

"Yeah," I replied as he looked at me, a mixture of horror and laughter in his eyes.

I have never really been a big eater. Sure, as I got older, I started packing on the weight. But that was mostly from lots of beer and eating too often, mixed with not enough physical activity. It's not like I sat down every night and had a 3,000-calorie dinner. Yes, at one point I could drink all night long. But I had never been able to put away a particularly large amount of food in one sitting.

"Why not?" I asked

"Because it is huge and there's no way you can eat it all," he told me.

"We'll see," I replied right before he closed his eyes. "Besides, I doubt I will ever get the chance again. Might as well give it a shot while I'm here."

Glen fell asleep for a couple hours as I shuffled through the channels on the television. It was strange trying to waste time without my phone. I still had an iPad with me but did not bother trying to connect to the hotel Wi-Fi. I am not sure why. Maybe so I could get a feel for the good old days. Maybe I was just being lazy. Whatever the case, I watched some *Wings* reruns and the five o'clock news before my uncle finally stirred. Once he was fully awake, we decided it was still too early for dinner, so we headed down to the lobby to get drinks from their small bar. An hour passed, as well as a couple rounds. Then another hour and a couple more rounds. Finally, about seven thirty, Glen declared himself ready for dinner, so we headed outside and made the short walk from our hotel to the restaurant.

If you have never seen it, the Big Texan is truly something to behold. It is a kitschy steak restaurant on steroids. The type of place a child or a Hollywood executive might dream up when you ask them to come up with the typical Texas steak house. There are all kinds of things to see in the lobby. Rattlesnakes and slot machines as well as a gift shop filled with all the crap your wallet can handle. Once inside the dining room, you find yourself face to face with a bunch of animals who are probably not that happy to be hanging on the wall. Glen and I were seated fairly quickly, as it was a weeknight, and soon a girl named Amber was standing next to us asking for our drink orders. I could tell Glen had his eyes set on Amber as he made small talk about his beverage options. We were about five drinks into the night and I was starting to wonder how I was going to get through the giant steak dinner. After Amber returned with our drinks and was getting ready to take our order, Glen asked if I was sure about what I was planning on doing.

"You only live once," I said to him, before telling the waitress I wanted to take the challenge. She seemed excited by the prospect as she informed us only two other people had tried it that evening, and she was hoping to see someone else give it a shot before she went home. Glen told her I was the guy for the job and then hinted about going home with her when we were done. She slapped his arm and giggled, as I stared in silence. He had always had more charm than most humans and being dead had only seemed to add to his arsenal.

Soon they came to lead me up to the stage where the people who take on the big steak sit, so everyone in the restaurant can watch them. As I stood up to leave, I thought about saying it was a bad idea and sitting back down, but I chose to stay silent and press on. It was something I had thought about doing for a while now and I was here, so I might as well give it a shot.

I was on the stage, waiting for my meal. Glen sat just below me, waiting for his much more modestly sized piece of meat. My entire dinner arrived rather quickly, and I was a little taken aback by the amount of food placed in front of me. In addition to the steak, I was staring down a shrimp cocktail, baked potato, salad, and a roll. In order to accomplish the feat of gastronomy I was attempting, I would have to consume all of the food in an hour. If I did, then I got my meal for free. If I failed, I had to fork over seventy-two dollars for the whole thing. After giving me a minute to cut into and try the steak, Amber pushed a button on a clock on my table, which was facing the dining room. It quickly showed fifty-nine minutes and fifty-nine seconds, and the trial had begun.

As there was now a clock involved, I decided to take Sheridan's words to heart and dive right in. I attacked the food with unbridled vigor. I wolfed down the salad and the shrimp, then started in on the steak. I would say I was maybe an eighth of the way into it when my pace slowed way down and I began to worry. I still had forty minutes left as I took a couple more bites before putting my fork down on my plate. Was I giving up or just taking a break? Amber seemed to wonder the same thing as she came over to check on me and to ask if I was done. I opened my mouth to answer her, but words would not come. Unfortunately, something else did. The steak and appetizers as well as most of those old-fashioneds were soon pouring out of my mouth, with the majority of it ending up on Amber's shirt. A groan came from the restaurant as I unburdened myself of all of that food, finally getting the rest of my vomit in the trash can the restaurant had provided for situations just like this.

Amber was long gone by the time I'd finished purging my stomach of its contents. Glen, sitting at our original table, looked a little sad as I sat on the stage in horror and shame. I was struck by the realization that not only was I not getting a free steak but that all these people had seen me throw up and I had probably ruined their meals in the process. I also knew that I'd ruined my uncle's chances with the waitress. There was no way he was going home with her now. A different employee eventually showed up on the stage to help me as two other guys hustled out to clean up the mess. The new guy asked the people in the restaurant to give me a hand for trying. Some of them complied. Although I feel like most of them didn't. I mean really, who wants to cheer for the guy who probably wrecked your meal by throwing up in front of you?

"I guess that didn't work out," I said to Glen as I finally made my way back to our table.

"No," he said, in between bouts of laughter. "It did not."

"You want to go back to the hotel?"

"Yes," he replied as he dropped some money on the table to settle our check. He took one more look around the restaurant, and then at me again, before heading for the exit. I followed, holding my stomach, and hoping I would not have a repeat performance of what had happened on stage on my way out.

BOSQUE REDONDO, 2016

We started the next day on Interstate 27 heading south toward Lubbock, but we did not stay on that road long. At Canyon, we got on US 60 and proceeded to drive southwest and then mostly just west, toward New Mexico. Eventually we crossed the border and were in Clovis, where I stopped to buy gas and ask exactly where we were going.

"We will spend the night in Albuquerque," Glen told me. "But first we need to make a stop at the Bosque Redondo."

"You mean the place by Fort Sumner?" I asked.

"Yes," he replied before closing his eyes and letting me know the conversation was over.

The Bosque Redondo is located next door to Billy the Kid's grave in Fort Sumner, New Mexico, and while the latter is the more famous of the two places, the former has far more historical significance. It is the place where, in the mid-1860s, almost the entire Navajo nation was relocated in what was one of the first attempts at creating a reservation by the government of the United States. It was the terminus of the Navajo "Long Walk" and as has typically been the case with

American forced relocation, it was an unmitigated disaster. Attempts to teach the Navajo to farm failed when their crops were destroyed by blight, and eventually the place was abandoned. Of course, later on Pat Garrett shot Billy the Kid there, which is why most people have any idea about the existence of the fort in the first place. The Bosque is located outside of the town of Fort Sumner, which is right off of US 60. Just make a left (if you're coming from Clovis) on Billy the Kid Road and follow the signs. It really is quite easy to find.

We arrived sometime after noon and made the turn down the road toward the site. This part of New Mexico is particularly dusty, making the trip to the Bosque something of a curiosity. You drive past agricultural fields on one side of the road and the arid desert on the other, with the lush Pecos River oasis up ahead as your final destination. There are plenty of trees and grasses coming from the banks of the Pecos and this is one of the reasons they decided to move the Navajo here in the first place. We drove past the Billy the Kid museum, which I remembered visiting with my parents when I was a child, then turned in behind it and drove up to the Bosque Redondo monument. The building itself is interesting with a single triangular shape rising from the middle of it, looking a lot like a teepee, which I found kind of odd as the Navajo were known for living in hogans, which look nothing like teepees. I later learned that the rectangular part of the building is there to represent the Navajo hogans, while the teepee is in tribute to the Mescalero Apache who were also forced to live at the fort before sneaking out under the cover of darkness some time before the Navajo eventually negotiated their own return to their ancestral lands. There were no other cars in the parking lot, so we took the space closest to the entrance and got out.

"We're not going in," Glen said to me as I began to walk toward the door. "Let's go this way."

He walked across the parking lot and past the building down toward the river. There were even more trees the closer we got to the water. We followed a tree-lined path, eventually coming to the banks of the river where we were greeted by a tall, sturdily built man wearing the traditional clothes of the Navajo. And by that, I mean he was wearing a breechcloth that fell from his waist down to his mid-thigh. He was also wearing longer buckskin leggings and a colorful blanket/poncho wrapped around his torso like a shirt.

"This is Narbona," Glen said to me as we approached the man. "He is the reason we are here."

Much like the Bosque, history has given short shrift to the Navajo headman Narbona. (I hesitate to call him a chief, because if you study the Navajo they did not really have what we have come to think of as chiefs. Instead, they had a leader who was selected by the tribal council. Instead of operating like a king, which I think is the way most people think of chiefs, the Navajo leader was more like an elected official. You know, just in case you were wondering.) Maybe it's because we just don't know that much about him. Maybe it's because the history books are written by the winners. Maybe it's because written American history is typically racist. Whatever the case, it's the truth. Narbona was one of the greatest of all Navajo leaders, who lived to the ripe old age of eighty-three before being killed by US soldiers while attempting to negotiate a peace treaty in 1849. He led his people for decades and was a well-respected and powerful man in the American southwest long before it was ever even a part of the United States.

He did not look that old as he stood in front of me. He was not young, but he did not look like a man in his eighties. Perhaps in his early sixties. He seemed to be older than Glen, but not as old as my father who, by this point, was an old man.

"Yá'át'ééh," he said to us as we stopped in front of him.

"Hello, friend," Glen said as he stepped forward and hugged the older man. "I hope you weren't waiting for very long."

"No," Narbona said, his English much better than it should be. I cannot explain this and I never asked. My assumption was there are language classes in the afterlife, but I cannot tell you this with any real conviction. I suppose we'll all find out one day.

"I have been here for only a few minutes," he continued. "This is the land where they sent my people. It is not a good place." He turned away from us and stared out at the river. "Many of them died here. But I needed to see it for myself. It makes me very sad."

"Do you want to go?" Glen asked. "We have a car back in the parking lot."

"Yes," Narbona replied. "I think it is time."

We walked back up the tree-lined path toward where the car was parked. Narbona lagged behind us, looking around as if he were seeing things we could not. "What's the deal here?" I asked Glen when I was fairly confident Narbona could not hear us.

"He'd told me he would be here around this time, so I offered him a ride," Glen answered. "He needs a ride home and it's on our way, so I did not think it would be that big a deal."

"And you know him how?"

Glen laughed at this question. "You would be surprised, the people you meet. After . . ."

He drifted off just as I thought he might actually shine some more light on where he had been. At this point I knew I would never get all the answers I wanted, so I did not pursue the line of questioning any more. I just accepted that my uncle somehow knew the great Navajo Narbona and that we were now going to drive him to his home. Wherever the hell that was. After road tripping with Robert E. Lee and Phil Sheridan, this was not any sort of surprise to me, so I figured I would just go with it and see what happened.

We got back to the Volvo and Glen immediately got into the back seat. "You're taller than I am," he said to Narbona. "You can have the front."

"Thank you, Glen," Narbona said as he opened the door.

I was already in the driver's seat when he sat down and shut the door carefully. "You go for a lot of car rides?" I sarcastically asked him, as he fastened his seat belt.

"I've been on a few," he remarked in what can only be described as a matter-of-fact manner. "You?"

"Oh, I drive all the time," I snidely replied.

"Good," Narbona seemed to laugh as he slapped me on the shoulder. "I would not want to be at the mercy of a bad driver!"

"I guess not," I said as I pushed the button to fire the ignition.

"I am glad to see you are driving a Volvo," he added. "It is the safest car on the road!"

Again he laughed and I began to consider possibly hating him. But his good-natured manner seemed to make that too hard. Especially here on the Bosque.

ALBUQUERQUE, 2016

We made our way back up Billy the Kid Road and took the left onto US 60. We drove through the town of Fort Sumner. It bills itself as a village, and I think that is probably appropriate. There may have been one stoplight. Or maybe it was one of those flashing yellow lights. And there was a gas station and a few restaurants and lots of stuff about Billy the Kid. But we did not see many people or cars really, other than the ones parked in the lots at the restaurants. Neither Glen nor Narbona wanted to eat, so I turned onto US 84 and headed west back toward Interstate 40.

We rolled through the high desert, past Lake Sumner and lots of cows, before finally intersecting with I-40 about thirty minutes later. There is a town at the intersection of the two roads called Santa Rosa. It apparently was once part of US Route 66, so it has a few museums and restaurants themed to this famous American thoroughfare. Because Glen is sort of a sucker for this type of Americana, we stopped and ate in the Route 66 Restaurant. The food was good enough for a roadside diner. Glen thoroughly enjoyed his green chile burger, but said his fries were a little underwhelming. Narbona drank a milkshake that he said was the best he'd ever had, which made me wonder how many milkshakes he'd consumed. I daresay the Navajo were not making ice cream in the first half of the nineteenth century. I ate some. The disaster at the Big Texan the night before was still weighing on my mind and my appetite. Eventually I gave up on the idea of consuming my lunch and took a self-guided tour of the kitsch while Narbona and Glen let their food digest.

Soon we were back in the Volvo and headed west on I-40 to Albuquerque. Glen told me we would stop there for the night, which was fine by me. I was doing all the driving, and while we hadn't really gone that far on this day, I was beginning to get road-worn from the weeks I had now spent roaming the country. The first mileage sign we passed said Albuquerque was 120 miles away and I made the trip in less than two hours. There is not a whole lot of scenery out there in central New Mexico. Not until you get to the Sandia Mountains, which you have to drive through in order to get into the Rio Grande Valley where Albuquerque is located. It was close to dinner time when we reached the Hyatt Regency in downtown ABQ. It is right across the street from a plaza where they shot one of the pivotal scenes in the final season of *Breaking Bad*. The one where Hank gets Jesse to try and trap Walt in a confession. You know the one. Jesse freaks out and can't bring himself to meet with Walt because he thinks Walt is planning on killing him, so he runs off before they ever come face to face. I won't go any further here; either you know what I'm talking about or you don't. If you fall into the latter category, then I suggest you do yourself a favor and go binge-watch that entire series. Just as soon as you finish listening to me tell my story.

The guy at the desk said nothing about the man in traditional Navajo attire who was going to our room with us.

He issued him a pass for breakfast the next day (thanks Hyatt Diamond membership!) and told us to have a good day, then pointed us toward the elevator. I had to prod Narbona and Glen away from the pitcher of complimentary pineapple-infused water by the check-in desk that they did not seem that interested in leaving.

"This is fantastic," Narbona told me at one point, handing me a small plastic cup full of the stuff. "Have some!"

"He's right," Glen added before refilling his glass.

I took a drink, and it was good. But maybe not as good as these two thought it was. "Let's go to the room," I told them. "I want to drop off the bags and then I'd like to get some drinks."

"Wash the trail dust from your mouth, huh?" Narbona asked.

"Something like that."

"Fine," Glen said as he finished off a final cup of the pineapple water.

We unloaded whatever stuff we had in a fairly nondescript suite with a floor-to-ceiling view of Sandia Peak in the distance. I still had my small bag of clothes which were in various states of cleanliness. Glen had picked up a few things along the way and carried them in one of the *Star Wars* grocery bags I kept in the back of the Volvo. Narbona toted a large Tumi suitcase with all kinds of things in it. I did not want to stare as he sorted through his belongings, but I could tell, from the brief glances I could steal, that he had been buying souvenirs from wherever it was he'd been. I asked him if he was going to change and he looked at me like I was crazy, finally saying, "I'm fine," before heading toward the door.

We camped out in the hotel bar for a while. Glen drank his gin and tonic while I sipped an old-fashioned. Narbona was content with some sort of local chardonnay. I am not sure of the vintner, but I know it was a New Mexico wine.

"What's with the wine?" I eventually asked him.

"It's good," he replied. "Would you like a glass?"

"No," I laughed. "I am just surprised you are drinking a chardonnay."

"What did you expect?" he smiled. "Firewater?"

"Maybe," I said, looking down because I thought I might be offending him. "But really," I tried to cover up what I felt might have been an insult. "I just figured you'd drink something stronger."

He chuckled and I could tell I had not hurt his feelings. "You will see when you get to be my age that those things that are stronger are not always what are best for you. This is a nice glass of wine and, who knows, maybe I will have one more glass. We'll see."

We stayed there for a couple hours. Glen got progressively drunker while I fought the urge. I knew where we had to eat dinner and it involved a car ride and I had no interest in driving around drunk. Narbona eventually had that other glass of wine, and he and Glen enjoyed a pretty long conversation about the movie *The Big Lebowski*. Much like me, Glen was a fan and had been since he'd first seen it. Narbona did not understand the appeal of the movie at all. He argued that the plot was silly and contrived and that the Coen Brothers were capable of so much more as they'd shown in *No Country for Old Men*. I wanted badly to interject myself, but they were so completely involved in their debate that I kind of felt like they forgot I was even there.

Eventually the time came for us to eat dinner, which meant I got to go to one of my favorite restaurants in the world. The Range Café is a small New Mexico chain with six greater ABQ locations that makes, perhaps, the best chile rellenos on the planet. Okay, maybe not as good as this little hole-in-the-wall place in Taos, but I was nowhere near Taos and if I'm in New Mexico, I must eat rellenos.

We rolled to the downtown location and after maybe a twenty-minute wait were shown to our table. We had a waiter named Trent who took our drink orders. Glen seemed a little upset by the fact we had a man waiting on us, which may have been why he changed his drink order to a margarita instead of his usual gin and tonic. Narbona switched from wine to iced tea and I decided to join him. I had spent most of my time on the road either in the haze of alcohol or recovering from that haze, and I liked the idea of keeping a clear head tonight and also of not having an aching head tomorrow.

Talk at the dinner table had little to do with the greater meaning of life and more to do with the topics of the day. Politics, the weather, movies, children. I let it all go. I may have been on a quest for answers, but sometimes there are answers in the mundane parts of life. I went ahead and accepted this, as I ate my rellenos, drenched in a combination of red and green chile that the people of New Mexico call "Christmas style." Narbona picked at his salad while Glen stuffed himself with meatloaf, and after an hour or so our meal was complete.

"What now?" Glen asked as he finished the rest of his frozen drink.

"I know a place we could go," I told them. "I don't know if you'll be able to get any alcohol. But it's a good spot for people-watching. Just to hang out, you know?"

"It sounds good to me," Narbona said as Glen nodded in agreement.

Soon we were up and on our way out of the restaurant and back in the Volvo. We took the short trip down Central to the Old Town section of the city. This is where the earliest settlers of Albuquerque had lived, and the adobe-style buildings and grand Catholic church that surround the central plaza do an impressive job of helping you feel like you have stepped out of the buzzing twenty-first century and are back in the frontier days of Albuquerque's past.

For the most part, the square was deserted, as it was later in the day. There was some activity in the central gazebo and a few tourists walking about. Some coming from dinner, others touring the various shops which all seemed to be selling the same things. We took the quick trip around the central block and then walked toward the gazebo to see what was going on there. When we got closer, we could see two local men breakdancing on the smooth concrete surface, underneath the roof which must have kept the floor cool during the heat of the day. That was not a concern now, as the sun was setting, but I am guessing they were enjoying the effects of it anyway.

The whole scene was very old school, complete with a boombox. However, the small group of children standing around watching them may have given away the ages of the dancers. On more than one occasion the kids called the men dancing "dad," hinting at the fact that maybe they'd been out here doing this for the better parts of their lives. I noticed an empty bench with a good enough view of the dancers and decided to have a seat. We sat, mostly entranced by the popping and locking and spinning in the gazebo, as the last rays of the sun set behind the dancers. At some point, one of the kids came over and pointed at Narbona and said, "Indian." He just laughed while I tried to shoo the kid away.

"Go watch your dad," I told him.

He replied by looking at me and saying, "You're fat," before running back to where his much more svelte father was dancing.

Eventually, the older of the two dancers seemed to tire and walked over to us while wiping his face with a towel. "Where you from?" he asked me as he approached.

"Texas," I replied.

"Right on," he said. "I've got a brother in Dallas. Don't get out there very much though. Where do you live?"

"Austin."

He smiled the way every youngish person smiles when I tell them I live in Austin. Of course, I never go into the fact that I live in the suburbs, or that I hardly ever go out on Sixth Street, or that I don't listen to live music every day. "Nice," he said. "I've always wanted to go there. You like it?"

"It's alright," I told him. "I think I like it here better."

He laughed. "You wouldn't if you lived here," he told me, although I did not believe him. "Well, I'm gonna get back to it," he said as he turned around.

"Anywhere around here to get a drink?" Glen called out as the man started walking away.

He turned and looked at us and then pointed to all of the buildings to our right. "Anywhere over there," he said as he smiled and then walked back to the gazebo.

"You guys want to go?" Glen asked. "I'm getting thirsty."

"I am cool sitting here for a while longer," I told him. "Go get a drink and come back when you're done."

"Okay," my uncle said. "You want to come, Narbona?"

"No," the Navajo said. "I am going to go in the shops though. I have some things to buy before I go home tomorrow."

The two of them then walked away, together briefly, then separately, as Glen headed toward La Placita Restaurant while Narbona went in the other direction, to the souvenir shops.

I spent the next hour watching the two men breakdance as the shadows of the waning day descended on their gazebo. Every once in a while, the men would take a break and get a drink from a cooler they had placed by the stairs leading up to their improvised dance floor, and their children would come back from their games of tag or hide and seek and join them for the refreshment. There was a sense of joy I could glean from them, not only during their dancing but also in the interaction between the fathers and their children every time they would take a break. The kids seemed so happy in those moments to have any of their parents' attention, while the fathers seemed to find it funny to tease their children to the point where they appeared angry, and then to relieve that anger with a well-timed hug or perhaps a quick tickle or tussle of their hair. Eventually it grew too dark, and I suppose the kids had to go to bed, because the men packed up their gear and the five of them all headed off, away from the light of the gazebo, and into the now blackened park.

Shortly thereafter Glen and Narbona showed up. The former with the glow of alcohol in his cheeks and the latter with a blue plastic bag full of knickknacks and whatnot. We loaded up into the car and I made the short drive back to the hotel. After leaving the car with the valet we went inside, where Glen informed us he was going to the bar. I knew this was coming but declined his invitation to join him. Narbona told him he was too old for such activities and would, instead, head upstairs to go to sleep.

"Don't wait up," Glen smiled at me and said as I stood waiting for the elevator. "With any luck, I won't be back until tomorrow morning."

"I doubt you need luck," I replied. "I will see you at what eight? Nine?"

"Make it nine," he said. "It's already late."

The Navajo and I rode the elevator up to our suite on the top floor in silence. I saw some of the things in his blue bag as he stared at the ceiling. There was a ceramic coyote and a cactus that said "New Mexico" as well as some turquoise jewelry. There were a few other things as well. Maybe a Heisenberg t-shirt on the bottom, but I was not sure, and the elevator brought us to our floor before I could look any further. We walked silently back to our room, and I waved the key in front of the reader and opened the door so we could go in.

"I guess I'm going to turn in," I said to Narbona as he entered the living room.

"Yá'át'ééh hiiłchi'į'," he said to me, which I assume means goodnight. Or something like that.

I glanced back at him, and he was standing at the picture window, staring out at Sandia Peak, the lights of the houses shining at the base as the moon illuminated the top of the giant which stands like a watchful protector over the city below. I closed the door behind me as quietly as I could and made my way toward my bathroom and, eventually to bed.

CANYON DE CHELLY, 2016

We left the next morning, headed west on I-40. Narbona had requested we drive him to Canyon de Chelly which is in northeastern Arizona, not far from the New Mexico border. Canyon de Chelly has long been part of the Navajo homeland and to this day it is part of their reservation, so the fact Narbona wanted to go here did not seem all the surprising.

Glen had arrived at our room around nine a.m., holding fresh coffee for himself and Narbona as well as a bag of pastries. It seemed he had been successful in finding somewhere else to spend the night and he was in a particularly jovial mood as he gathered his things. When the valet pulled the Volvo around he took the spot in the backseat again, offering the more spacious accommodations to the larger man. It seemed like this meant I was driving. Which I guess was fine. Better to drive and be distracted, than to be left alone with my thoughts and the scenery.

The drive west from Albuquerque leads through Grants, New Mexico, and eventually to Gallup. It is here that you leave I-40 and get on New Mexico 264, which will turn into Arizona

264 when you cross the state line. The entire drive through the high desert, past the peaks of red and orange, does not really take that long. It's a little over two hundred miles with over half of it being on the interstate. As was typically the case, silence ruled the car for most of the drive. Well, except the radio, of course. We'd hit a patch where my iPod seemed to play nothing but Wu-Tang Clan. Or the various solo efforts of the members of the Wu-Tang Clan. As expected, Glen did not seem all that interested in the music, but I felt like Narbona was. He nodded his head through most of it and from what I could tell, out of the corner of my eye, he actually appeared to dig it.

Shortly after we left the interstate and turned onto the more rural roads, Narbona decided to speak. I don't know if it was because he was bored by the Jimmy Eat World song or if he finally decided he had something to say. Whatever the case, he began to talk. I could not make out the first part as the radio was too loud, so I turned it down.

"My people have lived on this land for thousands of years." I caught him mid-sentence. "I never imagined we would be forced to leave. But we were."

"They came back though," I told him.

"Yes," he said. "That is true. But they never should have had to leave in the first place."

"Sure," I agreed.

"Glen tells me that you are searching for something," he said. "But you are not sure what it is you are looking for. Is this correct?"

"I guess. I mean, I think I have an idea, but it's very abstract. Like maybe there's no way to really find it."

"I see," he said. "I believe I can help you in your quest. You have been very kind to give me this ride. I know it's not exactly on your way. So I would like to try at least."

"It's not out of my way," I told him. "Shit, I don't even

know where I'm going."

"Los Angeles," Glen chimed in from the backseat. I looked at him in the rearview mirror and his eyes were closed. But I guess he was listening.

"Well," Narbona continued. "As I said, I believe I can help." With that, he reached into his pocket and produced a plastic ziplock bag full of something brown. He undid the zipper and pulled out two brownish-green things I immediately recognized as peyote buttons. How, you ask? Well, I once got some peyote from a fellow in Yuma who claimed to me a shaman. I took it and something happened, but not the vision quest I'd expected.

"My people sometimes use this when they have lost their way," Narbona told me. "Maybe it can help you."

"Is that peyote?" I asked, even though I knew the answer.

"Yes," he said. "Like what Lou Diamond Phillips gives to the other *Young Guns* in the first movie."

"You've seen *Young Guns*?" I asked.

"Sure," he told me. "I love Lou Diamond. He is one of my favorite actors! I look forward to the day when I can meet him."

I continued to laugh and reached out and took what he was offering me and put it in the empty cup holder closest to my seat.

"I cannot promise it will work," Narbona added. "But I figure it is worth a try."

"Thank you," I told him. "I'm willing to try anything."

"You get one for me?" Glen questioned from the back. "I'm not really looking for anything, but I am not going to pass up the chance to take peyote with you."

"Yes, Glen," Narbona said. "I gave him one for you, too."

Silence then prevailed in the car for a while. We were approaching Burnside, Arizona where we turned north onto US 191. From there it was just about thirty miles to Canyon de

Chelly and it seemed like Narbona could sense his journey was nearing an end.

"It has been nice to be out here," he spoke in almost a whisper. "But I have missed my family. I do believe there is no greater joy than being with your family."

"I don't know about that," I muttered.

"Why do you say that?"

"I don't know. Maybe because it's impossible to be who you want to be when you are stuck being something different to someone else."

Narbona chuckled. "That seems silly," he told me. "There is no reason you cannot be yourself and still be someone's father, or husband, or grandfather. I have always been a great warrior. You should know that. But it never took away from me being a father to my children or a husband to my wives . . ."

"You had more than one?" I interrupted.

"Yes." He laughed. "It was not a big deal."

The conversation paused for a second. Then he continued. "My point is, you can be yourself and still be the person your family needs you to be. If there is one thing I think you should remember, it is that your family are the people who will always be there for you. The very fact they are still around should tell you that. Think about it. They are with you more than anyone else. If they didn't like you, they would leave."

"That's a good point," Glen again made his presence known from the back seat.

"That's not MY point," I said. "Sure they like me. But I don't know that I like me. I never signed up to be a suburban dad, driving my kid around and hanging out at neighbors' barbecues where people drink three beers and then stop themselves because maybe they're getting a little too tipsy in front of the kids. I was supposed to do something else . . ."

"What?" Narbona asked.

"I don't know," I told him.

"That's a lie," Glen's eyes were still closed, but he was apparently a part of the conversation. "Tell him what you used to tell me."

Sheepishly I admitted, "I was supposed to be dead. I was supposed to write as much as I could, right up until I turned thirty. Then I was supposed to die. Of liver failure or some other disease related to the fact I was drunk every day from the time I turned twenty until that fateful day after my thirtieth birthday."

Narbona and Glen both laughed at me. I realized my teenage dream of living fast and dying young sounded particularly stupid coming from the mouth of a middle-aged man who was now far too old to die young. But in a lot of ways, it was the only life plan I'd ever come up with. So even now, fifteen years after I should have passed from this mortal coil, I was clinging to it. Because it was all I had.

"Being dead is not all it's cracked up to be," Glen said from the back seat.

"So you're admitting you're dead?" I looked at him in the mirror. His eyes were open, and he was looking back at me.

"I'm not saying I'm not dead," he laughed.

We were now very close to the entrance to Canyon de Chelly, and I began looking around for a place to pull over or park the car. Narbona pointed to a turnout on the side of the road and told me to stop over there. He reached out and touched my arm as I turned the car from the road and brought it to a stop.

"Things do not ever go as planned," he told me. "You have to adjust to the changes and then proceed. So you will have the best life you can. It will not be perfect. But it is all you have."

Narbona said nothing else as he pulled his belongings from the back seat. "You get enough souvenirs?" I asked him once he was standing outside the car.

"I think so." His face wore a gentle smile. "They are for the children. They like them." He backed away from the car and, as he did, he looked inside at me one more time. He raised his hand and said, "Hágoónee," before pushing the passenger's side door shut. Glen was now out of the car and the two men said something which I could not hear. Soon Glen was sitting next to me and Narbona was walking toward the entrance of the canyon.

"Why'd he get out here?" I asked my uncle.

"Don't know," Glen said. "I guess this was his stop."

I turned the car around. We were on Indian Route 7 and you have to follow that back to US 191. We backtracked down that same road for a while. Through the eastern Arizona desert, brown and orange and yellow in just the right light; it provided an impressive backdrop to our drive. At Burnside, instead of going east back toward Gallup, we remained on the 191 South toward Indian Wells. Here we merged onto AZ-87 and proceeded west. Eventually the desert turned into the mountains, which brought with them forest, and sometime around dinner time, we were back on I-40 and then in Flagstaff, Arizona.

FLAGSTAFF, 2016

We opted to stop here for the night. When I got out of the Volvo to go check into the hotel, the nip in the air was noticeable. Flagstaff is almost seven thousand feet in the San Francisco Peaks which means it is one of the cooler places you can be during the summer. I was pleased with the change in climate as we'd spent so much time in the sweltering heat of the South and then the desert southwest. Glen too seemed to notice the difference as he made some remark about it being cold during our walk into the hotel.

We had dinner at the Coco's next to our lodging, then found our way to the nearest bar. This one was attached to the building we were staying in. It was called the Amigo Room. I am not sure why I remember this as the bar was fairly nondescript. The decor was dated and there was a jukebox and a few tables. There were no waitresses for Glen to hit on and the bartender was a man, so we spent the next couple hours drinking and talking about the things we enjoyed discussing. Glen told me a couple ghost stories I had not heard since I was a kid, and I particularly liked that. There was always something otherworldly about my uncle. Even when he was not actually from some other world. So the ghost stories were a welcome distraction.

At some point in the night, a group of women came into the bar and, well, I am sure you know what happened. I lost my uncle's company and spent about thirty minutes by myself, before one of the ladies split off from the larger group and approached me. I assumed this was because I was literally the only other person in that bar, besides the bartender, and he was an old man. She looked out of place even before she left the group. Her dress resembled something from the turn of the twentieth century and her hair was pulled up in a rather severe bun.

"Hello," she said as she sat down on the chair where Glen had earlier been perched.

"Make yourself at home," I sarcastically greeted her.

"Sorry," she said as she pushed the chair back like she was going to stand up.

"I'm just kidding," I reassured her. "Please. Sit."

She smiled as she drew the chair back closer to the table. "I'm Charlotte," she said as she reached out to shake my hand. I did not bother standing. I had no manners. Not now anyway. I am sure my mother would be embarrassed, but it seemed pointless. I wasn't trying to impress anyone. Shit, I was still wearing the same black t-shirt and shorts I'd had on in Nashville. And my hair and beard had only gotten longer (obviously not a lot, but still, it's not like I'd cleaned them up any.)

"You want a drink?" I asked her, unsure if I was really willing to get up and get her one if she said yes. Still, I felt like I should ask. So, I guess I wasn't quite as impolite as I'd earlier stated.

"I have one," she said, holding up a glass filled with something that looked medicinal.

"Cool."

"Your uncle sent me over," she said, pointing back to Glen, who was busy charming the three other women. "He was telling us about your trip. It sounds wonderful!"

"It's been something," I told her, unsure that wonderful was the correct word for it.

Nondescript modern country, the kind of garbage they play on CMT and GAC that is as disposable as a McDonald's napkin, interrupted her for a second; then she continued and I was no longer forced to hear the music.

"Glen told me you are a writer," she said.

"Not really," I answered.

She was confused now, as she looked back toward my uncle. I swear that he somehow saw her glance and waved at her, as if telling her to go on, but how could that be? Maybe it was just a coincidental part of his conversation with those other three women. I don't know.

"So you didn't write *A Season in Hell*?"

Her words were like a slap in the face waking me from an opiate-induced slumber. Someone who'd actually read my book.

"I'm sorry?" I asked, sure that she must have said something else.

"*A Season in Hell*," she said. "The novel. You wrote it, right? I recognize your face from the back."

She recognized my face from the back!

That stupid portrait the publisher had made me take, standing in front of a tree.

Me in nature. Not holding a drink. Or a gun to my head. Or perched seductively in front of an expensive sports car. No, in front of a tree, wearing a suit coat and a tie.

Truth be told, I was also wearing shorts and flip-flops. But they only shot me from the waist up, so that didn't matter. They told me I would sell more books if I looked respectable on the back cover. Even made me shave, which has never been a favorite pastime of mine. Obviously, they were wrong. But that did not prevent a copy from ending up in the hands of this particular woman, who was sitting at my table on this particular night.

"Yeah, I guess I did," I told her, trying to hide my pleasure with the fact someone had recognized me.

"I thought so!" she exclaimed in her reserved tone. "I knew it!"

"So you read the book?"

"Yes," she said. "Not that long ago."

"Cool."

"I have to tell you something," she said as she set her drink on the table and leaned towards me. "And I don't mean to be rude. But I thought it was awful."

Just like that my ego deflated like a balloon, struck by a dart thrown on the midway at the state fair.

Perhaps she sensed this when she added, "It wasn't the writing. I thought the writing was good. It was the plot. The main character's obsession with the girl who doesn't like him. And all his complaining about living in that town he didn't want to live in. I just thought it was all so contrived. I mean, why didn't he just move? And, seriously, how could anyone be that infatuated with someone who didn't seem to care one way or the other about them?"

"You obviously have the soul of a poet," I remarked, my defenses up.

She laughed. "Perhaps not a poet. But I do know something about writing."

"Do you?"

"A little something, yes." She replied.

"Do you know how hard it is? Do you know the loneliness that comes from what is a solitary task? Do you know what it is like when it is gone?"

"Oh yes," she said. "I believe I do."

I simply sighed. There was obviously no getting through to her.

Again she laughed. "I'm sorry. I am not here to harangue you. I just thought it would be nice to have a conversation, writer to writer."

"When did you even read the book?" I asked. "It has not been in print for years."

"Oh, a couple weeks ago," she told me. "I picked it up and read it one afternoon. I really liked the idea of the title, but as I said, the plot did nothing for me."

"Thanks," I sighed again.

"Have you written anything else?" Charlotte asked.

"Not really," I answered. "I have tried, but it's just not working for me anymore. That's a big reason I am here . . . trying to figure out what to do next, you know?"

"As I said before, I do know," she said. "Tell me, why don't you write anymore? There must be a reason."

I looked at this strange-looking woman over again. She looked familiar, like I should know who she is, but I could not place her. I was more than a little drunk now which meant I was more than willing to discuss my favorite subject . . . me.

"If I'm being honest," I told her, "I think I lost my muse. I don't have the inspiration I had when I wrote *Season*. Shit, I don't have the inspiration I had when I wrote the column that won first place at the Texas Press Association awards five years ago. I don't really have the inspiration to do much of anything anymore."

"Then why not find it?"

"What?"

"Your muse," she told me. "If that's what you are missing, then it would seem prudent to me that is what you need to locate. Inspiration is a wonderful thing, but I know how fickle it can be. After the birth of my daughter, I spent an entire year confined to my bedroom. It was there that I found my greatest inspiration, in the wallpaper of all things, if you can believe that."

I looked her over again. Her words had seemed to jog something in my memory. It occurred to me that her dress was not simply some vintage fashion, it was in fact period garb, from the turn of the twentieth century, and then I knew who she was. "You're . . ." I exclaimed.

"I am," she told me. "Don't give up. I eventually found my way out of that room. You will find your way out of this."

"Okay," I replied as I gulped down the remainder of my drink.

"I wish you the best of luck," were the last words she said to me before she stood and left the table, as I sat in stunned silence.

Soon Glen had taken her place across from me. "How about that," he said, his eyes full of excitement. "We found one of your fans!"

"I wouldn't say that exactly," I told him. "Did you bring her here?"

He looked confused. "No, I think she came with those other women. Why?"

"So you don't know her at all?"

"No," Glen replied as he finished the last of his drink.

"Okay," I said. "So what's next? Let me guess—you're going home with one of those other women and you will see me in the morning. Say, nine a.m."

"No," my uncle said to me. "I'm going back to the hotel with you. Maybe we can find some *Twilight Zone* to watch."

"Okay," I told him before I rose from my seat and followed him out of the bar.

BLYTHE, 2016

It is a fairly straight shot from Flagstaff to Los Angeles, but we did not go that way. For some reason, Glen told me to go south, straight down Interstate 17 and on to Interstate 10 which would lead us into the megalopolis that is Southern California. You pass Sedona, its red rocks off in the distance, at some point when you go this way, and then you are back in the desert. But this one is a much hotter version than the one in New Mexico and I was not surprised to see the outside temperature rise to well over 110 as we entered the Valley of the Sun. We did not go all the way into Phoenix, choosing instead to take the 303 which loops around the city and finds the 10 in Goodyear. From there it is a pretty direct line west, through a bunch of Arizona towns whose names are fairly forgettable. Across the border at Quartzsite and into Blythe. We arrived in this particular California desert community sometime after one p.m. and decided it would be a good time for lunch. As we were in California, and I was in fairly familiar territory, there was only one option for me for lunch and it was Del Taco.

For the better part of my life, Del Taco had been a friend to me. As I was pretty broke most of the time when I was a young adult, it was always one place I could count on to get plenty to eat for just a few bucks. And the food was good. Don't let anyone tell you otherwise! The chicken soft tacos are as delicious as any chicken soft taco you are going to eat. The same is true for the bean and cheese burrito. My wife thinks I am crazy, but I honestly think the food at Del Taco is some of the best food I ever get the chance to eat.

The Del Taco in Blythe is right off the interstate. Just take the Lovekin Boulevard exit and proceed north. It's right up the street. That is exactly what we did. Because I never miss the chance to eat at DT.

Seventeen years earlier I had eaten at this very restaurant. It was the day after I'd run off to Las Vegas to get married and we were on our way back to the Imperial Valley to break the news to everyone we knew. Well, most everyone anyway. I suppose some people had already been alerted by drunken phone calls the evening before. I remember we stopped though and I am sure I ate a bunch of chicken soft tacos. I remember the restaurant was very dirty that night. Maybe because it was New Year's Day. And the food was not all that great. I also remember the rumble in my stomach somewhere around Glamis and the hundred-mile-per-hour sprint to the nearest gas station in Brawley. The last thing anyone wants is to have to take a shit on the side of the road in the dunes. I also remember the mix of joy and terror that swirled around inside me, both at the Del Taco and during the entire drive back from Vegas. And no, it was not the food. Smart-ass. It was the fear of the unknown, mixed with the limitless possibilities, of a relationship born so quickly between two people who barely knew each other. Obviously, it worked out. To some extent anyway. Seventeen years later we were still together, and we had Lucy. But that feeling was long gone, limitless possibilities replaced by a mortgage and multi-vitamins and the creeping fear that everything good that would ever happen to me was in the past.

I pulled the Volvo into the parking lot and shut off the car.

"Let's get some lunch," I said to Glen once the engine stopped.

"Sounds good to me," he replied. "But first I think we might want to expand our horizons."

"You want a better choice of restaurants?" I asked. "Because Del Taco is awesome."

"No, nephew," he laughed. I'd forgotten all about the peyote buttons Narbona had left in the cup holder, but Glen had not. He picked them up and handed me one before putting the other one in his mouth. I took the hallucinogen from him and proceeded to consume it. It tasted like shit. But I expected that. As soon as it became clear we had both swallowed our drugs we looked at each other, both of our eyes asking the other "what's next?" But neither of us spoke to offer up any sort of answer. Instead, we reclined in our seats and waited for something to happen.

It took a while for me to realize something was going on. I would say when the taco on the facade of the building in front of me started waving I knew the drugs were kicking in. I looked over at my uncle and he looked sort of crazy. His eyes were wild and his skin translucent.

"I'm going to get some food," I told him. At least I think I did.

"I'm going to walk over to Carl's," Glen said as he got out of the car. "I don't feel like tacos."

"Cool," I said. "Meet you back here then."

"Sure."

I watched him walk away. Not exactly in a straight line, but it's not like he was swerving all over the parking lot either. Then I got out of the car and made my way inside the restaurant. It did not seem like it had changed much. The decor was still vintage 1990s Del Taco. It was cleaner though, which I appreciated. The lights on the menu swirled as I looked at them. That was different, but I don't think that was a feature any of the other customers were privy to. I had a hard time focusing on the menu, but I did not need it. I always ordered the same thing at Del Taco, so when it was my turn to talk to the cashier I moved to the counter and told the fellow exactly what I wanted—three chicken soft tacos, small bean burrito with red sauce, and a spicy jack quesadilla. Oh, and a drink! I almost forgot. And I was pretty sure the peyote was somehow making me thirstier. Soon my food and that empty drink cup were on the tray in front of me and, after filling the cup with Cherry Coke, which seemed to want to escape the cup the entire time I was getting it from the soda machine, I took a table near the window.

"Still eating that shit?" a voice, not unfamiliar, said from across the table.

I was halfway through my first chicken softy when they showed up, interrupting what had been a pretty satisfying meal up until that point. My wife silently stared at me as the black-masked border collie with the predominantly white body sitting next to her continued to chastise me. "You know that shit is going to kill you, right?"

His name was Morty, and he had been our dog for fourteen years before he died two years ago. We had purchased him from a farmer out of the back of a pickup truck a few years before Lucy was born. He was the light of our lives right up until we had a kid, and then he sort of became an afterthought in the backyard. A couple of years after that he went blind; some sort of border collie genetic thing robbed him of his sight, and he got bitter after that. He spent the better part of his life sulking in the corner, or lying in the middle of the floor, waiting for someone to try and step over him so he could jump to his feet and attempt to trip them. He got me once. I kicked him for it. But that did not stop him from trying the same ploy day after day, week after week. My wife once pointed out I should just quit trying to step over the dog, but I was stubborn and so was he. I wept when Morty died though. We may have been adversaries, but he was still my best friend. He had kept me company those first few years I spent alone in the house. Lying in wait for me in the middle of the hall. But he was always there, and his presence was what I missed when he was gone.

"I will eat whatever the hell I want," I told him as I stuffed the rest of that particular taco into my mouth. "And what do you know anyway? You, sir, are a dog."

"True enough, dickhead," Morty said to me. "But even this dog knows enough about a good diet to know yours sucks."

"Whatever," I answered as I unwrapped my next bit of chicken goodness. I carefully applied three sauce packets as he continued to speak to me.

"Seriously, look at you," Morty continued. "You look like crap, you old fuck. When was the last time you took a shower?"

I considered his question but did not have an answer. I honestly did not know. Thus, I did not respond.

"I am fucking shocked you are still alive," the dog said to me as I continued to eat my food. "If there was ever a poster boy for an early death it was your miserable ass."

"I cannot disagree with that," I replied.

"Listen motherfucker, it is time for you to come home. You have responsibilities. You have a fucking child. You need to get home and take care of your child! She fucking needs you." Morty shook his furry head before he continued. "And what about your fucking wife? Who is making her dinner? Also, the neighbors are throwing a barbecue next weekend and it would be nice if you could make a god-damned appearance. Do you hear what I am fucking saying to you?"

I had finished the second taco and was working on preparing the third before I answered him. "What do you know about it anyway? And you," I turned my gaze to my wife who continued to sit across the table staring daggers at me. "Don't you have anything to say?"

She opened her mouth as if to speak, but only a single "woof" came from her lips. Then she closed her mouth and resumed her eye assault on me.

"Tell me this then," Morty continued. "What are you doing? Why are you driving around the country with your degenerate uncle?"

"I am trying to find myself."

"You're almost fifty years old. You should have found yourself thirty years ago,"

"Maybe that's the problem. Maybe I never knew who I was."

"I know who you are. You're the guy who abandoned me in the backyard."

Morty's words stung, because they were true.

"There," he continued. "Now you know who you are. So get your ass home and be a god-damned responsible adult. Take care of your shit, dick!"

"God, you're an asshole," I told him after washing down the third taco with some of the Cherry Coke. "You were really trying to trip me on purpose, weren't you?"

"Of course I was. It was always funny to watch your fat ass almost fall. I'm just disappointed I never really got you."

"Why? I thought you were my best friend?"

"Is that right?" Morty asked. "Do best friends lock their best fucking friends outside for the entire day? It was hot out there asshole! That never seemed to bother you."

"I guess not," I told him before stuffing one of the quesadilla wedges in my mouth. None of us said anything. The two of them looked on as I finished the rest of the quesadilla and the majority of the bean and cheese burrito. I was pretty full now and I wondered if Glen was going to show up soon and maybe run these two off.

"Well, I think I need to get going," I said to them as I pushed my way away from the table, hoping they would get the hint and go back to wherever it was they'd come from.

"Going home?" Morty asked.

"No," I told him. "We're going to Los Angeles. Then who knows."

"You fucking dick!" Morty was now yelling at me. "You need to get home! You have responsibilities!"

"Quiet down, man! You're going to cause a scene."

"God, I hate you," he finished. "You were the worst best friend of all time."

"I'm sorry you feel that way," I told him. "But how could I ever trust a guy who hid behind a mask his entire life?"

"Ha!' Morty exclaimed. "You want to see what's under here asshole?"

"I do."

With that, he reached up with his paw and peeled the mask from his face. Inside I saw nothing. And then he was gone.

"I hope you're happy." She finally spoke. "You made the dog mad again." Then my wife stood up and slowly walked out of the restaurant, disappearing as soon as the door closed behind her.

I took a minute to compose myself and finish the rest of that burrito and my Cherry Coke. Soon I was outside, where it was much later than it should have been. The sun was actually on the decline in what was now the evening sky when I found Glen leaning up against the Volvo. He seemed to not be bothered by the heat.

"I am tripping so hard," he told me. "What about you?"

"I don't know," I replied. The lights on the building were

no longer swirling, but the taco seemed to be waving, at least a little bit. "I think maybe we should hang out a little while longer. I don't really want to drive like this."

LOS ANGELES, 2016

We finally regained our senses sometime in the middle of the night. I knew I was alright when the taco quit waving at me. Glen was asleep in the passenger seat by this point. I waited a while before getting back on the road though, making sure I was not going to have some other reaction while I was driving. As the sun rose in the east, we headed west.

The drive from Blythe to Los Angeles is a pretty straight shot west on Interstate 10. It takes a little over three hours depending on traffic, which will grow increasingly awful, the closer you get to the City of Angels. It starts getting bad right around Palm Desert and then the farther west you go, the worse it gets. When I lived in LA I would often leave the 10 and get on the 60 at Beaumont. Back then, many years ago, this was a good way to avoid some of that gridlock, but that is not the case anymore. There are just so many people in the greater Los Angeles area that it is now impossible to escape them. Unless you turn around and drive back to Blythe.

It was the middle of the day when we arrived in the city of Glen's birth. I had been driving the entire time, as he contented himself with looking out the window as the barren desert morphed into a much more crowded desert, full of strip malls and houses and so much stuff that it no longer looked like a desert at all. We did not take the 60 shortcut, choosing instead to drive through San Bernardino and Upland and West Covina. Then we were past El Monte and downtown was staring us in the face.

"Let's go to Oakhurst," Glen told me when I asked for direction. "Then we'll find a place to stay."

I knew exactly where he wanted to go. My grandparents' house was on Oakhurst Avenue. It is where Glen had grown up. In some ways it was where I'd grown up. At least it was the lone safe harbor in a childhood filled with tumultuous change. My father was a vagabond for a good part of my younger years, which meant we moved around a lot. Sometimes it meant a new school, new house, and new friends on a yearly basis. But the house on Oakhurst never changed. Nor did my friends who lived down the street. They were always there to welcome me every summer when my father drove us out to visit his family, so in a way that place became the home I needed. When I thought of going home, I thought of going there. And that was where I would see Glen, on those special occasions that he actually showed up. It was in the street in front of the house that we would play our strange games of stickball and it was in the back bedroom that we would stay up late watching the *Twilight Zone* and whatever other weird programs he could locate on the television.

Instead of driving into downtown, I followed the 10 south and then back west, heading toward Santa Monica. Eventually we hit the Robertson Boulevard exit where we drove past Hamilton High School, where both my uncle and my father had gone. Through the streets of million-dollar bungalows, their perfectly manicured lawns glistening in the sun, we proceeded until we were parked in front of our ancestral home.

It was no longer ours. So we could not go in. Not long after Glen's death, my father and his sister had decided to sell the old house. They claimed it was because no one wanted to live there, but that was a lie. I wanted to live there. But I did not have the absurd amount of money necessary to purchase it from them. So they sold it and, just like that, my safe place was gone.

I wondered if the people inside knew we were out there looking at their house as we sat in the car. It looked different now. They had removed the black-and-white awnings and painted the formerly white stucco a different color. But familiar things remained. The block of bricks at the end of the driveway where I used to sit when I was not allowed to come inside was still there. As was the hedge on the side of the driveway we used to dive into. Cosmetically it was different, but at its heart it was the same. I suppose that's all the matters.

"I wish we could go in," I told Glen.

He turned his gaze from the window to me. "So do I," he said. "I miss this place. I miss coming here in the summers and eating one of your grandmother's delicious dinners with everyone around the table in the dining room. I miss visiting with your dad and playing with you and your sister. Those were good days."

I could see tears welling in his eyes and could feel them coming into mine as I listened to him talk. For the first time on this trip, my uncle was no longer the stoic comedian, back from the other side. Now he appeared to be older and sadder and missing something that he lost a long time ago.

"They were," he said to me. "I miss them too. But days pass, nephew, and you do not get them back. If there is one thing I wish I could get through to you, it is that you never get any of it back. So do not waste them. For your sake, I wish you lived here too, but do you think anything would be different if you did?"

"Maybe," I muttered. "I like to think so."

Glen just smiled at me and put his arm around my shoulder. "That's enough," he finally said, his voice breaking a little as he spoke. "Go up to Century City. We can stay at the Hyatt there."

Once again, I knew exactly where he wanted me to go. Century City was a favorite spot for me to waste my time when I lived in Los Angeles. There was a movie theater there. That was a big reason why. I was generally alone when I lived in LA and when I went to the movies at least I was surrounded by other people. That was something. Something to relieve the anxiety and loneliness. Something to pass the time anyway.

I'd never stayed at the Hyatt Century Plaza before, but I'd driven past it many times. The hotel itself appears to be a monument to 1960s architecture and, in some ways, it is actually a landmark of those heady days. It was in front of this very hotel that Vietnam War protesters clashed with police during a speech by then-President Lyndon Johnson. A couple years later, then-President Richard Nixon hosted a gala at the hotel to celebrate the Apollo 11 moon mission. The inside still gave off this 1960s vibe as we walked in after leaving the Volvo with the valet. As had been the case earlier in the trip, the doorman nodded at Glen as if he knew him, but I felt like that could not be the case. Perhaps he was just being polite. We breezed through check-in and were soon in a double room on the top floor, a view of the vast expanse of Los Angeles to the east greeting us from the floor-to-ceiling windows.

"Do you want dinner?" Glen asked, almost as soon as we entered the room.

"Yeah. I could eat," I told him. "You want to eat here?"

"No," he said. "I know a place. Let's go get the car. I will drive."

We headed west on Pico until it intersected with Sepulveda and Glen turned left. We traveled down the busy Los Angeles thoroughfare, surely driving past memories, both shared and solo as we went, until we came to one of Glen's favorite Los Angeles eateries—Tito's Tacos. Located at the intersection of Washington and Sepulveda, and right next to Johnny's Pastrami, Tito's Tacos might not look like anything special, but the line coming out the door and wrapping around the building will probably convince you otherwise. It serves pretty standard SoCal Mexican fare which means it is inherently delicious. It is an added bonus that they are good at what they do, and the food is actually better than many similar restaurants you can find on most corners in the southland. Glen had long been a fan of Tito's and it was with his recommendation that it became one of my favorite places to eat when I lived in Los Angeles.

We arrived late enough in the day that the line was not that long. Soon we had a tray full of tacos and chips that we took to a seat at one of the few tables they have available outside.

"These are great, yeah?" Glen asked, in between bites of his crunchy taco.

"Best in the city," I agreed. Although I can no longer say that with any certainty. Maybe it was the case twenty-three years ago when I lived there, but who knows now?

"I am going to miss all this," Glen told me. "I have really enjoyed our time together."

"Do you have to go?" I asked.

"Soon," he told me. "But not yet. We still have some time."

I was relieved, as I was unsure what I would do when he was gone.

"What will you do next?" he asked me as I was unwrapping what would be my third taco.

"I don't know," I told him in between applications of hot sauce.

"It's hard to figure out," he added.

"What?"

"What to do next. I wish I could go with you."

"So do I."

We finished our meal in silence and then Glen spoke. "People see what they want to see," he told me.

"What?"

"People," he repeated himself. "They see what they want to see."

"Okay . . ."

"You asked me a few days ago how all of this happened. How the generals walked around Virginia dressed as they were, and no one really said anything. Or Narbona in Albuquerque. Do you remember? You wanted to know why it was people were so accepting of the fact Robert E. Lee was eating blueberry pancakes in Bob Evans with Phil Sheridan. The answer is, people see what they want to see."

"Is that one of the mysteries of the afterlife?" I asked him.

"Hardly. It just is what it is. People saw us, or they didn't. And if they did, then they just accepted the fact we were there, dressed however we were dressed, and they went on with their lives. Most people were too busy to notice anyway. They have too much going on to even care about what is right in front of them."

"What about the women? They all seemed to see you."

"Maybe more of me than they wanted to!" Glen laughed.

"How did you pull that off?"

"Like I said, they saw what they wanted to see."

I considered his explanation, and it did make some sense. Maybe not as much as I'd liked, but I felt a greater under-standing now of how and why the things that had happened to me over the past week or so actually occurred.

"Okay then, let me ask you one more question."

"Sure."

"Why not Grant or Sherman? Why did you bring Sheridan

and Lee?"

Glen laughed. "They were busy. Those two were the best I could do."

My uncle eventually drove us back to the hotel. We stopped for a couple drinks in the lobby bar and soon Glen was chatting with a pretty Japanese woman. I knew this was my cue to disappear and I dutifully did. He woke me the next morning when he came into the room around his usual nine a.m.

"They have a champagne brunch downstairs," he told me. "I think we should try that. Then we can leave."

I was barely awake but managed to say "okay" before pushing myself from the bed and heading to the shower.

The spread downstairs was absolutely fantastic. In addition to actual champagne, there was crab and smoked salmon and bagels from one of Los Angeles's finest bagel shops. I drank my fill of the bubbly while eating a bagel with lox. Glen seemed to try and eat everything they had laid out before finally surrendering after an hour. We settled our bill with the front desk and waited for the valet to bring the Volvo to us. Soon we were back on Pico heading west. You don't have to turn from Pico if you are going to Santa Monica. It will take you all the way to Ocean Avenue and from there you can go north to Malibu or south toward Venice. Glen told me to turn right, which meant we were headed north. Eventually we lucked into some street parking not too far from Santa Monica beach and the pier.

"Let's go down to the water," Glen said to me as soon as I'd finished putting money into the parking meter. "It might be nice to wade in a little bit."

It was later in the morning and was becoming clear that the day was going to be a hot one. For Los Angeles. I add this qualifier because it is necessary. An 85-degree day that would be perfect most places is considered hot by many of the residents of LA. So, while it was going to be warm, it probably wasn't going to be actually "hot" by the standards of the vast majority of humans living on this planet. Glen immediately began to cross Ocean Avenue, despite the fact we were not by a crosswalk. I hurried after him, trying not to get hit by the many cars driving up and down the quite-wide avenue. Soon we were on the other side in the park, where the homeless people live. Glen hustled past their camps and descended one of the staircases that lead down to the beach.

I was unsure what day it was, so I do not know if I can say whether the beach was crowded for that particular day or not. As it was still fairly early it did not seem that bad, but as it is Santa Monica beach, it was not exactly deserted either. At the bottom of the stairs, Glen removed his shoes and socks. He stuffed the socks inside the shoes and held them both in one hand as he trudged through the sand toward the water. I continued after him. My shoes were still on, and they grew more and more filled with sand with each step I took. Shortly we reached the water's edge and Glen walked forward into the shallow surf. I kicked off my shoes and stepped onto the wet sand, eventually finding myself standing next to him in a spot where the water would reach our ankles every time the waves broke.

"I guess this is it," my uncle said to me as he reached over and put his arm around my shoulder. "This is where I get off."

"No," I told him. "You can't go. I . . ." I was unsure what to say. "What am I going to do now?"

For the final time, Glen laughed at me. "Keep going," he said. "Eventually you will figure it out. You've gotten this far. I am confident you will be alright."

"I am glad we got the chance to share this time," he continued. "It has meant a lot to me."

"I love you, uncle," I told him, tears on my face and in my voice. I knew there was no way I could stop him from leaving. No more than I could have summoned him in the first place.

Life gives and takes, and it took him away from me much too soon, and then, miraculously, it gave him back, but only for a short time. I'd known all along it would take him away again. I did not like the fact that it was happening so soon, but it was going to happen. Nothing I could say would change that.

"I love you too, nephew." His eyes were now watery, but he was not crying. "We will meet again. Don't worry. I will see you someday." Glen kicked at the wet sand as the water retreated. "Now go do what you have to do. Take care of yourself."

"You too," I said as someone behind me yelled something at his child who was apparently too close to the water. I turned to see what was going on and caught a glimpse of a thirty-something man pulling a toddler away from the surf. When I turned back to look at Glen he was gone. And again, I was alone.

✗✗✗✗✗

I spent the rest of the day driving around Los Angeles, looking at the places I had hung out, either when I was growing up, or during the time I lived there when I was in college. Sometimes things were different. Sometimes they were the same. Often they were gone completely (Tower Records). It was getting late in the day so I decided I would stop and get some food at the Shakey's Pizza in Culver City. It is on Sepulveda—actually not that far from Tito's Tacos. Or the airport. Depending on which way you are driving. As far as pizza buffets go, I don't think any place is better than Shakey's. Their pizza is great, plus they have mojo potatoes. If you are unfamiliar with the mojo potatoes, they are thick slices of potato, battered and fried. They are typically served with ranch dressing, and they are so good that you could probably spend an entire day eating them. If you were so inclined.

I did not do this, although I did eat my fair share. As I am also a fan of the pizza, I had to save room for a couple plates filled with it as well. After about an hour I was full but, having no plan, was unsure about where exactly I was headed. I eventually ended up back in front of the house on Oakhurst. Except this time I did get out of my car and eventually sat down on that little brick square at the end of the driveway. It had been a spot for me to clear my head when I was a kid, and again when I was a young man living here. I figured I might as well give it a shot and see if it could possibly work its magic on me now. In my middle age. The smell of the hedge next to the house was exactly the same as I soaked in everything around me. That shrub, the trees, the houses across the street. All of it was the same as it had always been. I was the only thing that was different.

And as I sat there, lost in a world of self-pity, I remembered what Sheridan had told me that day at Arlington. "Try and remember a time you were happy," he had said. "And try to recapture it." Then, it was Charlotte Perkins Gilman's words in Flagstaff that seemed to mix with Sheridan's: "Your muse. If that is what you are missing, it would seem prudent to me that is what you need to locate." And in that moment, on the thinking square I had utilized so often as a child and even as a young man, I finally realized where I needed to go. Unfortunately, there was a good chance I was twenty years too late.

"Hey, what are you doing in my yard?" the owner of the home called to me from the house's side door and awakened me from my trance.

"Get out of here!" he yelled as I slowly rose to my feet. I was not interested in a confrontation, so I retreated to my car, not bothering to say a word to the man.

I-5 SOUTH, 2016

There can be a cruel irony about social media. It can do wonders for you. It can reconnect you with lost friends. Give you people to talk to when you are bored or alone. It can provide you a place to espouse your deepest held beliefs, assuming you are not afraid of the blowback that is certain to come from your choice to discuss your religious or political views with the entire world. It is a wonderful way to share information, and pictures of your children, pets, vacation, and food with anyone on your friends' list. But it also can provide you with information you never wanted. Or needed, for that matter.

This is how I found Claire Grace Taylor. This is how I knew she taught science at Grossmont Community College in El Cajon. All thanks to Facebook. You see, somehow one of my friends ended up marrying a girl who was close friends with Claire's best friend in high school. This meant that every once in a while I would see one of this girl's posts because my friend had liked it. And, on an even rarer occasion, the posts in question would include a comment from my ex-girlfriend.

Now, it didn't happen that often, and when it did I tried my best to ignore the fact that I'd seen her name on there, but eventually curiosity got the best of me and I had to click on her profile. Don't get me wrong. I did not turn into some virtual stalker, but who's not curious about what became of an ex-flame? I am guessing most people are. And so was I. So, eventually I found out. She was married, but she'd kept her last name. She had a kid and she taught science at the aforementioned community college. And, as I sat in the lobby of the Hyatt Place by LAX, breathing in that weird smell all Hyatt Places have, I decided she was the one who would give me the answers I was seeking.

What's that? Why are you shaking your head? Are you wondering how I came to this monumental conclusion? It was on the thinking stone on Oakhurst! Didn't we go over that? It was there that I realized what Sheridan and all the rest of them were talking about. I was pretty sure there had been a time when I was happy, and I was certain there had been a time when I had the inspiration to write, and that time had been my late twenties. It had been when I lived in that town on the border of California and Mexico, when Adam and I would drink the nights away, and when my affair with Claire ignited and then flamed out. And since Adam was still around, the missing piece had to be Claire. She would get me back on track. I just knew it.

I spent the night at the aforementioned Hyatt Place by LAX but did not sleep much. For the first time in a long time, I knew exactly where I was going, and I was anxious to get there. I finally drifted off to sleep a little after five and when I awoke at nine a.m. I half expected to see Glen walk through the door grinning from ear to ear, holding his cup of coffee, and telling me to get up because we had places to be. That was not the case. Instead, all I saw was the clock telling me the time and a small sliver of sunlight making its way through the room's blackout curtains. I jumped from my bed and got into the shower, intent on making myself look presentable for my meeting with destiny. There was no way I could remove the years from my face or the fat from my belly, but I could at least wash my hair and put on some clean clothes and that is what I did. Half an hour later I was in the lobby checking out. Shortly thereafter I was in the Volvo, heading down Interstate 405, switching back and forth between listing to Josh Tillman sing "Leaving LA" and Guy Clark sing "L.A. Freeway" as I careened southward.

Past Inglewood and Hawthorne and Gardena I drove, each city looking a hell of a lot like the city before it. Eventually Long Beach was on the right and then Irvine was on the left, right before I merged onto Interstate 5. I drove past San Juan Capistrano and San Clemente, the small beach communities where I had passed many a happy day, but had no time to stop.

Things thin out once you get past San Clemente. For a brief moment you are no longer in the urban sprawl that is coastal Southern California. It all starts when you hit the San Onofre Nuclear Plant, with its two domes rising like giant breasts from the beach floor. The mighty Pacific is there, on your right if you are going south, but there is little on the left, just brown hills and dried grass. Mostly because this is all part of Camp Pendleton, which means no one can build strip malls or McDonald's or houses. Despite the proximity to the nuclear plant, I am sure all of these things would be there, if only the land were available for development.

Past Pendleton, you reach Oceanside and then Carlsbad and it was here that I decided to take a break for lunch and a rehash of my game plan. There is a fish taco place on the beach in Carlsbad that makes the finest fish tacos I have ever eaten. Anywhere. And that includes multiple places in Baja. I wish I could tell you the name of the restaurant, but I can't. Which is strange, because I have been eating there for close to twenty years. It is not hard to find though. Just drive through downtown on Carlsbad Boulevard, then continue south. As soon as you can see the ocean, you will see the restaurant. It is an open-air place with limited parking, but it's worth the aggravation. Trust me. Just get the fish tacos. You will not regret it.

I suppose I was lucky because I was able to find a spot to leave the Volvo in their small parking lot and made my way up to the restaurant to get a table. Soon I was seated and I'd placed my standard order. I guess this is where I should tell you that I was sitting in the very same restaurant when Claire Grace Taylor had broken up with me all those years ago. Maybe you remember? The one where she'd ordered the lobster just hours before dumping my ass. Yeah, that one. It is funny because we had discovered this place together on some day trip north from San Diego and up until the time we broke up I'd always kind of thought of it as one of "our" places. However, once we split, I was quick to change that mental picture to see it as one of "my" places. As such, I'd eaten here with plenty of other people; with my father, with my friends, and even with my wife. There were no painful memories tied to the wonder that was the fish tacos I was waiting to consume.

"Business or pleasure," the waitress, whose name was Brandi, asked me as she refilled my glass of Dr Pepper.

"I'm sorry," I said, her words pulling me from the trance the ocean had put me in.

"Are you here on business or pleasure?" She repeated. "You're alone, so I assume it's business."

I chuckled for a minute, then told her, "Business. Definitely business."

"Oh yeah, what kind?" she asked. Her arms were now crossed, and it was apparent she was going to have a conversation with me. Whether I wanted it or not.

"The personal kind," I answered. Hoping that would end our exchange.

"I see," she told me. "Then I better get your order so you can get to it."

Soon she returned with my tacos and placed them in front of me. I muttered, "Thank you," before grabbing one and shoving it into my mouth. I was hopeful this would stop her from trying to make any more silly small talk and the ploy worked. At least until I was done with the food.

"You want anything else?" About fifteen minutes after she'd put the food in front of me, Brandi was back. Because my plate was empty.

"I don't think so," I replied.

She poked around in her apron and eventually pulled out my bill. "Good luck," she told me as she placed the piece of paper in front of me.

"What?" I asked.

"With your personal business," she replied. "I hope you find whatever it is you're looking for."

"Who said I was looking for something?"

She smiled at me. It was not a smile of warmth, but more a smile of sadness. "It seems pretty obvious," she said. "You pay at the counter," she added, before walking away.

The Grand Finale

EL CAJON, 2016

It did not take me long to get to Grossmont College. It is located in El Cajon, just to the east of San Diego, which is around forty-five miles from where I ate my lunch. I stuck to Interstate 5, so I could look at the ocean on my right as I drove. Eventually I had to make the turn east, away from the water and toward the place where I hoped I would find the answers I was seeking.

I was familiar with Grossmont College from my time covering sports in El Centro. I'd been there a couple times to watch volleyball and basketball games and had a general idea where everything was. That did not mean I had any clue where the science classes were, so my first stop was in the main office to ask where I might find Professor Taylor. After assuring the lady at the desk I was not up to no good, I was directed to her office. Once there, the science department secretary told me that Professor Taylor was teaching a class and that she would not be back for an hour or two.

"Can you tell me where the class is?" I asked. "I'd like to go see her teach."

I suppose this lady did not take me for the danger the lady at the main office had suspected I might be, because she was happy to tell me the class was in room C-7 and even drew me a little map so I could find my way there. Soon enough I was standing in front of the door, wondering whether or not I was doing the right thing. There was no window on the classroom, so I could not see inside. I could hear some talking though. Maybe it was her voice. I was not sure as I'd not heard her speak in something like twenty years. I slowly opened the door, revealing a fairly large lecture hall with seats descending toward where the professor was talking. I could not see the person speaking as I slipped inside and moved as quietly as possible toward the first empty seat I could find. Quickly, I was seated and had a clearer view of the person at the dais and sure enough, it was Claire Grace Taylor. Professor of biology.

There were probably twenty to thirty people in the room, listening intently and typing notes on flickering computer screens. Down below, Claire was talking about covalent bonds or something like that. I don't know. I wasn't there to learn science. For a minute I regretted my decision and thought about slipping back out the door. She had not seen me, so really, at this point it was kind of a no harm/no foul type of situation. But I could not bring myself to move from my spot. Transfixed, I sat and watched her talk, studying her appearance as she moved around, writing on the whiteboard and then turning back and messing with the computer that was controlling her PowerPoint. In many ways she looked the same. Her hair was a similar color and length. Her smile, flashed a couple times when one of her students asked a particularly funny question, was the same too. But of course she had changed. There were lines around her face that had not been there when I'd left her that night in Kensington and her body was very much that of a woman who had given birth. Obviously, I was not one to talk when it came to the powerful effects of aging. In fact, I was kind of concerned she might not even recognize me if I did speak to her after class.

It took about twenty minutes for the opportunity to arise. That was when the class ended— about twenty minutes after I walked in that door. She turned off her projector and switched on the lights in the classroom as the students began to file out. One of them approached her and they had a brief conversation. Then he too headed for the exit. Claire was now by herself, putting her things away in a brown briefcase. I slowly rose from my seat and, for a brief second, once again considered going back out the door I'd come in. But I did not. Instead I pressed forward. Down the stairs, up onto the dais, until I was standing about five feet from her. Her back was still turned to me, so she was unaware of who it was that was behind her when she said, "How can I help you?"

"I'm not sure," I answered.

When she turned around, there was a smile on her face. When she locked eyes with me, it immediately disappeared. "Jack?" she exclaimed. Her voice was full of shock and questions I would never be able to answer. Perhaps there was even a little bit of fear in there. I wasn't sure. Maybe she thought I'd come back to send her to some sort of dark end. Honestly, why else would I be standing there?

"Hello, Claire," I told her as a brief smile crossed my face.

"Hi!" Again her voice was full of emotion. For a moment it seemed like she might want to move in to hug me. But she did not. And I was relieved. "What . . ." Her smile reappeared for a second, then was just as quickly gone again and confusion controlled her face. "What are you doing here?"

"I don't know," I told her. "I was in the area. So I thought I might come see how you'd been."

That confusion quickly turned to anger. This was a woman I'd broken up with via email once. I'd told her I had gotten married just a few weeks after she'd ended our relationship via the same medium. I went over all that earlier. So I am not going to rehash it. What I'm getting at though is she had no reason to have any sort of warm feelings for me. And I was quickly getting the idea she did not.

"Huh," was her only response as she went back to putting her teaching supplies away. "So you were in the neighborhood?" Despite the fact I could not see her face, I could tell by the tone of her voice she was getting angrier with each word she spoke. "And you just thought you'd stop by?"

I shrugged. Even though she couldn't see me. And I sort of made the Brodie face. The one Jason Lee makes a lot in *Mallrats*. (If you don't know what I'm talking about, then you should go find a picture right now. Otherwise you won't understand.) "Yeah," I said, infuriating her further.

She now had her bag in her hand and was facing me. "It's nice to see you are still an asshole," she told me as she walked past me toward the exit.

"Hey, wait." I attempted to grab her arm but thought better of it. "I came to see you. You're just going to take off?"

"Yeah," she said. "I am. You fucking dick. What makes you think, after twenty years, I want to talk to you? About anything?"

"Hey, you broke up with me!" I told her. As if that somehow mattered now. Or if that excused the way I'd chosen to completely end our relationship.

"Fuck you," she stopped, maybe ten feet away. Her face was turning red as she glared at me. "You have no right to just show up here and expect us to pick up like nothing has happened." I could see now just how much older she looked. And I wondered if she was thinking the same thing? At least in between fits of rage. She must have noticed all the grey in my beard. And the extra weight I was carrying. Shit, there was no missing any of that.

"I'm sorry," I told her. And I was. I obviously did not know what I was doing anymore.

"Does that make this alright? What were you thinking?"

"I don't know," I told her. "I just thought maybe you could help."

"Help you with what?"

"Figuring things out."

To that, she guffawed. Then she cackled and chuckled and belly laughed. "What is wrong with you? Do you need me to call an ambulance? Are you having some sort of breakdown?"

"I don't think so." I scratched my chin through my thick beard. "Maybe." I pondered further. Was she right? Was this some sort of break with reality? No. Couldn't be. I knew what I was doing. "I feel okay. I just . . . I don't know. Things just made so much more sense when we were together. I thought maybe if I saw you. If I talked to you. Maybe it would help."

"Help what?" She asked again. Now her look was one of actual concern. "Seriously, are you okay? Do you know where you are?"

"Yes, I know where I am. I am at Grossmont College in El Cajon, California."

"Do you know what day it is?"

I did not. But for good reason. Still, I think this further worried her.

"How about the year?"

"Yeah, it's 2016."

She looked me over and seemed to judge me mentally competent. "Now seriously, what are you doing here?"

"Seriously. I just told you."

This got her dander up again. "You want me to believe that after twenty years, after the way you ended our friendship, that you just came and found me because you think I can help you with your life?"

"You broke up with me," I muttered again.

"Stop fucking saying that," she said. "That doesn't even

fucking matter now. And you know as well as I do that you were still my best friend. We talked on the phone almost every day up until you ran off to Vegas to get married. And how did that work out for you anyway? I bet that didn't even last a year."

"We're actually still together."

Her hand went into her hair, and I think maybe she wanted to tear some of it out. But she did not. "Congratulations," she angrily responded. "Now, if we're done here. I have to get to my office."

"Wait, Claire." My words sounded like pleas, and it made her stop. "I don't know what I'm doing. I don't know where I'm going. I don't . . . I just don't know."

"Jesus Christ." She walked toward me. "You need help. I can see that. But I am not the one who is going to help you. Even if I wanted to. I am not the one who can help you. You need to figure that out on your own. Somewhere else. Now, please. I need to go."

She touched my arm and it reminded me of a time I picked her up from a car dealership where she'd dropped her Jetta off to be serviced. We'd not seen each other for a week when we met that day, and she ran toward me, a look of pure joy on her face. I remembered the way it felt when she wrapped her arms around me and kissed me on the cheek and then on the mouth. I remembered that electricity and the promise of what would come next. There was none of that now. There was just the hand of a soon-to-be middle-aged women resting on my middle-aged shoulder. She pulled me toward her, and again I thought she might be moving in for a hug, but instead she just pushed me in front of her, toward the door. Soon we were outside in the sunlight. I waited behind her as she locked the door to the room.

"I guess this is it," she said, unsure whether to offer me her hand to shake, or how one exits what was probably the most awkward situation she'd experienced in a long time. So she just smiled at me before turning to walk back in the direction of her office.

"What's the point?" I asked her, causing her to stop and turn around to look at me. "To all this? I mean, really. What are we doing?"

She looked at me, confused, and offered no response.

"Do you remember that little house you lived in in Kensington? Do you remember when we used to lie on the sofa in that living room and we'd listen to those mix CDs I used to make you?"

"Yes, you gave them some stupid name, but I don't remember what." She smiled. I knew she remembered.

"Yeah," I said as I put on my sunglasses. "And we'd lay there and I would sing along with those songs and we'd just do that, for hours sometimes, and the day would pass so quickly. It was all so perfect. I mean, nothing else mattered. Do you think that was it? Maybe that was just as good as it was going to get?"

"I don't know," she said. "I have to go."

Claire gave me one more look and another sad smile. I too was unsure how to end such an encounter, so I just held my hand up as if I were waving. I turned to walk away and was a few steps down the sidewalk when I heard her call from behind me. "Hey," she shouted. "I am going to get some lunch. Do you want to come with me?"

I turned around almost immediately and headed back towards her. I honestly felt as if I were running as I made the approach, although I don't think I actually was. I certainly hope I wasn't. "Seriously?" I asked when I was in front of her again.

"Yeah." She sighed. "We can do that."

I followed Claire back to her office, neither of us saying anything. She walked a couple steps ahead of me and I felt like she was trying to get away the entire time. She asked me to wait outside when we got back to the building that housed her office and I was pretty sure she was not going to return. Much to my surprise, five minutes later, she did.

"There is a Crocodile Café up in Grossmont Center," she told me upon her return. "Is that good for you?"

"Sure. Anything." I answered.

"Okay. Do you have a car? Or you can ride with me. I am parked over there." She gestured in a rather general direction—where, I was not sure.

"I'll go with you," I quickly decided. "I've been driving for a while now."

"Where did you come from?"

"Texas. By way of Virginia, Nashville, New Mexico, and Los Angeles," I answered.

She genuinely laughed for the first time since I had spoken to her. "That is not the most direct route."

"No. It's not." I laughed back.

Claire turned and began to briskly lead me toward the parking lot and her car. Once again, she was walking a couple steps in front of me, and I did not try very hard to catch up. Eventually we reached the parking lot and her red BMW X5. I honestly half-expected her to take me back to the same silver Volkswagen Jetta she had driven when we were dating. I was having a hard time wrapping my head around the fact that twenty years had passed since the last time I'd seen her. We were not the same people, and I am pretty sure she would not be happy if I were to grab her and kiss her. Then again, maybe she would be. Not that I was going to try.

When Claire started her car Morrissey began to sing to us. It was not surprising. He had always been her favorite singer and I found it comforting that some things never changed. The children's safety seats in the back of her car, on the other hand, were definitely different. I was not unaware that she had children, but these served as a stark reminder that we had come a long way from that night when I had walked away from her cottage in Kensington two decades earlier.

The drive to the restaurant did not take long and we were quickly seated, as it was later in the day and the lunch rush was long past. We made typical small talk—the weather, our shared memories of this restaurant, and our time working at the newspaper in the Imperial Valley—as we waited to place our orders.

"Tell me what you are doing here," she said as soon as the waiter had taken our order and was a few steps from our table. "Seriously."

"I don't really know," I replied. "I've been driving around the country with my uncle. Glen. I think you met him once." She nodded in the affirmative. "We've just been out there, on the road, living life, you know?" It was obvious to me by the look on her face she was not really sure what I was talking about. "I guess not . . ."

"Where is he?" she finally asked. "Your uncle. Where is Glen?"

"He's gone," I told her. "He left in Los Angeles."

"Where did he go?"

"Home. I guess."

"You guess?" she questioned. "You don't know where he went? Did he just disappear?"

My eyes got wide as her question soaked in. "Sort of."

Claire's expression changed from one of curiosity to one of concern. "I am still worried about you," she said. "Are you sure you're alright? You look terrible."

I laughed and her face became even more worried-looking. Then I laughed some more.

"I'm being serious," she continued. "This is not normal behavior."

"What's normal anyway?" I asked her.

"Not this," she assured me.

"Oh, Claire." I exhaled. "I am so glad to see you."

"Are you?" she questioned. "I'm still not convinced you even know where you are. You realize it's not 2000? We're not together. You know that, right?"

"I do," I tried to reassure her.

"Okay." Maybe she believed me. I wasn't really sure.

"So . . ." The waiter returned to deliver our southwestern salads and ask if we wanted anything else. We both said no and he disappeared again. "How can I help you?"

There she sat in front of me. Claire Grace Taylor, older, rounder, still pretty, sort of the same, but different. She was no longer the girl I left on that doorstep all those years ago; instead, she was a concerned almost-stranger, asking how she could be of help. "I don't really know," I finally told her. "I just got to a place and I got stuck. Do you know what I mean? I have a house and I have a wife and I have a kid. We live in the suburbs, and I am sure it would all seem ideal to some people. But it was never what I wanted. You know?"

Claire finished chewing a bite of her salad before she answered. "I guess." Her reply was more a question than a statement. "I have a house and children and a husband I love. I have a job I enjoy, so maybe I don't. What else is there?"

"That is exactly my point."

"What?"

"What else is there?"

"I think that is it," she said assuredly. "It sounds to me like you have a pretty good life. Do you still write?"

"Not really."

"That's too bad."

"That is debatable," I answered her.

"I guess," she said. "I always thought you were good at it. Why did you stop?"

"I think I lost my muse," I told her. "I think. Maybe. That was you."

"What?"

"I think you were my muse."

This time Claire's laughter was loud enough for the entire restaurant to hear. "Really?"

"Yeah," I told her. "I remember writing a lot when we were together and then when we broke up all of my inspiration sort of dried up."

"That's interesting," she answered. "Because I seem to remember it differently. Every time we had a fight, you would write something. Every time you tried to break up with me, you would write something. But when we were together, I don't ever remember you writing anything at all. You talked about it a lot. You worked on the stories you'd written during our time apart, but when we were together, nothing."

I looked at her, studying her face, making sure I understood.

"There is no way I was ever your muse," she finished. "If anything your muse is sadness, anger, angst, whatever you want to call it. I am sorry to say, but it was not ever me."

I continued looking at her and she was so sincere in what she'd told me there was nothing I could do other than believe her. The conversation stopped then, for a while, as we finished our lunches.

"Claire," I finally broke the silence after finishing the last of my strawberry lemonade. "If I were to ask you to run away to Paris with me, would you go?"

Again she laughed, heartily. "No. I have to go pick up my son from daycare. I have responsibilities. I can't just run away to Paris. Not to mention the fact I have a husband. I thought we'd already gone over that."

"We have," I said. "I just figured I would ask."

"Thanks," she said sarcastically as she looked away from the table. Her eyes seemed to be searching for something less crazy to lock on than the situation they found themselves currently in. "I am not sure what else I can do for you," she continued as the waiter placed the check on the table. I reached to get it and she tried to stop me. "Do you have any money?"

"Yes," I reassured her. "I have plenty of that." She pulled her hand away and let me pick up the check. I was relieved to see her salad did not cost as much as the lobster I bought her the last time we'd gone out to eat together. I placed my credit card and the bill back on the table and motioned for the waiter to come get it. He did, and when he left our conversation continued. "Are you happy?" I asked her.

"Yes," she almost gushed. "I love being a mom. I love my husband. I love my job. I still wish we lived in Los Angeles sometimes, but San Diego is great, perfect weather and so much to do."

"That's good."

"I'm sorry about whatever it is you are going through." She reached out and touched my hand, for the first time since I had literally shown up on her doorstep. "But I don't know what else to tell you. I don't know that there is anything I can do to help you."

I took a moment to breathe it all in deeply—the smell of the restaurant, the food and liquor and the scent of the people, her sweet perfume, the feeling of rejection all too similar to the feeling twenty years earlier. But it was more than that. The answer had been no. Or perhaps there had been no answer at all. I'd reached the end of the road and found nothing, except for maybe even more road . . . . I sighed deeply as I exhaled. Soon the waiter returned with my credit card and his gratitude for us dining with him.

"Are you ready?" I asked after I had placed my card back in my wallet. Claire nodded yes and I silently followed her back to her car. She made the brief drive back to the college quickly and I directed her to where I had parked my car.

"It's the Volvo," I sheepishly admitted after she'd asked where to drop me off.

"Nice," she smiled. "Safest car on the road!" She laughed as she slapped my knee. In that lone moment she was the girl I'd loved, smiling, her sense of humor silly and juvenile. She appeared younger in the waning afternoon sun, her eyes and smile looking all too much like a past I could no longer touch, no matter how hard I tried. Then, just as quickly, my Claire was gone and the woman she now was returned. "Good luck," she said as I opened the car door and pulled myself from her vehicle.

"Thanks, Claire," I replied as I moved to push the door shut. "Thanks for lunch and thanks for listening to me. It was good to see you."

"I still think you need help," she told me as I stood looking at her. The girl I had loved so much, now a woman I did not know. I looked at her for what would certainly be the last time as she concluded, "You should get some."

I slammed the car door shut and waved as she drove off, leaving me standing in the parking lot, alone.

A BRIEF INTERLUDE IN ROUND ROCK, 2014

"I really think this is the right car for us right now," my wife said to me as we strolled through the car lot at our local Volvo dealership. "It is nice-looking. It is in our price range and you know what they say? It's the safest car on the road."

I was staring at a silver Volvo station wagon. Not the small XC70 model, but the much larger V60 and, while I had to admit the cabin was luxurious, it was not the car I pictured myself getting when my wife had chosen to downsize her own SUV to get a Tesla for her daily commute.

I suppose I should give you a little context here. Ever since I was a kid all I ever wanted was a Porsche 911. I didn't care where I lived, as long as I could drive that Porsche. As I got older and learned firsthand what journalists made, I realized that the 911 was likely never going to be in my driveway, so I contented myself with a string of sporty cars. When we got married I was driving a V8 Mustang, and when I sold the rights to *A Season in Hell* I ran out and purchased an SRT8

Dodge Challenger. I eventually got rid of the Challenger because I became tired of taking my daughter in and out of the back seat, but I was fairly happy in the Chrysler 300 SRT I had settled into and was not necessarily looking to make a change on the day my wife came home and told me she had traded in her large family-hauling vehicle for a much smaller ride. After a few weeks of trying to use her electric vehicle as our main car, it became apparent this was not going to work and I began to search for a larger vehicle for the three of us.

This eventually led us to the Volvo dealership in Round Rock and that silver station wagon that I had never really even considered as a viable option. I should mention I grew up in the back of station wagons. My father was most definitely a fan. But I was a sports car guy. I wanted a car with two doors! At the very least, I wanted a car with a V8 engine. The 300 did not have the former, but it did have the latter, and for a while it served its purpose quite well. Unfortunately, it was not good for hauling all of our luggage and there was no way I was ever going to fit the Christmas tree in it. So I went ahead and shook hands with the Volvo salesman and agreed to purchase the V60 from him. At the time, it seemed like the right thing to do—and at that point in time, I was most definitely in the business of doing the right thing.

We picked out the silver one and took it for a test drive on the country roads of Williamson County. There was no doubt it drove quite well and at one point the salesman showed us its turn radius, which was quite impressive. After a brief conference back at the dealership, we decided we would take the car, and soon it was parked in our three-car garage, right next to the Tesla, which plugged in each night so my wife never had to buy any gas.

It was this car that I drove for the next two years, shuttling Lucy around to her after-school activities. It was this car we took on all our family vacations and this was the car used to haul the dog to the vet, cart the Christmas tree home, deliver the annual flowers we planted in the front yard, and bring home the groceries . . . .

JACUMBA, CALIFORNIA, 2016

And it was this car that I climbed into on the night I decided to leave, and it was this car that had carried me all over the country and eventually brought me all the way from Virginia to California. From sea to shining sea, like my grandfather before me, except my trip had not been financially motivated. But it was an escape all the same. Mr. Toad's Wild Ride in a silver Volvo station wagon, with Robert E. Lee and Phil Sheridan and Glen riding shotgun. The search for danger, excitement, and life itself, behind the wheel of the safest car on the road. A trip born of frustration, filled with searching and questions and some answers, but never the answers I was looking for.

It was into this car that I climbed that summer day in San Diego. Just moments after self-immolating in front of an ex-girlfriend I'd not seen in almost twenty years. As I had no more business in California, I figured it might be time to go home, mostly because I could not figure out where else to go. This meant back onto I-8 and pointed east. The sprawl of San Diego stretches farther than it used to. All the way to Alpine now. Or maybe even the Viejas Casino, if you want to be kind. But soon enough I was in the mountains with little around, other than the other cars making the trip out to the desert and beyond. I could see Mexico to the south and more of the brown mountains to the north as I crossed the big bridge right before the Mountain Empire rest area.

The weight of everything that had happened slowly sunk onto my shoulders as I drove. I remembered the times with Lee and Sheridan in Virginia. Was there an APB out on us? For burning down that bar? I wondered if Narbona's grandchildren liked the toys he brought them. And I wondered where Glen was. And why he'd had to leave in the first place. I had set out on this journey searching for something bigger than I could ever really hope to find and, as you know all too well at this point, I never exactly found any of it. But maybe, in not finding it, I actually found everything. Maybe the secret to life is there is no secret at all. You see, I think that's what Glen kept telling me, in his own way. These words, just like life, have no real meaning. It's just meandering chaos working its way toward an inevitably bad conclusion.

Joe Strummer sang "The Card Cheat" as I sped past the rest area and then the big windmills close to the second casino that is in the mountains. Soon I was in Jacumba, and I made a pit stop there. Once upon a time, Jacumba was kind of the only thing in this pass, which meant I'd made plenty of stops at one of the two gas stations before. They also have hot springs. In case you're ever in the area. I'd heard they are pretty nice, but I've never been. You can ask Adam if you ever see him. He knows. He used to hang out there with one of his girlfriends. I forget her name. Which I probably should, as they never invited me to tag along with them.

I drank a Mountain Dew while eating a bag of Cool Ranch Doritos in front of the Volvo. It seemed like the right thing to do, as it was probably something akin to what I'd eaten the first time I'd ever stopped there, back in 1989, shortly after my family moved to the Imperial Valley. Honestly, at this point in my life, I cannot stand the taste of Mountain Dew and I think I maybe managed to get through half the twenty-ounce bottle before throwing the rest of it away. The Doritos, on the other hand, still tasted great and were gone soon after I opened the bag. The air was cooler up here, which was nice, considering what I knew awaited me on the valley floor below. So I took some time to enjoy it before getting back behind the wheel and on the road.

Soon enough I was on I-8 headed east. Alkaline Trio's "If We Never Go Inside" played as the sun set behind me. I drove on, my past adventures replaying in my mind as I tried to remain focused on the road. Claire's words still swirled around in my head. But so did Glen's. And all the rest of them. If Claire wasn't my muse, then who was? And that business about sadness? That made no sense. If sadness was truly it, then I should be the most productive writer on the planet. I had been sad for the vast majority of my life. What if there wasn't anything more? What if I was out here searching for something I could not ever find? What if being a suburban asshole was all that was left for me? What if grilling on the weekends and drinking half a six-pack before retiring to the sofa for six or seven hours of television was as good as it was going to get? What then? I did not need to spend another twenty or thirty years just waiting around to die. This was not what I'd signed up for. This was, in no way, what I wanted. No muse, no point, nobody needs me . . . what the hell was I going to do next?

Shortly after Jacumba, you reach the descent from the mountains. The sun was gone now, and I was surrounded by the darkness of the moonless night. It was into this darkness that I pushed the Volvo, down the steep road that leads to the valley floor. They call it the grade and it is a pretty windy, treacherous stretch of highway, especially if you don't know what you're doing. Once, when I had a car that handled much better than the Volvo, I used to test myself to see if I could descend the entire grade without ever once touching my brakes. I eventually got pretty good at it. But only late at night when I had the use of both lanes of the interstate. There was no way I was going to get away with anything like that on this evening, so I proceeded with some caution, through the twists and turns in front of me until I was about halfway down and staring at probably the sharpest switchback of the entire descent. I took the first turn well enough and, as I came to the next curve, the valley floor, and the settlements on it, opened up in front of me like the night sky illuminated by a thousand brilliant stars. It was there that this all started. The book. The women. The booze. The drugs. The ennui. The anxiety and depression. Everything.

Despite the lights below me, the road was dark, but I knew most of it by heart. The next curve was a tight one—recommended speed forty-five, hard to the left. There were many times, in the past, when I wished my car would just drift into the oncoming traffic and get crushed by a semi. Sometimes I even let go of the wheel, with the idea that fate might pull me in that direction and get all of this over with. It never did. This time was different though. This time I was in control. I accelerated and pulled the wheel hard to the right. If I could find no answers in life, perhaps then I could find them in death.

For a second everything was as it had been in the seconds before. I was seated comfortably in the car, Townes Van Zandt was singing to me, but my hands were no longer on the wheel, and when the car hit the guardrail everything quickly changed. Soon I was upside down and then an empty Fiji water bottle, which had been laying on the floor in the backseat, hit me in the face. The car rotated a full 360 degrees before it struck the first outcropping of rocks. The rear windshield exploded on impact and I felt some of the glass slice the back of my ear. Then the airbags began to pop. First the one on the steering wheel, then the one by the passenger seat. Then the ones on the side and above my head. They call those the side-curtain airbags. The Volvo salesman was pretty proud of these. He called them next generation and said they would save my life. Fucking Volvo. Safest car on the road.

I do not recall much of what happened after that. There were a few more rotations of the car and then there was nothing. When I came to, I was on the valley floor, firmly secured to my seat, deflated airbags all around me. The car was on its side, and I could not open my left eye. There was blood, somewhere, running warm, and I was pretty sure something was broken. I did not know what, but I knew I could not move. I surveyed the scene with my one good eye. I was too far off the road for help to arrive quickly and I wondered if I would bleed out before anyone else got there. I could not see much. The headlights were pointed in a direction I could not look and, as I said earlier, there was no moon to speak of that night. There was little noise coming from the car. The radio had stopped, and I guess the engine had as well. I suppose I was unconscious long enough for the wheels to stop spinning, so all I heard were the cars driving past on the road above me. I noticed the side of my face was being scratched by the dirt on which it rested. I shut my one good eye for a second when I heard someone speak.

"You're next," they said. The voice familiar, yet disguised behind an obvious attempt to sound creepy.

I opened my eye and found myself staring directly into the smiling face of my uncle, who was lying on the ground next to me, his head no more than six inches from mine. "You're next," he hissed at me again before he started laughing, louder and heartier than seemed appropriate for the situation we found ourselves in.

"Where'd you come from?" I asked him. The taste of blood was warm and metallic in my mouth as I spoke.

"I have been here the entire time," he answered.

"Really?"

"Sure." He shook his head as I stared at him in disbelief. "I guess you went ahead and did it."

A tear finally came from my eye. "I fucked it up like I did everything else."

"That is one way to look at it." I could only see half of his face as the other side rested on the same ground that was serving as my pillow.

"I was ready," I told him, my words choked by tears and possibly by blood coming up from my throat. "I am ready!" I tried to shout at him. I was unsure if I succeeded.

"Not yet," he answered as his hand reached out and touched my blood-soaked head. He smiled as he looked at me. A smile of happiness. A smile of sorrow. A smile of hope. And he said to me one more time, "Not yet."

And lying there, my blood forming some sort of adhesive paste as it mixed with the dirt below my face, I finally understood.

AUSTIN, 2006

"Dad, I don't think I can finish this." Three-year-old Lucinda held up her half-eaten Pop-Tart as we got out of our car in the parking lot at our favorite park. It was a Friday, which meant I had Lucy all day, as I worked nights on those Fridays when I was a sports writer. She and I had a pretty set routine for our "fun" Fridays. We went to the local park for an hour or two and then we would go spend another couple hours eating lunch and playing at the local Chick-fil-A. After that we would go home and lay down on the couch to watch some kid's movie and eventually fall asleep for our afternoon nap. Every Friday pretty much happened the same way. And every Friday was pretty much perfect.

"Then you can throw it away in the trash can," I told her. She let go of my hand and raced forward on her short legs, her thin brown curls bouncing on her shoulders as she ran. She tossed the Pop-Tart into the garbage can and laughed as she did it. Then she returned to me and grabbed my hand to pull me quicker into the park.

It was still summer in Texas, even in early September, so

the trees were very much green, which contrasted greatly with the brown grass that had fallen victim to a two-year drought and the watering restrictions the city had put on itself and its citizens. Lucy dragged me behind her as she ran past the playhouse where we once spent fifteen minutes riding out a particularly heavy rainstorm, toward the playground that sat in the middle of a grove of post oak trees that provided a welcome respite from the rising afternoon sun.

"Push me," she squealed as she dove headfirst onto the first swing she came to.

"Get in it right," I told her as she jumped from the swing. She quickly grabbed it and sat back down the proper way.

I spent the next fifteen minutes pushing her and listening to her talk. I do not recall what she was talking about, and I cannot honestly tell you that I even heard most of it. When Lucy was younger she woke up talking and did not stop until her head hit the pillow. In order to cope with the incessant drone of her voice, I had to learn to tune her out for vast periods of time. I found that when she really had something important to say she would repeat herself, forcing me to apologize for not listening. But she never seemed to take it personally, as she almost always replied, "That's okay," and then went back to her nonstop chatter.

She eventually tired of the swing and ran off to play with the other kids on the huge play structure that was the centerpiece of the playground. I found my usual seat, on a green wooden bench underneath one of the large trees, and settled in to watch her. For the next thirty minutes, she chased other kids, slid down the two slides, and spent plenty of time yelling, "Hey, Dad," at me from inside the wooden fort, letting me know she was up there. After a while, the other kids left, as they always did, and once she tired of playing by herself she came to get me.

"Do you want to go on a walk?" she asked when she was

finally in front of me.

"If you want to go on a walk, then I want to go on a walk," I responded. She confirmed that she did indeed want to go on a walk and grabbed me by the hand, pulling me from the bench. We headed away from the playground, toward the paved path that led to the creek. We descended the trail and found the creek swollen from a recent, rare, rainfall. The water swept over a small portion of the trail and I could tell Lucy was afraid to cross it.

"Just jump," I told her as she stood looking at the swift-moving water. "You can do it."

"I'm scared, Dad," she told me. "I don't think I can make it."

"Yes, you can," I tried to reassure her. "Come on, I will help you." I grabbed her hand and told her to jump. When she did, I stepped across the flooded area and lifted her over as well.

"We did it!" she exclaimed proudly as she landed on the other side.

"Yes, we did," I answered.

"I love you, Dad," Lucy said as she again began to pull me forward, along the trail, toward the next stand of trees that it curved into.

"I love you too, Lucy."

"Dad."

"Yes, Lucy?"

She turned and looked at me, her hands rose above her head, and she jumped in the air, her face a giant smile as she said, "I wish we could stay here forever."

I caught her before her feet touched the ground and I pulled her up so she was eye-to-eye with me. "So do I, Lucy," I told her as I hugged her tightly. She gave me a dirty look that let me know she did not want to be carried, so I set her down and she ran ahead. Her little legs churned as fast as they could, taking her forward around the bend in the trail and eventually out of sight.

APPENDIX

1. The best tuna salad:

1 can tuna, preferably StarKist in water, although Bumble Bee works alright too. DO NOT buy the tuna in oil. That shit is gross!

1 tablespoon mayonnaise. Use Duke's. Hellmann's is also acceptable.

At least 1 tablespoon pickle relish. You can get creative here. Sometimes I use sweet, sometimes I use dill. It is up to you, because they are both good. I say at least 1 tablespoon, but I always use more. Again, it depends on how you like it.

Dash of black pepper

Bigger dash of onion powder. I cannot get enough of this stuff, so I use a lot. Besides the relish, it is the most important part of the tuna salad.

Stir together in a bowl and enjoy on some wheat bread. Or right out of the bowl. Maybe standing over the sink eating it, like I do.

2. Top secret rib rub recipe:

1/2 cup brown sugar
1/4 cup paprika
1 tablespoon black pepper
1 tablespoon sea salt
1 tablespoon chili powder
1 tablespoon garlic powder
1 tablespoon onion powder
1 teaspoon red pepper flakes
1/2 teaspoon cinnamon

Mix all ingredients together, then spread by hand over pork back loin ribs. Make sure to rub mixture into pork and let sit for thirty minutes or so. Smoke, or cook over indirect heat, at 300 degrees for at least two hours. Meat should easily come from bone when ribs are done.

3. The scourge of Chip and JoJo

There is a terror going around these parts that is proving itself to be a detriment to good people everywhere. This terror masquerades as something good, something benign, something to aspire to. But it is much more insidious than all that. The terror I speak of is the terror of Chip and JoJo, and it is a terror that must be stopped.

When Chip and JoJo first showed up on my television screen, I found them to be harmless enough. They did not appear to be much worse than any of the other hosts of the home-remodeling shows my wife liked to watch in the evenings on HGTV, and the fact that they lived in Texas actually made them a little relatable to me. While I myself did not reside in Waco, I was at least partially familiar with the place they lived, and the houses they worked on looked similar enough to the homes around my town.

But then things changed. The more success Chip and JoJo achieved, the more their supposedly perfect relationship was brought to the foreground of their program. No longer was the show simply about remodeling homes; now it was some sort of manifesto on the power of family, with undertones of Christianity running rampant through everything they did. And this is dangerous, dear reader; do not doubt that. In a day and age where almost twenty percent of marriages end in divorce, forcing this picture-perfect family on the world does nothing to calm the strains many marriages are under. How many of us have the chance to eat pizza nightly with our spouse and children while we are at work? I know for a fact, most people would be in a whole hell of a lot of trouble if their family showed up with bags of food, expecting to eat dinner, while they were in the middle of their shift. Yet, if you watch Chip and JoJo on a regular basis, you know this is a big part of their lives and you begin to wonder why you cannot live this way as well.

And don't get me started on their ever-expanding empire. This dastardly duo is not content being happy with the fortune they have made as television stars. No, they also want to sell this lifestyle, and JoJo's one-note decorating talents, to the world. I would tell you that Chip and JoJo will not be happy until every person in the world has multiple words like "love" and "family" and "eat" plastered on the walls of their modern country homes. This is nothing we need, friends! We do not need everyone's home to be decorated in the same way. What would be the next step? Will all the men be forced to dress in jeans and boots and t-shirts and ballcaps? And will the women have to wear a uniform chosen from JoJo's subdued closet? I, for one, hope not!

Do not take this warning lightly. Chip and JoJo are at the

forefront of an insidious movement to make us all the same, and they must be stopped. Take off that ball cap! Tear those words from your kitchen wall! Leave the popcorn ceilings and 1980s shag carpet in your houses! Do not conform! We are the last line of defense, those of us who have not fallen under their country-chic sway. We must stay strong and make a stand before it is too late. There is a scourge in this land, but it is a scourge we can rid ourselves of. One piece of shiplap at a time.

4. A good pimento cheese recipe

8 ounces cheddar cheese—grated coarsely
8 ounces other cheese—white cheddar, jack, even mozzarella can work—grated coarsely
1 cup mayonnaise—use Duke's!
One jar pimentos
Salt/pepper, garlic powder, onion powder, and hot sauce to taste

Combine all ingredients in a bowl and then let sit in refrigerator for at least an hour. Then enjoy on white bread or crackers or whatever else you like to put pimento cheese on!

5. Glen Grant's gin and tonic

Fill highball glass with gin and ice. Add splash of tonic and squeeze in juice of lime. Enjoy repeatedly!

6. A really basic old-fashioned

Bitters, sugar, bourbon, cherry. Orange for garnish. Enjoy figuring out the ratios yourself!

TRAVEL GUIDES

Memphis

Where to stay: The Peabody, 149 Union Avenue. The grande dame of southern hotels; be sure to check out the ducks as they make their daily march from the roof to the lobby fountain.

Where to eat: Charlie Vergos' Rendezvous, 52 South Second Street. Directly across the street (and down an alley) from the Peabody, Vergos has been in business since 1948 and serves world-famous dry-rub pork ribs, which are the must-order item on the menu. The beans are also particularly good, although I was not that impressed by their slaw.

What to see: Sun Records, 706 Union Avenue. Right down the street from the Peabody, Sun Records was the place Elvis Presley, Johnny Cash, Carl Perkins, and Jerry Lee Lewis started their careers under the guidance of the legendary Sam Phillips. Take the chance to sing into the microphone they used during recording and check out the cigarette burn Lewis put in the keys of the piano.

Graceland, Elvis Presley Blvd. This is a bit of a journey from the Peabody, but worth the trip. The people-watching is as fun as the tour of Presley's home, which is something you have to see to believe.

National Civil Rights Museum at the Lorraine Motel, 450 Mulberry St. The museum is a sobering trip through America's racist past. It is located across the street from the hotel where Martin Luther King Jr. was assassinated by James Earl Ray in 1968. The exhibits inside the museum are fascinating with plenty of evidence from Ray's trial, including the gun he used and a recreation of the room he was in when he shot King.

New Orleans

Where to stay: The Royal Orleans, 621 St. Louis St. This hotel is to New Orleans what the Peabody is to Memphis. There are no ducks, and the rooms are a lot shabbier, but the rooftop pool is one of the best places to hang out in the French Quarter. The central location of the building makes getting to Jackson Square a breeze.

Where to eat: There are more good restaurants in New Orleans than I could possibly name. Commander's Palace, 1403 Washington Ave., is the place to go for fine dining. But I want to focus on a more reasonably-priced place, with food that is just as good. Mandina's, 3800 Canal St., is a neigh-borhood institution in Mid-City. It serves a variety of food, from Italian to Creole. The chicken parmesan is not to be missed!

What to see: The French Quarter is your main tourist spot. Go outside and walk around. You will see plenty, and it will all be free.

Chattanooga

Where to stay: The Chattanoogan, 1201 Broad St. Nice hotel with big rooms. Ask for a room with a view of Lookout Mountain.

Where to eat: The Public House, 1110 Market St. The pimento cheese is the star of the show at this restaurant just a short walk from the hotel. Or the fried chicken. Or the craft cocktails. Honestly, I don't think you can go wrong with any of it.

What to see: Lookout Mountain Battlefield, 110 Point Park Road, Lookout Mountain Road. The Battle Above the Clouds was a key part of the larger Battle of Chattanooga. Even if you aren't that interested in battlefields, the view of the city and the river below make the drive up the mountain worth it.

Richmond

Where to stay: The Jefferson, 101 W. Franklin St. Another historic southern hotel. Maybe you are catching onto a theme here. The lobby is spectacular. The rooms are fine, but hardly special. The hotel restaurant, Lemaire, serves some of the best food in the city.

Where to eat: Tarrant's Cafe, 1 W. Broad St. A short walk from the hotel, Tarrant's offers a cheaper alternative to dining at Lemaire. The restaurant is housed in a former drugstore, which was in operation for over a hundred years. Both the shrimp and grits and the fried chicken and waffles were excellent.

What to see: The American Civil War Museum, 1201 E. Clay St. The former Museum of the Confederacy now has a more politically correct name, but still is home to the most impressive collection of southern artifacts from the Civil War. As an added bonus, the Confederate White House is right around the corner.

Nashville

Where to stay: The Hermitage Hotel, 231 Sixth Ave. N. Another spectacular southern hotel with the nicest lobby of any hotel I have ever been in. The Hermitage also gives the weary traveler the type of service you would expect from a five-star establishment. Personalized stationery, bedtime snacks, slippers, robes; you get the feeling this is the kind of place that will get you anything you want, as long as you say please when you ask for it.

Where to eat: The Capitol Grille, in the basement of the Hermitage Hotel. Farm-to-table is the star of the show down here. The menu seems to change with each passing season, so I can't give you a go-to dish. The craft cocktails from the bar are spectacular, as is the men's restroom, which was voted the best restroom in America in 2009.

What to see: The Hermitage, 4580 Rachels Ln., Hermitage, TN. Love him or hate him, Andrew Jackson's home is something to see. The museum accompanying the house is worth a look as you wait for your assigned tour to start. The house itself is not the biggest, or most impressive, plantation house in the South, but it is still worth the trip.

Oklahoma City

Where to stay: It really doesn't matter.

Where to eat: Eh, it's Oklahoma. You're probably not getting a good meal anyway.

What to see: The Oklahoma City National Memorial and Museum, 620 N. Harvey Ave. This is really the only reason to come to OKC, but it is a great reason. The grounds are somber as the monuments to the people who were killed when Timothy McVeigh blew up the Alfred P. Murrah Federal Building stand solemnly to the side of a large reflecting pond. The survivor tree is a place to ponder the senselessness of McVeigh's actions before going into the museum which takes the visitor through the entire day of April 19, 1995, and everything that followed.

Albuquerque

Where to stay: The Hyatt Regency, 330 Tijeras Ave NW. Centrally located downtown, the hotel is across the street from a large city square where *Breaking Bad* shot one of its most famous scenes. It is a pretty standard Hyatt, but if you can get a view of the Sandia Mountains, then you will have something nice to look at while you plan your ABQ adventures.

Where to eat: The Range Café, 320 Central, Southeast. The purveyors of "ordinary food done extraordinarily well," the Range Café has been in business for close to thirty years. The great thing about eating there is they will fill you up and not drain your wallet. This is probably the closest location to the Hyatt, but any of their restaurants will suffice. Make sure you say "Christmas style" when they ask how you want your chile. You have to eat the chile rellenos, but, if you don't, you will not be disappointed by whatever else you might choose.

What to see: Old Town Plaza, 200 N Plaza St. NW. The center of the settlement at one point, the city has spread away from this area which still serves as the western border of downtown. Lots of fun shops and restaurants. If you are looking for local art, look no further than Santisima, 328 San

Felipe St. NW #F, where local artist Johnny Salas sells an assortment of work from other local artists. The shop focuses mainly on Day of the Dead-themed items but has lots of great stuff to look at and purchase, if you are in the mood.

Los Angeles

Where to stay: Andaz, West Hollywood, 8401 W. Sunset Blvd. As the Hyatt in Century City is undergoing an extensive renovation (and has been sold to a different hotel chain), you will probably need a different place to lay your head at night. The former Riot House has a rich rock-and-roll history, but is much more chill these days. Have drinks on the roof by the pool and stare at the homes in the adjacent Hollywood Hills or the LA skyline which is in the other direction. The rooms here are big, and the minibar snacks are free, just as long as you don't take the booze!

Where to eat: Tito's Tacos, 11222 Washington Pl., Culver City. No-frills Mexican taco stand where everything is delicious, even if you aren't sure why. There will probably be a line, but go ahead and stand in it. Then get some food and try and find a spot to eat it. Just make sure you get enough. Because you won't want to get back in that line.

What to see: Start with the Getty Center, 1200 Getty Center Drive. It's free and has an incredible collection of art that is matched by its incredible views of the Pacific Ocean. Once you are done there, drive up the coast from Santa Monica to Malibu on PCH. Be sure to make a stop at Will Rogers State Beach and take some time to get up close with the Pacific. After that you can find your own way. It's Los Angeles. There is no shortage of things to do.

ABOUT ATMOSPHERE PRESS

Atmosphere Press is an independent, full-service publisher for excellent books in all genres and for all audiences. Learn more about what we do at atmospherepress.com.

We encourage you to check out some of Atmosphere's latest releases, which are available at Amazon.com and via order from your local bookstore:

The Swing: A Muse's Memoir About Keeping the Artist Alive, by Susan Dennis

Possibilities with Parkinson's: A Fresh Look, by Dr. C

Gaining Altitude - Retirement and Beyond, by Rebecca Milliken

Out and Back: Essays on a Family in Motion, by Elizabeth Templeman

Just Be Honest, by Cindy Yates

You Crazy Vegan: Coming Out as a Vegan Intuitive, by Jessica Ang

Detour: Lose Your Way, Find Your Path, by S. Mariah Rose

To B&B or Not to B&B: Deromanticizing the Dream, by Sue Marko

Convergence: The Interconnection of Extraordinary Experiences, by Barbara Mango and Lynn Miller

Sacred Fool, by Nathan Dean Talamantez

My Place in the Spiral, by Rebecca Beardsall

My Eight Dads, by Mark Kirby

Dinner's Ready! Recipes for Working Moms, by Rebecca Cailor

Vespers' Lament: Essays Culture Critique, Future Suffering, and Christian Salvation, by Brian Howard Luce

Without Her: Memoir of a Family, by Patsy Creedy

Emotional Liberation: Life Beyond Triggers and Trauma, by GuruMeher Khalsa

ABOUT THE AUTHOR

Hall of Fame sportswriter Chris Grant has a daughter and a dog, both of whom reside in central Texas. He has published short stories, history articles, and true crime research, in addition to his journalism, which has been featured in newspapers from coast to coast. When not writing, he goes to punk rock shows, curates the baseball history website Letters From Home Plate, and dreams of running away to Iceland.